JANE FROST

Published by Mindstir Media, LLC
45 Lafayette Rd | Suite 181| North Hampton, NH 03862 | USA
1.800.767.0531 | www.mindstirmedia.com

Printed in the United States of America
ISBN-13: 978-1-7361190-3-7

MINDSTIR MEDIA

JANE FROST

BRIAN WEBER

This book is dedicated to all the *Janes*.

In the words of winter mogul Darryl Richardson, "Go get 'em!"

Jane Frost

Once upon a time…you've heard it before…usually at the beginning of fantasy stories. Stories with kings and princesses, where dashing knights save helpless maidens. But let me tell you, this story is no fantasy. And it has no dungeons or fairy godmothers.

I'm not big on spouting out tales of The North and all its glamour and glory. There are enough of those stories goin' around. They *are* mostly actual accounts, with little exaggeration. But there's another side to The North. A darker side.

Because folks are uncomfortable with this place of wonder being linked with confrontation and struggle, the life-story of a powerful woman has been hidden away…stuffed *far* back into the deepest corners of closets. As if purposely set there in a place where eyes would never *dare* to look. I'm speaking metaphorically of course. Nobody has *ever* written her story before. Ever.

Don't feel bad for *her*, though. If you had the chance to ask her, she would let you know she would *want* her story to be buried. That's why it's a story nobody has written until now. As age begins to get the better of me, I feel like I have to tell it, because nobody else will. Fear? No one's gonna say a word about me tellin' Jane's story. I'm a strong woman too. I'm not taking *a thing* from anybody, child. But we'll get more into me later.

To be honest, I think lots of folks 'round here have been wonderin' when I *would* put this story in text form. You sit down and listen. Pull up a chair, because you're about to learn a few things. Life's greatest lessons are not always learned from triumphs. Diamonds don't polish themselves either, *hear?*

This is the true story of Jane Frost. And I can tell you this… without knowing her story, you can never know the *whole* story of The North. More to it than wrapping paper and mistletoe.

As you're reading, I'm sure there will be times when you'll want to close my words onto themselves as you curse, "This could never happen!" I wouldn't blame you.

Neither would Jane.

1

"Jenny, don't forget to put your library books in your schoolbag!"

"'kay!"

It was about 20 years ago. Jenny was in her room getting ready for school. She ignored her mother's request and reached for the oversized thermometer by the window.

"Forty-seven degrees!" she whisper-yelled in anguish while holding her head with her free hand.

This was a common temperature for St. Louis, Missouri in early December. But Jenny and *common* would knock heads every now and then. An exasperated strand of her jet-black hair dropped down over her eyes, sharing in the anxiety of the moment. Jenny used her forearm to push the strand to the side of her smooth brown face. Her grip on the thermometer grew tighter. At times, Jenny would hold that thermometer as if it were the only thing she had. Nothing could be more true and more false at the same time, than that notion right there.

Jenny shook the thermometer, rotated it, and twisted it anxiously in every direction, begging the number to change. The mercury was unforgiving. She glared at the thermometer and blew on it fiercely.

"Thirty-four degrees!" she quietly celebrated.

But *that* didn't last long.

"No, no no no!" Jenny whispered in frustration as the mercury rose back up to forty-seven.

Her mom called up the stairs, "Can you find them?"

"I have 'em!"

Jenny blew on the thermometer again. The mercury dropped to thirty-two degrees, before slowly rising to its origination once more.

"C'mon Jenny!"

I'm sure the same tug of war was going on between all of the parents trying to get their eight-year-olds out of the house that morning. Minus the thermometer.

Jenny sighed, swooped her arm through the strap of her white pleather schoolbag, and hustled out of her bedroom. Her library books lay abandoned on a side table, underneath a box of crayons.

11

Form-fitting, knee-high white boots take a few final steps toward the peak of a forest-covered mountain in the Alps. Sliding above the shaft of the boot, legs covered in a glossy white fabric. Legs a bit thicker than those of a track star. And less muscular. Natural. Just above, a jacket tailored for the sturdy frame of a five-foot-seven-inch, twenty-eight-year-old woman, who could do her own work. The sleeves of the jacket lead down to smooth brown hands, exposed to the cold, yet showing no effects. Peeking out from beneath the right cuff, a brilliant diamond bracelet.

Black hair drapes down to the woman's toned shoulders, contrasting harmoniously with the pure white of her jacket. A small scar under her right eye. A diamond necklace eases down her neck like a soft stream...trickling down until captured by a snowflake pendant resting in the middle of her chest. Flawless diamonds, glistening brighter than sunshine on snow. Flawless in the fact that they do not detract from the scar on her face. *Jane Frost.*

There she holds her ground, sturdy, in a wide stance. Overlooking what is to come. Behind her...what already was. For if she glanced back she would see, stretching down the hills and mountain peaks as far as the light would show, a snow-covered winter world. In front of her lay a brown forest floor, expanding over all the hills and valleys, complete with evergreens...still green...and standing firm. There is an exact line between the white and the color. On that line, stands Jane, breathing in and out. The frozen mist of her breath gives an icy warning to the untouched landscape before her.

With a short sprint and a hard twist, Jane becomes a snow squall. She moves as swirling snow, in and out of the trees, taking human form intermittently. Brown and white wolves join her, flanking her sides, seemingly as guardians. The wolves' pads and claws make a distinct sound every time they grip down into the icy snow that Jane spreads everywhere she travels. Next, gray and white wolves filter in, on watch.

Like a runaway train on mute, Jane Frost's breathing is all that can be heard. Hands straight, arms pumping. Her snow holds the sound of the wolves and preserves the peace of the high mountains. In and out, in and out, breaths on point. Running like a track star, Jane knifes down the steep ground. Until poof! She transforms into a compact snowy blizzard, taking over new territory with each rampant turn. As a fierce whirlwind of snow, Jane is still able to maintain close contact with the ground. She ramps up the next mountain, delivering harsh surges of white powder along the way. The light gets brighter as Jane moves farther uphill, closing the distance between herself and the blue sky above her. Then back to human form. Breaths like ice razors, firing out, then dissipating. A new air inhaled. A blow. Inhale and blow. Arms pumping. Poof! Jane whips into a snow squall once again, before spinning and morphing back into human form at the top of a steep cliff.

Jane has covered the forest in snow. She looks back. Her brown eyes have an opportunity to assess her masterpiece. She proudly exhales. Wide stance. Sturdy. Wolves behind her, asking, *What's next?* Wondering if they'll be able to keep up.

Satisfaction. A rare feeling for Jane. Fleeting. Her eyes catch the edge of the next highest cliff. She sprints toward it and leaps off! Jane's legs continue to churn as she runs through the air, but gravity reaches up to grab her. A hard rip twist and fwoo, she becomes a spiraling snow blizzard again, before rising…and dissipating into the sky.

The wolves have discovered their limit. They gather at the precipice and howl in support of Jane. Not even snow can muffle the sound of a heartfelt howl. Owooo! Owooooo! For once, the wolves stop to see their *own* breath expand over the icy air. They pant as they track the edge of the cliff in awe. And the dusk begins to steal away the light.

III

A brand new, pure white SL 65 Mercedes convertible exits a ramp and enters downtown Miami. Across the airwaves, radio host DJ Krane introduces the new day. "We were skateboardin' on the sixties for a minute. But ya have no fear, mon. 'Cause we'll be jommin' high into the seventies today! Could creep into the low eighties inland."

Cohost Kelly T. breaks his groove, "That is such a bad Jamaican accent."

"So all you lovely ladies get your caliente back on, and show us fellas some looove!" DJ Krane forges on, now butchering a Mexican accent.

Kelly T. quickly surrenders to Krane's lazy, yet comical shtick. "Do it ladies! You know what he's talkin' 'bout! Bring that Miami *heat*!"

The unflappable DJ finishes his lead-in. "And this one is to all my fly baby girls of every make and shade. We're gonna skip right over this winter thing and take you straight through to summer!" Krane proceeds by spinning an old school summertime rap song.

Jane lets go of the steering wheel for a second, before tightening her grip again. She ponders driving off the road...into a ditch.

"In December? Heck no," she curses.

With no one else in the Benz, Jane knows she is only sharing her disapproval with herself. Yet her trigger finger won't pull on a station change. Almost in an act of self-mutiny, she listens to the Philadelphia rapper glamorize the summer like it was a red carpet event. Surprisingly, Jane remains composed as she pulls her car over to the curb and parks. She taps the *open trunk* button and exits the low bucket seat of the Benz, one leg at a time. Then she kindly sashays around to the back of her car, grabs a tire iron from under the fabric cover in the trunk, and walks over to the passenger door. She loosens her grip on the tire iron, and then re-grips it. Grips, loosens, re-grips. Calm.

Jane opens the passenger door...leans down...and smashes the entire radio with the tire iron. Smashes and smashes. Bang! Bang! Crunch! Smash! That radio is dead. She pulls back for a second. But then she proceeds to smash and crack the radio a few more times. After laying the tire iron on the passenger seat, Jane grabs the entire stereo with both hands, heaves at it, and pries it from the console. A few wires refuse to let go, but Jane gives the stereo one last tug and rips it out of the car completely. Then she peacefully transitions it to a nearby trash can, her steps unhindered by the dangling cords.

Jane's sleek, all white outfit is unblemished from her act of vengeance. She straightens her top and whips her hair. Then she takes a deep breath and strolls back to her car. Her delicate fingers push the passenger door shut. She presses the lock button on her key. Chirp!

The rivets on the 65's rims reflect the Miami sun. The white glass coat finish on its body mirrors the fabric of Jane's outfit. Even when Jane handled business, there was a flawlessness to it. To her, and *whatever* she did work on. She promptly put the tiny radio episode in her past and walked the Miami sidewalk. She had a cute little walk. Not to digress too much into looks, but Janey *was* cute.

She really was. Not overdone either. Cool. And she was centered once more. Centered enough to start talking to herself, again.

"Skateboards?"

Curb hopping skateboarders were doing tricks in the park across the street.

Jane continued, "Didn't they go out in the eighties? Tony Hawk. Parents won't buy their kids sleds, but they'll buy them a piece of wood with wheels bolted to it." Jane's irritability heightened as she desperately tried to contain her words to the air in front of herself. "Break an arm faster on the pavement! What is it then? The temperature?" She sarcastically ranted in baby talk, "If it gets cold, we're all going to have to go inside and huddle up with our tablets."

Jane wandered onto Coconut Grove. Her mind continued to run away from her.

The perfectly pruned palm trees rising skyward above the boutiques, the professional shoppers, the early warmth of the south Florida sun…these things didn't check any of Jane's boxes. It was showing.

All of her self-talk began to catch the attention of the fashionistas walking the strip. People began to stare at her as if she were crazy.

"I'm not talking into a Bluetooth," Jane spouted toward an innocent bystander. "Talking to myself. You ever talk to yourself?"

She breezed by, not caring for a response. However, in Jane's self-conscious state, she was fully aware that she was beginning to unravel. Beads of sweat began forming on her forehead. But she wasn't interested in cooling off. Okay, Janey did tiptoe her little white booties to the shade-covered sidewalk across the street. There, a wanna-be-player homed in on her, with his boys behind him waiting for the unfold. Jane opened her palm toward the pavement beneath the rookie, and covertly sprayed a patch of ice.

"Waaa!"

The nicely dressed gentleman went down hard. All of his friends fell out. Arms waving, finger pointing, the whole bit! Not one put out a hand to help him up. Jane...didn't give so much as a backward glance. She kept it moving. If you were staring down the edge of making yourself look foolish, Jane wouldn't mind giving you that extra little push from behind.

There was an outdoor café halfway up the block. It caught Jane's eye...called to her in a way. She walked up to the open gate of the classic, weathered white picket fence, which ran across the street side of the café's patio dining area. The fence was covered in an elegant, purple flowering vine. As Jane walked through the gate, she made an exaggerated effort to avoid the vine and each one of its colorful flowers.

She sat herself at a small, round table off to the side and put her head in her hands. If Jane had a minute to herself, she may have had a chance to pull herself together.

"Did someone seat you, Miss?" the waiter asked.

"Uh, no I–"

"That's okay. No problem, honey. It's just sometimes they sit people at my tables and don't tell me. Then I have to go back there and say, '*I can't wait on them if I don't know they're there.*'" The waiter completed his finger wag, pursed his lips, and seemed like he was about to bow to an adoring audience.

Jane lifted her eyes above her fingers. The waiter laughed to himself and sighed, but Jane offered no response.

The server sailed on, "...that sort-a-thing." Then he released one of his dainty hands from his hips and pulled a pen from behind his ear. "Do you know what you want already? Can I get you a menu?"

"An ice latte."

The waiter brightened, "A Chilly Lat?"

Jane tilted her head and popped up quizzically.

"It's our ice latte."

"I'll have that," Jane responded. But her mind was already fifteen steps from the current conversation.

"Are you okay?"

Jane motioned *yes* with her hands.

"One of those nights?" the server empathized, offering an open ear.

Jane shook her head, not having the energy for a clear response.

The waiter lent her a consoling glance. "I'll put that in for you right away, darling." Then he hurried off.

Jane mimicked him, "*Are you okay? If you're sitting at my table, but I can't see you, because nobody told me you were sitting here…*" Then she repositioned herself. "Ain't nothin' good about me settin' here."

Two stylishly dressed African American ladies were sitting at a nearby table discussing each other's glamorous sunglasses. Their attention was drawn to their hot lattes.

"Look at the heart in it!"

"The heart?"

"They made a heart with the crème!"

"Aww."

Jane shifted uncomfortably as she mocked them under her breath, "*Aww. Wook at da widdle hawt. They used the cweme to make a widdle hawt.*"

"Excuse me," one of the ladies called across the café.

Jane straightened up. Her eyes widened.

The woman continued, "Sammy? Excuse me. We ordered hot lattes."

Jane's heightened emotions and proximity had caused both of the women's lattes to freeze.

Sam, the waiter, scurried over to the ladies. "I did bring you Hot Latts. Can I heat them back up for—"

"This is like a milkshake," the woman's friend comically interrupted.

"Ohh. This *is* a Chilly Latt," Sam agreed as he lifted the drink and inspected the bottom of the cup. "You wouldn't even put a Chilly Latt in this. I'm so sorry. I swore I put in for hot. Be right back…"

Sam offered an additional, "Sorry," before rushing off.

"It seemed hot," the woman's friend shared, somewhat confused.

"Anyway, I'm gonna be hangin' with my sister up in New York on Christmas."

"*Alright.*"

"We haven't spent Christmas together in a minute."

"I knew it had to be a stretch. Your momma gonna be there?"

"Girl, she's on a cruise in the Bahamas!"

The women burst into laughter while exchanging high fives.

"I think it's gonna be wild thinkin' about it bein' just me and my sis' together. Except I know it will be colder than all get-out."

"Maybe you'll have a white Christmas."

"Ha! White Christmas? The only touch of white I want in my Christmas is some Bradley Cooper."

"Right?…or Brad Pitt!"

"Ya hear me?"

Jane's mind was logging and tracking the dialogue at adjacent tables. She took in a surveillance-style view of the quaint Coconut Grove café. Eventually, she locked in on a cute woman in her twenties with a high ponytail. The woman's honey brown legs were crossed in a ladylike fashion, teasing a short, yellow, flower-patterned sundress. She flicked one of her orange platform sandals up and down in a flirty manner while making eyes at her man. The kind gentleman across the table from her was wearing an untucked orange and baby blue plaid shirt, which was draped over his natural-colored, linen drawstring pants. Yes, Jane's obsession with her surroundings had become intense.

The woman led in, "I know you don't care about the flowers, but..."

Her man put up a half-hearted defense, "I care...a little."

"Do you want to try any of our Chilly Drinks today?" their waitress stepped up and asked.

"I know they're makin' you say that, 'cause ain't no way. Feels like it's sixty degrees," the woman laughed.

"Lisa," the man scolded.

"No, she's right." The waitress was relieved she could let *that* out! She lowered her voice and leaned in, "You know I can't stand carrying those frozen drinks. Freezes my hands just to walk with 'em."

The young woman tossed her ponytail proudly. "See."

The waitress flung her wrist down, "Cold is for the devil."

"What? Crazy! For the devil?" Jane mumbled to herself.

The server launched into her spiel. "We have Hot Latts. Several different..."

"I'll have a cortadito and a slice of lemon cake," the woman cut in.

"I'll go with the Chilly Colada!" the man said, broadening his chest.

Jane pumped her fist. *A vote for the cold! A small victory in this god forsaken–*

"Eh. Know what? Call me a sissy, but it is too cold! I'll have a hot Caramel Cortado instead."

The waitress and her two new confidants let loose a cloud of laughter that carried across the café.

Jane whipped her body around and sank down in her chair. "Aoww!"

The people in the outdoor seating area clearly took note of Jane at this point. Her gyrations had become seriously awkward. Her high investment in the casual conversations around her had made Jane's internal conflict an external one.

"Sorry, just looking for my contact lens...down here. Got it!" Jane shared, holding up nothing with her pointer finger and thumb pressed together in the air. She had heard enough. She decided to pay her tab and leave. "*The devil?*" Jane repeated to herself in disbelief.

"Look, I can see my breath," a customer joked to his friends standing in line with him.

Jane left out through the weathered gate of the café. Escaping while she still had a morsel of dignity left.

IV

Jenny was walking home from school, flanked by her best friend, Reggie. They both looked down at the sidewalk, measuring their steps, as though they had never been there before. As Reggie walked along, his knobby knees frequently bumped into each other, leaving his skinny body to wriggle back and forth with each step he took. His comforting brown skin and thick natural hair erased some of his awkwardness, but the rest was hard to hide.

"You got to be home?" Jenny asked.

"No," Reggie replied.

Jenny preceded Reggie through a tall wrought iron gate, which was suspended by rusty, broken hinges. This was the once majestic entrance to a park in an area of St. Louis where folks struggled to make ends meet. There was a playground tucked deep in the back and a basketball court positioned in front. Regardless of the appearance, there was a comforting community feel to that basketball court. Money wasn't everything...folks did their best to get by. That's just what it was. The court wouldn't have held more value if it was plated in gold. People came from all over the surrounding neighborhoods to prove themselves there. Steppin' on that court, everyone was the same, for the most part. Was about who could beat who.

Jenny and Reggie both took up a seat, elbow-to-elbow and knee-to-knee, on the second row of bleachers. Jenny was always on Reggie's right. Reggie was always on Jenny's left. Reggie peered down toward the playground at the opposite end of the park. *Eight years old. Too old for that now.*

He thought it, even if he didn't believe it.

There was only one entrance to the playground, and they had just passed through it. To get to the swings and slides, everyone had to walk past the basketball court. They had to leave out in the same manner. This put the hoops on center stage at all times.

After school, there was a slow period, prior to things heating up. Younger kids could steal some court time, before they were bumped off by the twenty-somethings, the players in their thirties, or the old heads. Reggie always wanted to steal some court time. Consequently, it *was* December. And the court traffic would usually slow down when the temperatures dropped. Therefore, Jenny was sure that if there were *ever* a time for Reggie to get out there and play, this would be it. But she wasn't going to say anything.

Four kids were bouncing around the court, playing with a ball that had become fuzzy from wear. They moved swiftly around the three point arc, along the baseline, and through the lane, unobstructed by the cracks in the surface and the dried out weeds reaching out from within them. As for the other end of the court, it didn't even have a rim. But Reggie kept staring at it like it was going to fix itself.

"Why are we sitting here?" Jenny zinged.

"I'm going to play," Reggie returned unconvincingly.

"It feels like we've been doing this forever…sitting beside the court, waiting for them to let you play."

Reggie faced Jenny to add an air of confidence. "I am going to play."

But Jenny, of all people, could see right through him. She piped up. "Then go ask them, already."

Reggie was challenged. So he mustered up all of the bravado he could, to let out a timid request. "Trev. Hey Trevor…can I play?"

Trevor was only nine years old, but he acted as though he'd been running the court for years. Ultimately, he decided who would or wouldn't play on *that* court everyday…at least until four-thirty. His friends, Lonnie, Corey, and Clemon, were always riding on Trevor's coattails. This time, the three of them intercepted Reggie's court time request, feeling that they could answer it on their own.

"Hey Trevor, Can Iiii plaaaay?" Lonnie mocked, imitating Reggie's melodic voice.

"No!" Clemon flared up in disgust.

Lonnie continued, "You can play after Santa comes."

"When's that, Lon?"

To which Corey jumped in with perfect timing and shouted, "Never!"

The boys' chortles tore across the basketball court, through the park, until they became mangled in the playground a hundred feet away.

Lonnie finished the parody. "*Cause Santaw ain't wheel.*" His dynamic white smile reflected off his fresh-out-of-the-box shell tops. The orange and navy stripes crossing his pristine, unwrinkled Polo, remained parallel. No matter what Lonnie threw into the atmosphere, none of it ever circled back to put a smudge on him.

Clemon raised up and shot the street-worn ball at the basket. His left hand remained elevated with his wrist turned down in a finished position. It didn't make a difference if the shot went in or not. He was going to hold his form like a champ. His chin tilted up. His lower lip pushed his upper lip toward his nose. Clemon smugly waited for *the comeback*, which he was fully aware he and Lonnie had incited.

"He *is* real!" Jenny blurted out desperately. "Yes, he is!"

With this one response, Jenny knew she was giving the boys everything they could have ever dreamed of. Their day was made. The boys all turned to Corey. He was the only eight-year-old of the group. He had the *quick draw* for any moment. The cutest round little face ever, but boy could he let you have it. Whether it was a one-liner, a facial gesture, or part of his physical comedy…Corey's timing was on point. After Jenny posted her regard for Santa, Corey took the ball, heaved it into the air, and began skipping circles around the imaginary cylinder below it. As the ball bounced and bounced, Lonnie, Clemon, and Trevor added sarcastic, "Ooohs," and "Aaahs," to the dark euphoria.

"Look who has a bodyguard!" Clemon triumphed.

"He is real!" Jenny flared up again.

Trevor slid the ball between his legs, spun around, and floated a shot high off the backboard. As he wheeled under the basket, his dirtied extra large T-shirt rippled gracefully. He weighed in. "Clem, would you stop talkin'’bout Santa?"

Trevor took his time to use the bottom of his shirt to wipe the dirt-filled sweat from his face. He uncomfortably lifted his head halfway. His eyes barely linked with Reggie's for an instant. "C'mon. You can play."

"Yo, what? Trev!" Corey griped.

"Core. Shh. Shh. Shh…" Trevor returned, trying to back Corey down.

Reggie pushed himself up from the bench. Never had gravity worked so hard against him. He had wanted this for such a long time, but now he had the invitation…and a load full of doubts to go with it. His legs wobbled. He fought to stand up.

One foot in front of the other, he thought to himself. Reggie's arms were shaking, and so was his heart.

"Naa. Make 'im beg, Trev." Corey started flapping his arms in disgust, but he stopped abruptly when Trevor gave him a stern final glance to *cool it*.

Next, Clemon started in on Reggie. "Yo Lon, see how his ribs stick out?"

Lonnie jumped back in. "Yo momma feed you?"

"Clem, he's got clubfeet too!" Corey added while mimicking Reggie's walk. "Look at 'im hobblin' around. How he hobble, yo!"

Reggie surprised himself. He listened with precision to every cutting insult, yet he still found himself one foot inside the three-point line. Clemon was holding his stomach in heavy laughter. Lonnie and Trevor were tearing up and snorting.

As if part of a non-stop chain of rehearsed taunts, Corey began skipping and parading in front of Reggie's path. "S'okay, tho. Pass 'im the ball. 'Cause when he come through this lane…"

Trevor pulled his head all the way up to read Reggie. They now stood four feet from each other. "Core not gonna do nothin'. Don't worry, Randy. *He's shorter than you.*"

Corey's face wrinkled.

"*Randy?* It's Reggie." Clemon corrected Trevor, but not without finding great humor in his mistake.

"It's *Reg-in-ald*," Corey mocked in a singsong fashion.

Reggie nodded. He had to. And he had to stay. And he had to watch. The boys broke into such a triumphant arrogant laughter,

Trevor hurt his throat, trying to keep a straight face. The comedic blitz levied on Reggie soon forced snot out of Trevor's nose, and tears down his face.

Lonnie was reduced to one knee, but he made a half-hearted attempt to try and pull himself together. "Whew. Okay, we got Reginald."

The boys all snickered again.

Lonnie sounded off, "Check!" and Corey gave him a bounce pass.

Lonnie snapped a quick pass to Reggie, which hit him in the shin. The ball ricocheted out of bounds.

"He's got no hands, Trev. I told you!" Clemon celebrated.

Lonnie set his arm down around Reggie's shoulder. "Don't listen to 'em Reginald. But seriously, who cuts your hair?"

Jenny continued to oversee the whole event, but she knew any words or actions on her part would set things off on a whole 'nother level. Her eyes took notes, but her face gave away nothing. Not even a twitch.

Trevor became impatient due to the amount of court time being lost. He snapped, "Give 'im the ball, Clem! Let him shoot." Then he added in a mumble, "I'ma swat 'im."

Instantaneously, Corey scooped the ball out of Clemon's hands and turned from Reggie. Clemon had relinquished the ball, but he hadn't relinquished the jabbing. He leaned over Corey and spoke in a low tone.

All Reggie felt he could do was stand there as Clemon plotted against him.

Clemon's skin had a gentle shine. Spitting image of one of those wooden African sculptures with the dark finish. His hair was freshly cut, short. It was shaped perfectly, as though the lines were part of an architect's blueprint, drawing down precisely to a sharp point at the bottom of his sideburns. Someone had spent a lot of time taking care of him. Invincible, yes. Nothing was getting in. Clemon had the game on lock.

He encouraged Corey to proceed in a *not so secret* tone. "Jus' do it. Give 'im the ball and let Trev swat 'im."

Corey dribbled forward and purposely fumbled the ball into Reggie's midsection. Reggie took a short step, raised up, and smoothly released the ball from his hands—SWAT! Trevor knocked the ball out of the air with such force, it screamed to the bleachers before rattling underneath them. Clung, bung, clap!

The boys turned loose their demonic glee. "Oooooh!"

Lonnie clamored, "He's gonna cry. Clem, he got tears!"

Reggie awkwardly jogged to the bleachers. He self-consciously fixated on his skinny fingers and oversized knuckles as he attempted to pry the ball from under the first metal bench. At first try, he was unsuccessful. While he contorted his body to free the ball from another angle, he could feel his grapefruit sized knees wobbling erratically like an old fashioned toy.

In the background, Reggie could hear, "Yo, he bawlin'! Not ballin', but–"

"'Prised you even know about word play!" Jenny cracked back.

She had Corey's attention.

"What'd you say, princess?"

"Nah, Core," Trevor cut in. But this train had already derailed.

Clemon continued to jab, "Reginald, I think there's napkins over there! If ya need some tissues!"

The four boys thundered once more. To Reggie it seemed like there were eight of them. Jenny...she would've been happy to get her hands around the throat of just *one* of 'em. Her hands were balled, her lips were pursed, and she had a lot to say. But she refused to give the boys the satisfaction.

Reggie finally gathered the ball. He tossed it back into the lane and gave a subtle gesture to Jenny. Then the two friends walked out of the courts, through the rusted wrought iron gate, together.

"*That your girrrrrrlfriend?*"

"Let 'im go, Lon. That's enough," Trevor interrupted, severing the conversation for good. "Gimme the ball, Core. Ten-six."

Reggie and Jenny continued down the sidewalk. That sidewalk had a center city feel to it. Dried, dead leaves gathered along the edges. Crushed leaves lay scattered over the middle. And gusts of wind would take turns lifting them up, only to discard them in the same place all over again. Outside the row homes, people were often sweeping some combination of street dust and plant debris off their steps. Didn't matter what was going on around Reggie and Jenny though. They were always alone in their own little world, even if the rest of everybody else was synchronized in choreographed activities around them. Reggie put the courts behind him, if not for the sole reason that there were more pressing matters he wanted to discuss with Jenny.

"I have something to tell you," he began.

Jenny put her hand on the back of Reggie's neck.

"Oww!" he squealed. "Would you stop it, with your cold hands?"

"What do ya want to tell me?"

"I'm going away."

Jenny raised a confused eyebrow.

"To this space camp thing. Like to help save people or something. They're supposed to be training me to help…in space…kind of."

"Kind of?"

"I guess."

"You? You can't even save yourself!"

Reggie and Jenny released a camaradic laughter. No, camaradic isn't a word, so put down your spell-checkers, or your cell phones, or whatever you people are using these days. I can make up a word every now and then. Won't do any harm.

The two shared such camaraderie. They could poke fun at each other's true weaknesses without hurting one another. In fact, many times, as in this instance, it would turn to laughter. That's when you know you have a good friend, right?

"Really. It's kind of like helping people in space," Reggie continued.

"There are hardly any people *in* space. What are you going to do? Put Band-Aids on stars?"

Reggie and Jenny embarked on another round of friendly banter. I get such a warm feeling when I say those two names aloud together. I do that sometimes, remembering how it was. Then I do seem to tighten up a bit. Get a little somber. Childhood friends... if you could bottle that. Close your eyes for a second and you can take yourself back there, I bet. Timeless memories. Just laughin' for no reason. Finishin' each other's sentences while walkin' around the neighborhood all day. Where were we walkin' to anyway? Everyday, it was like you had all the time in the world. Your best friend *always* right beside you. *Hm.* But we can't stay children forever now, can we?

V

Jenny and Reggie sat down on a park bench at a playground close to their homes. The bench had been painted over several times. Each layer of forest green paint glazed over the chipped coating on the paint job before it, giving the old bench a clean and glossy look. This playground had more of a quaint, cozier feel than the one they had just left. The red slides and sleek black swings looked new, and the mulch still had a fresh smell to it...even in December. The playground was empty, though. In this middle class St. Louis neighborhood, things slowed late in the fall, just the same as it did on the courts down the street. Folks mostly stayed inside, right on through winter. Every once in a while somebody would break out a grill, but that was it. Quiet. A couple of lone leaves dangled high on a tree branch above Reggie and Jenny.

Reggie pulled an envelope out of his schoolbag. This was why he led Jenny to the bench. Not just to talk, but also because he had never mastered the art of pulling items from his schoolbag and walking at the same time. In the past, when Reggie attempted such a feat, he would end up spreading a chaotic mess of papers fit to cover a 33.1964286-square-foot area around himself. I only know this, because Jenny proudly did the math one day and shared it with a few people. Most notably Reggie's parents.

Having Reggie's papers all over the ground was only the half of it. Afterwards, Jenny had to help him get everything back into his schoolbag again as well. The two of them sitting on the sidewalk puttin' Reggie back together. Happened more than once, I can tell you.

Reggie handed the bent-up, fully-sealed envelope to Jenny. "Here."

Jenny tore open the letter and read aloud, "*Your son, Reginald Randolph, has been offered a position in the North Post Aeronautical Engineering Conglomerate.*"

"Good, Jenny."

"I can read, ya goof."

Jenny read on, "*Our panel rated you highly in each* blah, blah, blah. Blah, blah, blah, blah, blah. *We eagerly await your response.*" Jenny pulled her eyes from the paper, lifted them up to Reggie, and fed him a programmed line. "Reggie, this is great."

Not a sound could be heard in the empty playground...until Jenny broke the silence again.

"*It is,*" she said, attempting to convince herself.

"I'm kind of excited about it," Reggie quietly responded while staring at his feet.

He noticed how his toes were awkwardly pointing toward one another.

"I'm excited too," Jenny added, trying to reassure him.

Reggie and Jenny had been hanging out for a long time. Reggie doubted Jenny's sincerity, only because he could imagine how *he* would react if the roles were reversed.

Jenny instantly decoded Reggie's suspicions.

"What? *I am!*" she repeated.

Jenny playfully patted Reggie on the back, before putting her arm around him and pulling him close. Then she released the pull without removing her arm, leaving her fingers to dangle in the void over his left shoulder.

"How long will you be gone?"

"I'm not coming back."

Jenny was clearly confused, but Reggie pushed on.

"I'll be back to visit. But I'm moving…"

"Did you talk to these people?"

"A little."

A tension-filled panic began to surface inside Jenny. She always watched out for Reggie. With all his quirks, she naturally took on the role as a sort of guardian for him. Making sure he didn't get taken advantage of, or get bullied too badly…didn't roam into a construction site…didn't keep walking right past his own house while he was talking away. She sensed in Reggie's opportunity an open-endedness mixed with finality, and the dots weren't connecting.

"This space medic, doctor thing…will you be trained to help astronauts if they get sick or something?"

"I think."

"You're only eight!"

"I mean…I don't know, but I guess that might sound kind of right. My parents think I might be a leader right away."

"Leader of what? To lead who?"

"They said to my parents, one day, I might even be the one to organize and lead special missions."

"*What missions?*" Jenny asked, searching for comprehendible answers.

At the culmination of her exasperation, Jenny was actually able to find humor. She arrived at an inner peace, realizing Reggie didn't know what he was talking about. But she recognized that there had to be *something* good there, and she was proud of Reggie.

Jenny sarcastically whapped him with the crinkled letter and shook it playfully in front of him. "How can you be excited and want to go, when you don't even know what this is exactly?"

"I just know we don't belong here, alright? Look at these people." Reggie motioned toward the pristine, cookie-cutter townhomes on each side of the playground. "None of these people are like us, Jenny. We're not like them. What are *we* doing here? What are *we* here for? You're talking about me. You said you wanted to be a professional ice sculpturer."

"Sculptor. And I was kidding."

"I know when you're kidding."

In this chess match between two friends who knew each other down to the last feeling in each other's hearts, Reggie had checked Jenny.

She was unable to move forward to her next thought.

Then Reggie added, "Mrs. Robbins asked about your life's dream. Asked, 'If you could do any job in the world, could be absolutely anything you wanted to be...on the whole planet...What would you want to do? What would you want to be?' And you said, '*I want to make ice that's prettier than diamonds.*'"

Jenny stared straight ahead.

"You ever hear anybody else around here say they wanted to sculpt ice for a living, Jenny? Is this your life?" Reggie extended his arms in front of himself, palms to the sky, and swung them outward. His pointy elbows angled out from his skinny arms, but his sermon was being served straight down the middle. "This is your life? What you *say*, and what you *dream about* doesn't match what's going on here."

"And later, Mrs. Robbins said, 'Some people already are the things they dream of being. They just need to find themsel–' I guess that's you," Jenny sadly conceded.

Reggie glanced down at his stick legs, before softly adding, "That's us."

Jenny swung her head in the opposite direction. "Pfshh."

Reggie tried to be more clear. "These people don't listen to you. They hear what you say, but they don't *feel it*. They don't *understand* what you're saying."

Jenny was melting. "You understand me."

"Well, it's just the two of us. There's got to be more of us out there somewhere. The way you picture things and speak on those visions like they're real. Those aren't daydreams. There's something true about them." Reggie squinted at Jenny. "There's hope in those pictures…in your mind."

Reggie, Jenny, and the forest green bench. At that moment, they were the only three things on the planet. This time Reggie spoke words that they both desperately needed to ring true. "We can't be the only ones."

VI

One block away from Reggie and Jenny, stood Reggie's townhome. Inside, Reggie's parents were moving throughout their bedroom, readjusting things, which needed no adjustment in the first place. His mother finally picked up the item in the room that they were both avoiding. The most valued piece. It was a framed photograph of Reggie, their only child. It had been sitting by itself on top of a long, sleek mahogany bureau. Dashawna sat down on the bed and trained her eyes on the picture. Suddenly the circling ceased.

"What's wrong?" Reginald's father, Earvin, asked with his eyes still tied to the wall across the room. "...He *is* different."

"If he's different there too..." Dashawna replied.

Earvin was finally able to turn and face his wife.

He spoke in safe, gentle terms. "Shawn...he will be. And you know what? Sometimes our strengths are also our weaknesses. It works the other way too. He is our son. He was chosen for this. You know, people..."

Earvin put his hand out softly.

Dashawna delicately handed him the framed photograph.

It was Reggie's school picture. His plaid shirt, with red and light blue stripes, accented his individuality. His grand smile, with gaps in his teeth, accented his innocence. His even-toned skin would make that finished mahogany bureau jealous.

Earvin's connection to Reggie's face in the picture could not be broken. His large ebony hands held the frame delicately, but it did not wiggle. His wiry arms gave more than ample support to the most prized possession in the room. As Earvin observed the innocent boy in the picture, he pushed forward, "People who are great... who are unique... special...just aren't liked by everybody."

The hardest reality for a parent to accept, isn't it? Coming to terms with the fact that anyone would *ever* see your child as an outcast. It's not in the parenting cookbook is it? I'm tearing up now just to think. I don't have kids. I think the Mister and I were so busy taking care of others, we figured it would take away from the whole production. Sometimes I think, *What would it be like?* And then the image of that day comes into my mind. Darlin', it's one thing you can be sure of...your babies will always be your babies, even when you can't hold 'em and protect 'em from the world anymore.

"He doesn't have to go where *anybody* doesn't like him!" Dashawna cursed, dropping her protective shell. "He doesn't have to go anywhere." Tears pushed heavy on her eyes as she turned away.

"He does, Shawn. You know the truth."

"Reg told your brother he wouldn't be coming back, except to visit once a year."

Earvin laughed lightly. "He's just really excited about this. He'll be coming back more often than that." Earvin handed Dashawna a tissue.

She dabbed a tear in the corner of her eye. "I know. Or I'll go right up there and drag him here again!"

They laughed.

"He'll drop in twice a year," Earvin winked.

"Earv, I'll lock him in this house!"

Earvin took the tissue from Dashawna and wiped her cheek. Then he returned the picture to the bureau. Back to the way it was...letting it stand on its own. "Neither of us wants him wandering around his whole life, trying to figure out who he is."

"We don't," Dashawna agreed, with both of her hands resting flatly on her lap.

"You'll take that job opening in Colorado and we'll be around all of your relatives again."

Dashawna gave a stuffed up laugh. "Ha! You're excited about that now?"

Earvin put his hands on Dashawna's shoulders and gave them a playful wiggle. Then he ducked down to meet her face to face with a wide smile. "I'm excited for *you*. Everything don' always gotta be about me. We came here for me. We'll go back for you."

"Reg seems a little twisted about leavin' Jenny," Dashawna remarked while standing up and straightening her blouse. She walked toward the window and peered down to see if Reginald and his closest friend, his *only* friend, were making their way down the sidewalk. "Jenny...what will she do?"

Earvin slid his palms down his face. "You just keep jumpin' from one thing to the next to worry about."

Dashawna's lips relinquished a smile, but she didn't lose focus. She craned her neck to sneak a further peek up the street.

VII

The two leaves lost their connection. Once dangling from the high branch of the tallest tree in the playground, they now fluttered and swayed through the air...in different directions.

"We aren't ever going to see each other again! We can dead that issue right now! I don't care where you go! We're not going to be apart, but together. We're never gonna be anything...so you can just start walkin'!" Jenny stood over Reggie as her heart poured over the pavement. Her desperate tears would not evaporate under the fire of her eyes.

Reggie could only stare at the ground while his heart was being stretched from his chest. He wished he could push out more. "I don't know what to say."

"You're talkin' a whole lot for someone who doesn't know what to say! Who is she?"

Jenny rose up over Reggie even further, but she was still able to tie his eyes straight onto hers. "How are you going to remember me? You don't even know my name! You just start walkin', 'cause I don't care! I don't care who she is. I'm going to learn about her." Jenny's finger swung in front of Reggie's eyes as her body lowered down in front of his face. She would make *sure* her message was hitting home.

Reggie's silence seemed like a self-incrimination. And in his soul, he felt a swirling anxiety, which he knew this moment would not cure. Reggie felt no guilt, but he didn't feel good...for his worst fear was taking shape right in front of him. He had made a mistake and there was no turning back now.

"I'm going to learn about her. I'm going to get to know her inside and out. You'll be gone, and I'm going to be her worst enemy! And you're going to hear about it! You're going to remember *my* name! You will *never* see me again. And you can put *that* in a letter and mail it to yourself!"

Jenny ripped up the letter and threw it at Reggie. Then she sprinted down the street and dashed down a nearby alley. Reggie stared solemnly at the ground. Motionless.

As Jenny ran, her arms were pumping and her legs were driving, but her lips only released short, crisp whisper breaths, *woo, woo, woo.* When she exited the alley, she swept around the corner with her white backpack barely clinging to her shoulders.

In little time, she had swooshed down the sidewalk, and up the steps to her front door. But what was there to win from this race? Where was the finish line? It couldn't have mattered less to Jenny, who made it from the front porch to her second floor bedroom, in one fluid motion, as if she were skating on ice.

"Jenny!" her mother called from the back porch. There was no answer. Only stillness. "Jenny?" Not a single floorboard creaked... not a drape whispered. Her mother didn't need her to answer, though. Because mothers *always* know...don't they?

40

VIII

Jane was a few feet past the entrance to the CocoWalk when her back pocket vibrated. She used her thumb and three fingers to slide her cell phone from its snug placement. Then she raised it up to eye level. There was a text from Rollo, which read, "Hit me up."

Jane scrolled through her contacts and tapped on Rollo's name to call him. Five rings sounded off, one by one, by one, by one, by one. If Jane was calling back anyone else, she would've hung up before the third ring.

Rollo finally answered.

"Jane Frost," he stated in a tone of professionalism mixed with controlled excitement.

Rollo had a big belly, which you could hear in the throat of his deep, raspy voice. His alluring dark skin would draw you in. Dark brown eyes, broad nose, full lips. Had a grin that could light up a room, nestled in a full black beard that could give midnight a run for its money. Bold, round hands...down for whatever. His body gave the impression he had done a lot of sittin' around, but you could tell them mitts had handled a thing or two. Sunglasses at night. A smooth brother. Always a group of his sidekicks circling around him too.

"What's goin' on, Snowman?" Jane mused.

"Jane."

"You need to talk fast, 'cause my cell's about to die."

"Jane."

"Yeees."

Rollo repositioned himself on the couch. His seven sidekicks drew closer to his phone.

"Do you know what my hat is doin'?" Rollo rhetorically bantered. "It's hangin' on the hat rack, Jane. Do you know the part of the song, *Frosty the Snowman*, where it goes, *Frosty is a fairy tale, they say*? That's gonna be true for me, if you don't come wit it. I'm going to be the fairy tale, Jane!"

"Yeah, come wit it, Jane!" Rollo's right-hand 'kick interjected, before starting up the *Two-Step*.

Rollo's sidekicks were little people, between four and five feet tall, and they were always gettin' in his business. One of the sidekicks joined the other in doing the *Two-Step*. The rest of the coterie were triggered into doing the *Cabbage Patch*.

"Come wit it, and bring that snow!" the first sidekick repeated as the whole sidekick posse deteriorated into the *Whip and Nae Nae*, which morphed into an unsynchronized, frenzied version of the *Macarena*.

Finally, all seven sidekicks were dancing around Rollo and his couch, chorusing, "*Come wit it, and bring that snow, come wit it and bring that snow!*" Global anarchy had broken out in a split second. Actually, living room anarchy. But to Rollo it might as well have been the same thing.

Rollo gave his 'kicks the *calm down* look.

That didn't work.

Then he tried to wave them away aggressively. But they were already hyped to a new level.

Jane was entertained by listening to the circus in the background. Her main source of pleasure was picturing Rollo in a distressed state, trying to make his point amidst the circling hysteria.

"Rollo," Jane called out calmly.

"C'mon Jane. Snap out of it, man."

"Rollo, I can't stir up a big blizzard just for three big lumps of snow and seven little snow bunnies."

All of the dancing came to a halt.

One of the sidekicks reached over Rollo, trying to pry the phone from his grip. "Who she callin' a *snow bunny?*"

The rest of the team chimed in, "Yeah, we ain't no snow bunnies! We ain't no snow bunnies!"

Jane decided to needle Rollo for further amusement. "I told you not to be putting me on speaker!"

"You're not...I didn't!" Rollo defended himself in desperation. "Git!" Rollo snipped as he whacked the sidekicks away. "You holdin' out. That *is* wrong, Jane."

"I'll be in touch. Stay cool, brother."

"B-b-b Jane!"

"Rollo."

"Yeah?"

Jane paused for effect. "Keep your scarf on."

"But I don't have a—"

Jane cut the call.

Rollo slunk down in his sofa. "Cold."

Jane had walked all the way back to her car.

She slipped her phone back into her rear pocket. Then she slid her legs down into the driver's seat of her SL 65, pressed the ignition button, and pulled out.

The orange sun brightened the sky behind her as she exited downtown Miami.

Yet, while the sun was setting on Jane's first excursion, it definitely wasn't setting on her day. A peek into her rear-view mirror revealed a sharp black luxury sports car, which seemed to be tracking her. This wasn't hard to decipher, what with the swarm of sport bikes trailing the sleek, black two-seater. Zzzzzeerm! Zzzeerm! Brrrmmm! Jane didn't need clarity on the situation. If she did, there was nowhere to turn off to see if the pursuit was a real one anyway. She was on a straightaway, with the Florida swamps on either side, and the next exit five miles away.

Jane kicked her Benz into the next gear, hoping she could shake free of the swarming vehicles. Her wheels kicked up a cloud of dust and loose pebbles that backed off the weaving sports bikes, but the jet-black supercharged nightmare of a luxury car still had a bead on her.

It didn't take long for Jane to hit eighty miles per hour. She was one mile from the nearest exit, but two of the black sport bikes had reached the rear wheel on her driver's side. At first glimpse, she could see their black helmets. She didn't have time to make out their faces.

Jane refocused on the road and quickly arrived at the exit. Errrr! Her wheels gripped hard on the loose asphalt. The two side-hugging motorbikes zipped past, unable to make the turn in time. However, the black sports car tore in behind Jane while the rest of the speed bikes flanked it like wings extending from a vulture.

Jane veered into a back-road, which digressed from granular asphalt, into a sandy, rocky, *used-to-be road*. None of the vehicles had traction now. They all began slithering from one side to the other. Within seconds, Jane had led the chase into an alley running between an abandoned warehouse and an empty, deteriorating parking garage. The sandy beige of the off-the-track ghost town was only cut by Jane's flashy white Benz and the black bullets chasing her.

Scooting down a side street within the contained quarters of the compound gave Jane the opportunity to shake free. She upshifted, and began to race in and out of the shadows cast by the withering structures. When a few bikes reappeared, she reached out with her palm extended behind her, and sprayed a cold blast in front of them.

"Mist?" she uttered in disappointment. "Come. On with this place!"

Where the sunlight shone through, Jane's mist shot straight up from the ground, sending two motorbikes on kamikaze slides in opposite directions of the complex.

"Okay," Jane stated in relief. "I'll take that."

One rider dove off his bike before it smashed into a wall. CRASH! The other rider regained her balance, but she was redirected up the parking garage ramp.

Where there were areas of shade, Jane's spray formed ice. Three of the bikes raced onto separate ice patches. They immediately hit the ground, before skidding sideways and smashing together, in a calamity of twisted metal, broken mirrors, and shredded rubber.

In the dusty rearview mirror, Jane could see the black luxury sports car was far behind, but a six-pack of identical black compact cars joined in on the attack from the bottom level of one of the buildings.

Jane shook her head. "Okay, you got jokes?"

Bumper Cars Gone Crazy ensued!

With one of the compacts accelerating toward her from head on, Jane slammed on the brakes and rode full throttle in reverse. She backed up around a pillar, causing a chasing compact to clip the side of another chasing mini. Plastic flew when the two cars broadsided pillars in opposite directions.

The black sports car reappeared. But Jane didn't need her mirror to see it. She could feel the black shadow closing in. She mashed the gas pedal to escape, but two compacts came from opposite sides, trying to squeeze her.

In and out, the carnival carried on as weaving cars moved forward and in reverse, navigating the entire complex with reckless abandon. Eventually, the jet-black two door and the squad of remaining compacts forced Jane up the spiral ramp of the parking garage.

"No, no no no," Jane pleaded.

Around and around they went, one turn after another.

Jane searched for another way out. She pushed the button to retract the hardtop roof of her 65. While the roof was folding back into the trunk, she pulled her foot off the gas, put the car in neutral, leaned back, and stuck one of her boots onto the armrest. Then she pushed herself up, and began to climb out of the convertible. SLAM! Jane's car was rammed from behind by the black sports car. But Jane continued to claw her way upward.

She moved one boot on top of her seat and the other onto the headrest. Somehow, she was able to stand upright and balance herself as her car was banged and thrust upward around the curving incline. SCREE-EE-EE-EEECH! The scraping sound of Jane's car being pressed against the walls of the tight ramp sent high-pitched metallic screams through the spiraling cylinder.

Jane was in a bad spot, standing on the seat of her car, until she seized the opportunity to jump onto the concrete ledge of the level above. She grabbed a railing and started to climb up the interior of the garage. The pursuing vehicles savagely pushed her vacated car around the spiral to the next landing. The other compact cars peeled off and ascended the ramp on the other side of the garage. In a brief moment, Jane realized that facing all of the vehicles on foot was probably a bad idea. When she looked down, she could see her car was still being charged up the curved ramp.

She closed her eyes…"Ugh!"…and dropped back into the driver's seat of her car!

Then she spontaneously hooked her car out of the ramp, onto the next level. The chasing cars missed the cut! Now, the black sports car was the only one left in pursuit. However, Jane's convertible had become coated with such a layer of dust and loose sand that her side view mirrors offered no view, and her windshield only presented a blurred image of what was in front of her. She nearly struck a pillar! ERRRR!

When the cloud of sandy dust cleared, Jane became aware that she was on the fifth level of the parking garage. She quickly chased the down-ramp arrows…descending to the fourth level, REEEACH, the third level, KAJUNG, the second level, CLACK CLACK, and then the first, before exiting into a central dirt-covered area, surrounded by the parking garage and three other abandoned building structures. Of all the right moves Jane had made during the chase, her last move…was the wrong one.

She was immediately closed in by the chasing fleet.

Dust from the furious car chase continued to billow above and throughout the surrounding buildings. Yet Jane could still make out members of the pursuing squad as they appeared from out of the withering structures on foot. Their vehicles had been lost to the pillars of the parking garage. Their racing gear was carved up. Their helmets were gashed and their face shields were cracked. Some of them limped forward. Some bared cuts and scrapes. But they *all* moved forward. Together.

I should tell you...Jane ain't one to play the role of sitting duck. Consequently, she got out of her car without hesitation, and scanned the whole scene.

Her hair was sleek with sweat.

Perspiration gathered on her forehead.

Jane breathed in, then released the air out through her pursed lips. Ebony wrapped in glowing white. That hadn't changed.

Jane's company *had changed*, however.

The bikers dismounted from their bikes and removed their helmets. The drivers stepped out of the dented doors of their compact cars. And then...

IX

One sleek leg emerged from the luxurious black sports car. A light-skinned hand wrapped around the edge of the door. Black nails tapped one by one as they met the glass outside of the driver's side window.

Another arm, draped in black pleather, slithered over the driver's side roof with an extended hand. Black-polished fingernails dug into the ridge on top of the car. A black ponytail rose up, before whipping fiercely to the side. Face down.

A second leg eased out. A glance under the long black car door exposed skinny light-toned ankles, forming a bridge between the cuff of the pants and shiny, untouched black stilettos. One step. Two steps.

Ice made a cynical announcement to her circle of followers. "Check it out, everyone…looks like Snow White has lost her way!"

Despite their mixed bag of ethnicities and backgrounds, Ice's cohorts were united in assisting Ice with whatever she had gotten herself into…no questions asked.

Ice was four years older than Jane. Her thin face and strong cheekbones guided Jane's attention to her shade-colored eyes, thick midnight lashes, and shaped eyebrows. Her poker-straight hair was wrapped tight into a ponytail, which dared for someone to make a move. Dared for someone to utter a syllable. Five foot three didn't mean a thing to Ice.

"Snow White? You know I don't like being called that," Jane clapped back.

"The chosen one," Ice taunted as her pointed stilettos took calculated steps in Jane's direction.

Jane widened her stance. "I wasn't chosen for anything."

"You're chosen now."

Ice's ponytail circled like a python.

Her long neck weaved in and out, synchronizing with the movement of her hair, as if they were one.

Jane leaned in. "That's cool. I'm glad you brought the extras."

Ice lowered her guard an inch. She strode to within a couple feet of Jane, but angled herself away slightly. She refused to make eye contact. "That's what everyone is to you."

Jane began to reason, "You were never an extra. You were always–"

"Turn up the heat on this..." Ice swung her leg toward Jane's ankles. She struck air when Jane impulsively jumped the daggered stiletto. The surrounding posse inched forward tentatively as Ice and Jane engaged in a rapid battle.

Jane swung, but Ice blocked her right hand practically before it left her side. Another swipe from Jane came as a white blur in front of Ice, who swiftly bent her torso backwards to avoid the hit.

"That's why you came," Ice spilled out, trying to release the fury burning inside of her. She thrust out a knee stab, but Jane lifted her into the air and flipped her in the opposite direction. Ice landed on her feet.

"I came? You came for me," Jane responded without losing focus.

Ice's onyx bracelet swiped millimeters from Jane's eyes, but Jane pulled her head back in time to avoid each stone as it passed by her face. The two battled relentlessly, regardless of their inability to land a direct strike. It appeared they knew every one of each other's moves before it came.

The heat began to work Jane over. Sweat flew from her face. It was as though she were fighting one against two, and the surrounding hooligans hadn't even stepped in yet. But Ice's disregard for the Florida heat created little advantage. She dropped and spun once more, before extending her palm toward Jane's feet and greasing the area around her with Florida ice. Jane's boot turned on its side and slid out from under her, but with a quick smack to her hip, she popped skate blades out from the bottom of her boots. SLINK! SLINK! Sparks were sent into the air as Jane regained her balance.

Ice closed in aggressively, paying no heed to Jane's palm extended in her direction. For good reason. Jane's effort to spray ice was futile. The ice immediately changed to drops of water and fired out as a heated, misty rain, drenching the two combatants in a murky haze. White and black strikes flashed like lightning among the expanding mist, leaving Ice's posse clouded on where or when to jump in.

Eventually, the droplets evaporated under the intense heat of the Florida sun, revealing Jane and Ice a few feet apart in a ready stance. Jane popped down her blades. Slink! Slink! An exasperated strand of her jet-black hair dropped down over her right eye.

"Forgot where you were…tryin' to play with your snow?" Ice blitzed, with measured breaths. "You been in a battle or two already, huh? Scarred that pretty little face?"

Jane's hands were still up. She had no interest in the dialogue. Her focus laid weight on Ice, who realized that she needed a second to regroup, herself.

Ice sucked in. And released. "Fighter now?" The opaque black stones in Ice's bracelet mirrored her eyes. She raised her hands and stared dauntingly through Jane.

Cunningly saved for this instant, Ice came from the left for the first time and slammed a midlevel kick straight into Jane's side. Jane went down on one knee. However, she reacted quickly and flipped flat on her back, avoiding Ice's next sharp heel, slicing by her cheekbone. With an immediate follow-up, Ice spun and lifted her knee, intending to drop the toe of her stiletto into Jane's torso. This time, Jane popped out her skate blades, bobbed, and delivered a sweeping roundhouse kick, which slashed through Ice's sleeve.

Jane let out a somewhat sincere, "Oops." But she straightened up nonetheless. She felt the need to ready herself for anything else Ice might throw at her. This proved to be a smart move.

Ice attempted a left hook, before firing off a roundhouse kick of her own. Jane dodged both. Ice gave her arm a sharp study. White strings dangled from the laceration in her black sleeve. Her skin definitely showed a mark from the impact, but there was no blood. She hunched over, gasping for air. This was *her* territory. She shouldn't have been the one sucking wind.

Ice lifted her head and narrowed her eyes at Jane...exhausted. But Ice wasn't about *the draw*. She was about *the win*. It's just that she had nothing left. It was then that she recognized her best way out was to give Jane an out.

"Go now. And take your internal demons with you," she cursed.

"I have an *external* demon..." Jane popped her blades in. Slink! Slink! "...but I'm not taking *her* with me."

Ice had no comeback. Her stunned posse opened a path for Jane, revealing Jane's banged-up Benz. This provided the opportunity for a few of Ice's antagonists to, at least, get in a little jeering from the shadows. Perhaps this could be a small victory for them to go home with.

Jane reached her palm out, and stretched her right arm high over the left side of her body. Then she ripped down, icing the shadowed roughnecks from their waists to their toes.

While holding her injured arm, Ice shouted across the battle-field of mangled bikes, cars, and bruisers, "Don't you have enough already? You need to be here?"

She let her arm hang limply.

Ice intended to drop the last hammer. However, the tone of her grand final statement came across as more meek than imposing. Cringing at the sound of her own weak counter, she balled up her fists and engaged Jane once more.

The cowards became aware that Ice was setting up for round two. They began to close the opening they provided for Jane. They were definitely coming for her this time.

In the brief moment Jane took to consider her options, Ice slipped in and the sparring began again. Jane popped out her skate blades and snap kicked two of Ice's posse members. UGH! OOF! They went flying!

Ice opened her palm to slick the ground, but Jane's blades grinded down, sending flashes through the air. This gave Jane the stability to lock in on two more ruffians rotating in on her. She knocked one off his feet with a right hook, and buckled the other with a knee to the midsection. Jane sucked in deep. The day's final rays of sunlight stretched shadows from the feet of her adversaries. This battle had carried on far longer than any of the parties expected.

Meanwhile, Ice was limited. She tried to keep her injured arm out of Jane's reach by working with her feet instead of her hands. The strategy was working. She used her spiked stiletto to take Jane's skate blades out from under her. From one knee, Jane grabbed Ice's other foot and twisted. But a follow up wheeling kick from Ice smoked past Jane's eyes, forcing her to let go of the stiletto pinwheeling in her palm.

Jane spun back to her feet.

And the two squared up again.

Jane was dripping with sweat. Only now did she realize that a setting Florida sun was still something to be reckoned with.

"Yep," Ice agreed, shifting from side to side with swagger.

Jane was low on tricks and on her last leg with the heat. This was it. She repositioned herself and smacked her hip. Slink! Slink! With her blades retracted, Jane weaved in close. POUND! SWIPE! In two quick moves, Ice was down. Jane took another step forward and stood over her.

Drips of Jane's sweat descended onto her fallen opponent.

Ice's posse timorously waited in the wings, unable to even think of faking a response. They sagged back. They knew better. Drip. Ice's face was smudged with dirt, but her intentions were crystal clear. Drip...drip. But she wasn't getting up from this.

Jane exhaled. Then she looked down onto Ice with the last word, "You should take a break. I think you're getting burnout."

Ice gave no response. She was back to passing up on eye contact as well.

Jane walked in the direction of her car. No counter.

She felt all eyes on her as the gravel crunched under her boots. But Jane didn't look back. She opened the door of her car, got in, and pushed a button to power the roof shut on her convertible. Then she ignited the engine and drove away.

Ice's posse began to man their dented vehicles, but the defeated scowl on Ice's face told them they weren't going to follow. They were all relieved. They didn't want another round. Instead, they watched Jane's license plate, "*32-F*," as it became increasingly faint, behind the whipped-up sand from her tires.

Jane passed a billboard, which read, "*Thank You For Visiting Miami. Hurry Back!*" Her eyes rolled. "Yeah, right."

She made a turn and cruised down a long, straight suburban road. Jane finally had a chance to ease off the gas. It was quiet. She could hear the granular pebbles crackling under her tires as her wheels made easy rotations toward a cul-de-sac at the end of a new housing development construction site. Too subdued for Jane, maybe? She gunned the car for fun, ran it hard, and spun it into a hard one-eighty at the end of the road. ERRREEEACH! The dust rose. She felt a release. And then, for a sliver of time…no.

A sound arose from the opposite end of the street. If it was another vehicle, it would have to be coming from straight away, because there were no crossing streets to that leg of the new development. There was only one way in. Only one way out.

The shells of unfinished houses stretched all the way down the street and horseshoed around the semi-circle pavement, capturing, and reverberating the sound of a truck rumbling closer. Pap! Rattle! Bump! Heavy chains clanked against the metal of the vehicle, which maintained its momentum as it progressed straight down the center of the road.

Jane stepped out of her combat-weary car. The noise of the truck increased in volume. She had a keen awareness as to what was going on around her, but she stood with her back to the approaching machine nonetheless. Jane ran her hand against her neck and lifted her hair up to let the air in. Then she turned halfway in the direction of the approaching truck. Sturdy. From her shoulders…to her belt…down to the soles of her boots. Not a wrinkle. Jane waited.

The last sliver of sunlight was erased, allowing the blue color of a virgin dusk to seize control of the sky. With the glare removed, the approaching vehicle became clearly visible. It was a flatbed tow truck. It slowed. Then stopped. Five men jumped out, bolted to Jane's car, and surrounded it. Simultaneously, Jane knifed between them, dashed into the nearby woods, and vanished...leaving the five men alone with her SL 65.

Working together like a pit crew, the men jacked up the car and replaced the tires on the battered Benz. ZIRRR! ZIRRR! SS! SS! ZIRRR! ZIRRR! SS! SS! They wiped the car over with urgency and shined it up to the best of their ability, before pulling a clear plastic film off the windshield, and releasing the jacks back down.

One of the crew members caught a glimpse of the hole in the dash, which once held a radio. He pulled the others in close and showed it to them. They all peeked their heads into the car at the same time. A tire iron rested on the passenger seat. Dusty sand was sprayed throughout the interior. They were perplexed, to say the least. *What in the name?*, they wondered. After standing there scratching their heads, sharing twisted expressions, the team shrugged indifferently and resumed their work. Knowing Jane, they weren't even going to try to piece that one together. They craned their necks to take a look around for her. But she was nowhere in sight.

"Take it away?" a crew member asked.

"Take 'er away," the leader confirmed.

Two of the men hooked a chain to the Benz. Another member of the crew hit a button, which pulled the car onto the flatbed of the tow truck. From the tow truck's cabin, the crew lifted out an immaculate white tarp. They carefully kept it from touching the ground as they stretched it over Jane's car and secured it. Then they jumped into the truck, turned out of the cul-de-sac, and sped away... taking their only way out.

Jane was already deep in the woods, running hard. Her open hands slashed through the air, initiating a breeze, which cooled her. As she paused within a collection of tall pine trees, large black crows swooped down and latched onto her arms, four to a side. The crows slowly pinched their sharp claws into her jacket...continuing to do so...millimeter by millimeter, simultaneously with each fraction of time she waited. Yet she felt no pain. She even lifted her arms up and stretched them out to observe her new company. You see, Jane felt a belonging to the woods...and in that way the crows respected *her spot*...as she respected theirs.

She tore ahead fiercely once more.

Jane's arms pumped aggressively, forcing the crows to extend their wings, release their claws, and lift up vertically among the infinitely rising pines. After a few more hard strides, she lined up a jump and performed a hard rip twist like a figure skater. POOF! Jane whipped and weaved as a snow squall until eventually dissipating into the darkness of the woods. Not even the night could find her now.

X

Jenny sat alone at her desk in her bedroom. She was solemn for a girl who was putting the finishing touches on a picture of her dream mansion. It was elegant and white, with columns and large crosshatch windows...all artistically highlighted with a cerulean blue colored crayon. Jenny was good at putting her dreams on paper. No doubt, she was an artist. By personality, skill...by her emotions.

Everyone has a part of his or her mind that dreams or invents. Get these ideas...visions that run through our heads. We try to process them. Tell people about them. Maybe get some feedback. But we don't always express our ideas in the clearest manner, do we? Sometimes people don't know what the heck we're talking about. But an artist...you can envision their dream, if you pay attention. You can see what they're saying in their work. In their paintings, sculptures, or whatever it is they create. It's in the lines, the shapes... *they* tell the story. You can learn from an artist's strokes...from the things they put their hands on. *Watch*.

Jenny reached for a sky blue crayon, and began drawing snowflakes on her picture. She started at the top and continued to add more until they stretched all the way down to the bottom of the paper. With each snowflake drawn, Jenny felt a greater comfort. Sadly, those snowflakes seemed to be her only friends in the world. And on that day, those new friends could only offer a quickly fading solace.

Jenny put the sky blue crayon back into the box and pulled out a denim color. She drew wavy lines that came to a point–icicles which hung from the roof of the mansion. Soon after, she drew more icicles hanging from the windows.

Jenny could think now. She could try to make sense of all the events which had occurred that day. She found warmth in what was cold for the moment. But then she looked out of her window again. There she saw a different kind of cold. One that had nothing to do with the temperature.

She sang to herself,

> *"A bird needs a nest,*
> *An actor: a stage,*
> *Yet, sometimes we all need to-*
> *Turn the page.*
>
> *A bike needs two wheels,*
> *A playground: a swing,*
> *Sometimes we all need to believe-*
> *In something.*
>
> *Angels don't do for show,*
> *They don't judge how you go,*
> *But they're walking right beside you,*
> *Look just like us I know.*

It's things like this I see,
For me that's enough,
Someone's looking over us."

Jenny put down her crayon.

"Blue needs the ocean,
White needs a dove,
At birth in the night–
A baby needs love.

Hope needs a saint,
A bouquet needs to be caught,
We need to keep giving–
What cannot be bought."

Reggie pried himself from the bench. It was hard for him to walk away. You know, a piece of him wanted to sit there forever. But he didn't have trouble grasping the blowout that occurred. It *was* his worst fear. Reggie could tell you he foresaw this scenario. That there was actually a high probability to it. Since that day, he would never trust anyone to handle *any part* of his personal business again. Good doesn't always come from bad, but as sure as *true* is to The North, Reggie became a stronger leader that day.

He grabbed the cuffs of his shirt and pulled them over his wrists. His shoulders sagged. Reggie was truly heartbroken. He didn't need to second guess. Had it to do over again, he would've done it differently. Still talks about it.

As Reggie left the playground, he sang to himself,

"Santa's warm heart–
Still yearns for the snow,
We need to have faith,
That's what I know.

It's things like this I see,
For me that's enough,
Someone's looking over us."

As if connected on the oscillating wings of uncertainty, Reggie's and Jenny's visions wove together in synchronized clarity,

"Open your hands,
And open your heart,
Every finish line–
Still needs a start.

Apologies need mistakes,
A stamp: A letter,
A child needs a hospital,
So they can get better.

A prayer needs a bible,
Tracks beg for a train,
Ornaments need a tree,
Cobblestones crave a lane."

Jenny placed her fingertips delicately onto the ledge of the window as she gazed into the empty sky.

She wondered aloud,

"When someone leaves,
What does it mean?
Does it mean they don't love you?
'Cause that's how it seems."

Reggie was almost home. He folded his hands in front of himself as he pondered,

"Do they know why you go?
Will they let you back in?
Do they know how you're torn?
How your heart is breaking?"

Jenny's left hand released from the windowsill and led her to the corner of her bed.

"Cause my heart is breaking."

At last, Reggie's and Jenny's voices synchronized one last time,

"Sometimes I believe–
Even in what I can't see,
And I do believe,
Someone's looking over us."

Jenny folded her hands in her lap and closed her eyes. She sat alone in her room, with only her thoughts and her song,

"...And I do believe,
Someone's looking over me..."

Jenny finished her picture. A magnificent blue and white mansion sat prominently on a snowy hill. Snow-covered pine trees populated the landscape as though they naturally grew there. Reindeer gathered at the lower right-hand corner of the picture while a fedora-wearing snowman stood slightly left of center, encircled by seven little rabbits. The majestic double-entry doors were attended by two butlers...one on each side.

"Mom! Mommy?" Jenny sparked.

"Yes?" Jenny's mom called up from the bottom of the steps.

"I need a red crayon!"

"What do you need that for, Snowflake?"

Jenny's mom had an easing tone to her voice. Sweet. That *everything's gonna be alright* sweet. Calm you to look at her too. Earth-toned, patterned scarf wrapped around her hair, blending seamlessly with her light skin. Vibrant clothing that glided along with her movements. Tiny thing, she was. But strong too. She could set the table *and* tell you where to sit. *Yes sir,* like that.

"Red for the lead reindeer's nose, so he can guide Santa's sleigh this year!" Jenny enthusiastically explained.

Her mom arrived at the top of the stairs with a laundry basket attached to her hip.

She popped her head into Jenny's room and lightly stated, "Jenny, you can't believe *everything* you read in books." Then she continued down the hallway, leaving Jenny to handle the rest of *that* problem on her own.

Jenny crossed her arms and wrinkled her face. "Hm."

She sagged down in her chair and blew upward, parting a few strands of hair drooping over her eye. She scanned her bedroom... all the wheels churning in her brain. Closed her eyes tight...thinking...thinking...

Then she got up, walked over to her door, shut it, and sighed.

XI

SASKATCHEWAN, CANADA

Jane blasted into Andre Branch's realty office. When people interacted with Andre Branch, they were sure they were getting consistency. Consistent slick talking, consistent brashness, and consistent self-indulgence. Can't lie about that, although I'd like to. Oh, you could trust him all right. Trust he had an agenda, and he was going to stick to it with zero deviation. If his agenda met your needs, then you had the right guy, complete with a snazzy suit.

Jane recognized a gathering of customers as soon as she walked in, so she muted herself by edging over to a rack of pamphlets on the side of the room. She flipped through Andre's propaganda, waiting for the last couple to leave. She crossed and uncrossed her feet. She paced. She anxiously surveyed the street from the storefront window. She peered down at her wrist to check the time even though she wasn't wearing a watch. Seemed like the wait was forever, but it was five minutes at most. Finally, Andre flashed his cheesy smile at his last set of customers, before thanking them with a nice, hearty *howdy neighbor* wave as they exited his store. Jing-a-ling-ling!

What a relief! Jane exclaimed in her head. Then she raised a hand and extended it, palm out, toward the wall of scintillating literature, which she had been forced to peruse for all too long. Andre stood behind the front counter, about ten feet from Jane, knowing he was too far away to stop her, but close enough to get encapsulated in the potentially pending havoc.

He threatened her, "Don't do it! I'll take a picture, post it online, and they're going to hate the ice and snow even more! I'm only giving the people the opportunity to embrace the *sunshine* and *warmth* that they love and crave." His snarky tone cascaded over his message like a polluted river over bedrock.

Jane held her position, but redirected her energy toward Andre's desk. It was covered in stacks of manila folders stuffed with brochures and documents—all begging to be organized. Paper trays were stacked five high on each side of the counter, filled with dog-eared papers and taped on sticky notes. Three mugs with dried coffee stains acted as paperweights for the pieces of paper deemed *most important.*

"Maybe I'm just going to have to start taking *your* customers away from *you*," Jane charged back.

"How are you going to do that?"

"If the planes can't leave the runways, people can't make their little realtor visits with you, to your little '*Turn your sunny vacation into your everyday destination*' spots...or your '*It's grand in the sand*' condos, or your '*It's greater at the equator*' communities...or your, your..."

"Reading my works, are you?" Andre proudly remarked.

"I'll cover the roads too!" Jane lashed.

"Ms. Frost, if you *selfishly* do something to *freeze* them out, you're going to drive them to me even faster," Andre sneered. The phone rang. "Let me take this."

"Mr. Branch!" LaQuinn bounced excitedly.

LaQuinn was Andre's *fabulous* secretary at his Miami office. He talked with his hands and vibrantly manicured fingernails, even if nobody could see him through the phone.

"Quinn!" Andre pompously championed, trying to blow his hot air of importance across Jane's face.

"I have good news!" LaQuinn bubbled over, "The Jensens signed the paper woooork!"

"Already?"

"Already, honey lamb!"

"You did it, Quinn! You brought them home!"

Andre pumped his fist and hopped with both feet.

LaQuinn batted his eyes, "Like a stork brings a baby, *my dear!*"

Andre flipped from hot to cold. He was confused *and* nervous. He was nervously confused. "Who's having a baby?" Sweat formed on Andre's forehead as his shirt soaked clear through. The phone slid down his clammy hand.

Jane grabbed a large gingerbread man paperweight from the side of Andre's desk and SLAMMED it down in front of him.

Andre snapped out of his trance. "Uh, LaQuinn, I gotta go. Keep makin' that money." Andre hung up the phone and motioned toward the paperweight. "Careful with that."

"Why are you doing this?" Jane questioned earnestly. She carefully placed the paperweight back on the desk. "What is it you truly don't like about the ice and snow? Hasn't done anything to you."

"It's…cold. Ms. Frost, NOBODY likes the cold."

Andre's four secretaries wove into the room from different directions. They swirled up to the front desk and arranged themselves
side by side behind Andre. Their big hair flowed out in natural
curls, framing their gorgeous smiles and jeweled glitter makeup.
Their diverse shades of brown skin proudly co-authored their glitzy,
gold outfits. Tube tops and short shoulder-padded jackets glamor-
ously reflected the realty office's recessed lights, while glittery gold
biker shorts set off the secretaries' long legs. The final detail...dainty
white tennis shoes, which dotted the "i" on the cute-as-a-button
performers, who slipped in to provide Andre's backup.

With the ladies in place, Andre began rapping,

"Amped up, Plug heat in? No need for that,
I send 'em right where the sun is at,
I'm doin' seventy-five to ninety on your thirty-two,
Paintin' yellow and green on your white and blue,

I'm a turn 'em over to The Source of course,
'Cause I'm the type that will find ya flaws,
I'll take 'em to the heat, bathe 'em in the warmth,
Pull up a seat, I'm a tell ya what they want..."

Thirty Broadway Dancers appeared out of nowhere and the roof
lifted off the office, as the intimate hip hop club set blossomed into
a grandiose Broadway Musical extravaganza! Andre was swept up
in the histrionics, but he would not be remiss in showing Jane the
scoreboard...

"Lotion on, we poppin' an umbrella for shade,
Now you left out in the sun, like a Maf' gettin' made,
Good or bad, who's who? I'm the one who planned it,
You mad, you blue, and I'm the gold standard,"

In Miami, LaQuinn was putting on a glam production of his own. He was backed by three latina dancers dressed in electric-orange tube tops and shorts. They followed their dance routine with a passion. Child, we could be surprised they didn't hurt nobody! And Janey couldn't do a thing, but just watch for awhile, 'cause Andre was straight on a roll.

"You act like a castaway, playin' runaway,
You a pro-fess-ion-al at takin' fun away,
You feelin' a certain way, I'm feelin' a certain pay,
Your distance is a disadvantage, now you dismayed,

Put that ice on ice, save the white for the rice,
I'm a sell 'em a place, where it's hot in the nights,
You gonna step to me? Betta step gently,
No need to be gettin' scratches on the Bentley,

Keep the lawn chairs out, deer in the stable,
'Cause the paperwork's in, deal's on the table,
I showed 'em the beach bash, they showed me the cash,
And I'll be out, 'fore the whole thing crash!
And I'll be out, 'fore the whole thing crash!
And I'll be out..."

Glitter fell from above as multi-colored streamers shot across the air, overtop of the *over-the-top* entertainers. Next, Carnival dancers pranced through wearing large jeweled headdresses and feathers that accentuated their bright cheery faces.

Not to be outdone, Andre's four secretaries stepped into the spotlight and started singing,

> *"It's gettin' chilly, we got your place,*
> *No need for boots or a fireplace,*
> *It's gettin' chilly, no time to waste,*
> *Now, come on down and don't be late,"*

The whole office was turned inside out. Soon after, Andre looped back in to take center stage again.

> *"It's the heat, yeah I'm bringin' it,*
> *In the spot, 'cause I'm king of it,*
> *Temp drop? Not thinkin' it,*
> *Jam hot? They all singin' it,*
>
> *I'm cruisin' Pacific Coast, you runnin' through woods,*
> *You deliverin' promises, I'm deliverin' goods,*
> *We eatin' like royals, move over, pass the pasta!*
> *Now catch me, if you can...catch a monster!"*

Jane had shown a masterful amount of self-control throughout the bizarre theatrical production, but she finally lost it when one of the Carnival performers breezed by and gleefully whacked her on the fanny. Once again, Jane sized up the disarray, which was Andre's desk. She put her hands on top of his manila file folders and began frantically swishing them around, catching other loose papers in the swirling mélange as she swiped.

"If. You. Can't. Find. Your. Records. You just. Won't be able to. Get in touch with…" Jane panted.

"Oh! Oh! Oh! Oh!" Andre cried. He was unsuccessful at guarding his folders from Jane's frantic frenzy. Each swipe by Jane, got another "Oh!" from Andre. But he couldn't block her or deter her from the other side of his desk.

All the more I can say is…THE CHASE WAS ON!

The Broadway extravaganza quickly dispersed when Andre launched himself over his desk in an attempt to preserve what was left of his cockamamie organizational system. Jane swung back and spun.

She serendipitously caught a glimpse of the wall full of brochures behind her.

"Stoooooop!" Andre cried in anticipation of Jane's next move. He reached for Jane. But in a crazy turn, she came to a complete stop. Her frenzy had left her in a near breathless state. Andre paused with hope. But wait! She wasn't stopping.

"Noooooooooo!" Andre pleaded as Jane brushed her arms over the shelves of propaganda. Brochures fired off in every direction. "Aaaaaaaah!"

It was a pandemonium of pamphlets!

Andre eventually edged around the corner of the desk with Jane lined up as his target, but his foot landed on a brochure, and his left leg slid sideways. He flopped onto his hip, propelling his left hand onto another pamphlet. WHAP! He dove toward Jane from the floor. Jane tried to spin out of the way, but she was brought to the ground when she slipped on an adjacent lake of glossy leaflets. WHAP!

With neither of them able to find proper footing, they both rose up onto their knees. There was nothing solid or stable they could use to get back on their feet. This brought the crazy flourish to a standstill once more. Jane was hot, literally. Now, I know what you're thinking. *Why wouldn't she just cool herself off at a moment like this?* We all used to wonder that. But we all know the answer now. When Jane was mad, she didn't *want* to be cooled off. And there she was, sweating and struggling to pull herself together, with her long black hair covering the side of her face. She brushed her hair aside with the back of her hand, but a part of her wouldn't have cared if it stayed. She could stare daggers through Andre either way.

"BRING IIIIT!" she screamed.

Andre had no response for that. To be honest...he was even a little bit scared. Ha!

Jane took a breath. "You mean to tell me, with all your talent for closing deals..."

Andre was dripping with sweat too. He used the sleeve of his sport coat to wipe his forehead, but his vexed state caused the beads of perspiration to quickly resurface.

Jane pressed on, "You could sell almost anything to anyone..."

"...could sell Father Time a wristwatch," Andre lauded. He never missed an opportunity to praise himself, regardless of the situation.

"Could sell *anything anywhere*..." Jane continued, gasping for air.

"...could sell a toy to an elf at the North Pole," Andre proudly attested with heavy breaths.

"...but you want to sell warm places to *cold weather people*." Jane paused. "Why?"

"Because that's the thing I can do to make the MOST MONEY!"

Andre reached over his desk with both hands, grabbed a glass of water, and put it up to his mouth. Before he could take a drink,

Jane froze the water. Andre held the glass upside down and shook it. Nothing came out. He angled his head sideways, trying to lick the inside of the glass, but failed to lap up any relief.

By now, the Broadway Show had long since been vacuumed from the room. Andre's four secretaries were back in their business suits…and their big hair…well, it was just a bit smaller now.

Andre broke off his futile chase. "Ms. Frost, why don't *you* do something different?"

"I am going to do something different," Jane confirmed. She recognized she wasn't accomplishing much with the whole *Andre fracas* anyway. She pulled herself to her feet.

Jane carefully navigated her way through the minefield of brochures on her way to the door. It seemed, with a flip of a switch, she had removed herself from the whole event. Maybe not. She spontaneously re-engaged Andre by opening a palm toward him. She sent an ice-cold shot at his hands from across the room, freezing them to the brochures he was picking up.

Andre raised both of his hands, affirming that each one had a pamphlet frozen to it. "Okay. That's not even funny."

Jane reached for the door handle, ready to leave somewhat satisfied.

"Jane!" Andre called in desperation.

He placed one brochure-frozen hand onto a paperless corner of his desk and propped himself up. Then he sighed as he rubbed his nose with his other *brochure hand*. Jane sauntered out the door, smirking.

Cling-jing-ling!

Andre's four secretaries could hardly contain their laughter. One of them had coffee coming out of her nose, another was under her desk crying, and the other two were making a run for the bathroom.

Andre put his *brochure hands* on his hips. "I could leave *you* in the cold!" he scowled.

The secretaries began hastily shuffling papers. They would attempt to look busy until they could regain their composure. The young ladies in the bathroom were going to wait for an "*All Clear*" text from the secretaries on the floor before returning to their cubbies. Andre avoided them all. He wasn't about to be within range of their giggles the rest of the day. He would clean up the mess on his own.

XII

It was December 18th. Jane stood on the front porch of Mother Nature's estate with her hands folded at her waist. She could hear Mother Nature's soft, but weighted footsteps move down the hallway toward the front of the house. When the front door opened, a sweetness filled the air. Jane remained there, in perfect posture.

"What can I do for you, honey?" Mother Nature asked.

"Needed to talk."

"No worries, baby, come in."

Mother Nature was a young looking woman. She had the skin of a twenty-year-old, though it was basic knowledge she had been around much longer than any of us. She was round in shape, with a soft, rich brown face, and pillowy hands. At first sight, you'd want to run into her arms and melt into one of her nice warm hugs. Her soothing vocals...they would take you away, even if you didn't totally agree with the advice she was giving you. Thing I know is—when Mother Nature speaks, you'd be right to listen.

Her home was a rancher built on rolling hills. Its construction tied together four remote directions into one central point. There was a North Wing, a South Wing, a West Wing, and an East Wing.

The home was set up like a cross, with the main portion of the rancher located directly in the center. In case you were wondering, if you ventured out of the North Wing's main door and travelled in a straight line, eventually you *would* end up at the North Pole. The other wings could be followed likewise.

Mother Nature stepped aside and led Jane into the house. From where she stood, Jane could see four glass doors, each one marking the entry to one of the wings.

"We're meeting in the North Wing, right?" Jane hesitantly asked. She knew that outside the door to the North Wing it was always winter. Consequently, she also understood that outside the South Wing door it was always summer.

Suddenly, Jane caught a glimpse of a figure flashing by the glass door of the South Wing. It was *The Source*. Just as Jane created snow and ice for the winter, The Source provided heat in the summer.

The Source was theatrical in every sense. He wore a loud plaid sport coat and a brightly patterned tie. His white shirt was the only neutral aspect to him, but he only used it to offset the colorful contrasts in the rest of his outfit, right down to his mustard-colored skinny jeans. This eccentric, energetic mid-twenties fella was indeed *The Heat Source*. We called him *The Source* for short. Nobody had time to spit out his full name, especially not with his fast talking self always babbling on. Wouldn't get it all out if you tried.

"What's *he* doing here?" Jane complained.

"He wants to show me a new trick he can do. Breathin' fire or something," Mother Nature replied.

The Source positioned himself in his self-imagined spotlight, directly in front of Jane and Mother Nature. He was only separated from them by the modern, transparent glass door to the South Wing. On his own cue, he proceeded to breathe fire through his mouth.

The glass pane immediately blackened.

And he began to scream, "Aooww! Aaah! Woo!"

The Source's mouth was burning. He pounded on the glass door, holding his tongue. Bang, bang, bang, bang!

Jane remained at peace. "Should we help him?"

Mother Nature was unphased as well. "Eh."

The Source continued his gyrations, spinning in circles like a dog trying to catch its tail, while the bottom of his sport coat flailed out around him in a cry for mercy.

"How you keep your skin lookin' so young?" Jane asked.

Mother Nature pointed to the clean white shelves in the next room, filled from floor to ceiling with equally spaced bottles of lotions, creams, butters, and oils. "All natural products, honey. The only way."

"I got you…" Jane nodded. Then she began perusing the shelves. "How's Autumn doin'?"

"She found a *new* man."

Jane chuckled, "She gave up on the King of Spring?"

"She falls, child, but she don't fall that easy!" The two of them shared a good laugh.

Meanwhile, The Source had worked himself up into a panic. The way his knees were rising up and down, he nearly tap-danced the mustard out of those skinny jeans! Moreover, his argyle socks were barely hanging onto his dress shoes through all of his, "*Ooches*" and "*Aaches*." Yet The Source's not-totally-planned demonstration continued behind the black smudges of the charcoaled glass without help from the audience.

But don't worry, Jane and Mother Nature could see enough. I mean, how could one miss The Source in that loud suit, holding his tongue with both hands as he pogo-sticked up and down?

Eventually, Mother Nature nonchalantly walked toward the South Wing entryway. She exhaled, before pressing a button, which opened the door. Pshht.

The Source barreled in, holding his mouth. Jane grabbed him by his sport coat and yanked him close to her. She put her lips within an inch of his lips. Then she supported the back of his head with her hand and breathed frigid air into his mouth. Ice vapor formed a mist between them.

The Source felt something. His mouth cooled, but heat surged through his body.

Jane felt a chill too. But it was a different kind of chill than she was used to giving others. The Source's heat waved over her, causing her jet-black hair to wetly shine.

The two of them gazed past one another as their minds drifted away in a swirling haze. They each tried pulling back, but it was to no avail. Instead, their eyes drew together once more, before blissfully closing again. Mother Nature put one finger on Jane's lips. Then she put one finger on The Source's lips...and delicately pushed the two apart.

"*Sugar, you're about to make me change my season,*" The Source sassed.

Needless to say, Jane had made quite an impression on him. But Mother Nature was losing patience. She circled in front of The Source. "Move on now. I know you got better things to do."

"Ladies," he obliged, with a curtsy and a tip of his imaginary cap. Yeah, I know. Shees. You'd have to see it, I guess. He *was* an original.

The Source shivered out a lip fluttering, "Brrrr," as he experienced the after effects of Jane's chilly breath. Nonetheless, he hastened his way back out through the South Wing door.

Honestly, he had turned the heat up on Jane a little more than she was expecting too. Yet, she *was* able to re-cool herself by delicately turning the back of her hand toward her body while guiding her fingers down her torso. Her skin showed hints of a red hue, then waved over to a cool blue, before centering on its original shade of brown.

"Come," Mother Nature directed, walking in the direction of the West Wing.

"Where are *you* goin'?" Jane questioned.

"Follow me...the West Wing."

"Spring? You told me we could meet–"

"Hush now, none of that," Mother Nature quipped.

Jane pulled back. "You too?"

"So you don't have to think about work," Mother Nature explained. Then she pressed a button to open the silver-framed West Wing door. Pshht.

"The Spring Wing," Jane muttered as she followed Mother Nature.

"Oh Jane."

"*What?*"

The West Wing door opened up to yellow wildflowers singing soothing songs of joy. As the yellows rolled freely over the broad fields at their own will, lavender wildflowers sprinkled in between to add the high notes. Mother Nature and Jane passed through the doorway and paused high on top of the hill. After taking a grand look at the life-filled landscape below them, Mother Nature inhaled a great wind of satisfaction.

Blue skies and fluffy white clouds filled the air above, ready to listen to anyone who needed to share, while the oak trees below showed an eagerness to grant their wisdom to those who needed guidance. Though the trunk of each oak held more than a thousand years of knowledge, their branches were freely extended with the youth of green leaves and budding dreams. A group of geese spread their feet and opened their wings as they began to land in that colorful place of hope and new beginnings.

"Fly south, you stinking ducks!" Jane blasted.

"Jane!" Mother Nature scolded over the ensuing sound of honking geese.

A flurry of feathers poofed into the air as the geese aborted their landing and swooped back into the sky.

"Geese. Not ducks."

"Same thing," Jane darted back, with a deadpan expression.

Mother Nature gave in to a wrinkled smile while shaking her head. She enjoyed Jane's candor, but it wouldn't stop her from thinking, *What am I going to do with her?*

Jane surveyed the fields for a spell as Mother Nature waited for the dust of Jane's last explosion to settle. Jane tried to remain composed, feeling pretty certain she was going to have to follow Mother Nature's lead if she wanted to get the answers she had come for. But to Jane, thirty seconds was a lifetime. Patience? No, she couldn't wait. Jane broke first, even though she had promised herself she wouldn't.

"So what do you think?"

Jane's upper body became rigid and her legs became weak. She began wringing her fingers. Mother Nature's wisdom...how Mother Nature felt...these were things Jane truly wanted to hear. But she wasn't sure if she really wanted to hear *all* of it. *Should* Mother Nature's response agree with her position? Or would Jane prefer to be told she was totally wrong? How was she supposed to feel after she got the answers to her questions? In either case, Jane had already opened up the dialogue, and Mother Nature wasn't about to sit there silently while Jane backed her way out of the conversation. No, that wasn't going to happen.

"What do I think about what?" Mother Nature calmly responded, pretending to be in the dark.

Jane knew she didn't have it in her to open up and tell it all. To express everything running through her mind...how she got to this point...what she was feeling. Her mind started picking up speed.

But Mother Nature bailed Jane out.

She often did.

"If it's worth buildin' up, it's worth fighting for," she counseled.

Just then, The Source trudged in from the bottom of the hill to their left, tripping over tree roots while juggling a collection of branches. Each time he took a stride, another branch began to slide out. Then he'd have to struggle to corral the sticks all over again. With both arms already occupied, he needed to use his knees to boost the pile every so often in order to make his way up the hill. But The Source didn't only come with sticks...he came with the gift of an unsolicited piece of advice as well.

"D'ya wanna know what I think?" he asked.

"My god!" Jane cringed.

Jane's level of irritation was on high, but that didn't stop The Source from huffing and puffing his way up to her, to give his opinion, "...Since you asked..."

"We didn't," Jane and Mother Nature interjected in tandem.

The Source persisted, unfazed. "Jane, they got me wearin' out. They got me doin' overload..."

"You look real busy," Jane responded sarcastically.

Mother Nature swiveled toward Jane in an attempt to support *and* hasten along The Source with his point. "We've got to have four seasons," she said sympathetically.

The Source continued, "The people…"

"The people?" Jane fired up, "Don't start talkin' about what *the people* want. The people want more heat and less snow."

"They don't know what they want," The Source chuckled. "Maybe you should go into air conditioning," he mumbled, "…if they want it hot on the outside and cool on the inside."

Jane was about to lock horns.

The Source pleaded his case. "Once the flowers bloom, they've bloomed. That's it for Spring. On the other side, fall doesn't start 'til those leaves start fallin', so Autumn waits. Speaking of leaves… that *leaves* me to cover the whole stretch in between. Now, I been coverin' that hole for as long as we can remember. But if you don't drop that snow somewhere between Autumn and Spring, people are gonna want heat and green grass for half the year! Do you know what that would do to my mental state?" he rambled.

"Your mental state can't get no worse," Jane responded dryly.

"Bye Sourcie," Mother Nature cut in, before shooing him away.

Jane popped backwards. "Sourcie?"

"A cute little name."

"He ain't cute."

"Heard that," The Source responded from just beyond the first oak tree.

Mother Nature redirected Jane, "He'll leave us alone. Come with me."

The Source carried on a conversation with himself on his way back down the slope with his pile of branches. Meanwhile, Mother Nature escorted Jane along the side of the house.

When they were clear, Mother Nature turned to Jane and spoke in her crisp, spiritual tone. "There are *forces of the mind*, and *forces of nature*…both interwoven. As much as people may try to harness them, to manipulate them…they will never be separated, hear? *Look at me, now.* People can carry out acts, which curtail the free flow of nature…build a dam…clear forests. And nature can carry out acts, which uproot humans. Such as sweepin' through with a tornado, or openin' up the ground and shakin' it to the point where *houses crumble*. Yet forces of nature and the mind *always* come together…*always* intertwine. It's not a pick and choose matter. It's what is meant to be. Snowflake, you are *not* one or the other. You are both. You are a *force of nature* with a *forceful mind*. Accepting that…is where your peace lies."

XIII

The Elves were all abuzz at the Community Room of Santa's Headquarters. On December 19th at the North Pole, things were always one wrinkled ribbon away from all bedlam breaking loose. However, there was an added level of tension that year, the magnitude of which nobody wanted to begin measuring. Although, at the Pole there were definitely devices to do that, if someone felt so inclined.

Pacing elves spoke jibber jabber as they grappled with the *hows* and *whys* of their current situation. But they didn't need to. Because in minutes, it was all about to be spelled out and re-clarified for them on live television. Many members of The North had gathered in that same room with the elves. *Everyone was concerned.* And there they all sat, fully concentrated on the television screen hanging high on the far wall of the Community Room.

A newswoman spoke in front of a map with trepidation, "Meteorologists define a *White Christmas* as a Christmas morning with at least one inch of snow on the ground. All across the country there are unseasonably warm temperatures. This will prevent snow from accumulating, even in places having a dusty covering to begin with. The persistent warmth in the East and Midwest has set the table for more of a *green* Christmas…than a *white* one." Upon finishing, the newswoman despondently turned to her right and waited for a response.

Her co-anchor tapped the news desk with his pen and sighed, "Aww. Kind of puts the hot cocoa back in the cupboard, doesn't it Rebecca?"

One of the elves swung his head so fast, his pointed green hat didn't spin with him. The two elves on his left glanced back at him in wide-eyed panic as the first elf whirled back toward them, hoping he wasn't hearing what he was hearing. The golden jingle bells on the tops of the elves' hats began whirring from all of the head whipping and puzzlement tearing through the room.

"Put the hot coe…?" the first elf stammered, "Put the hot cocoa back in the cupboard?"

A second elf held his head with both of his hands and yelled, "THAT MEANS THE MARSHMALLOWS TOO!"

"NOT THE MARSHMALLOWS!" a third elf wailed.

Three divas sat calmly on the couch amid the chaos. Yet, they too were trying to wrap their heads around the news. Vicki was the youngest…appearing to be about twenty years old. She had that vibrant brown skin—a perfect match for her colorful personality. Normally, there was at least one person in the room trying to flirt with her, but in this case, there seemed to be too many catastrophes going on…like the whole hot cocoa-and-marshmallow situation. Without the two young ladies sitting next to her, she would've been totally on her own. That didn't stop Vicki from sharing this brief note about herself, "No disrespect, but *SHE* is not going to be traveling all over God's *GREEN* earth on Christmas Eve."

Endearing little Dani sat on the other end of the couch, looking all of twenty-two years old. She had big brown eyes and long,
lovely lashes. She patted the side of her enviably thick natural hair
as she piggybacked on Vicki's complaint, "This hair was not made
for humidity."

"And *I* don't like to sweat. *All-of-this...*" the third diva, Daija,
poured on, sliding her fingers along her exquisite braids and then
down the side of her body, "...the 24th... the heat? Oh no, playa.
That math just ain't gonna add up."

The first elf was now meandering in circles with his fingers
intertwined over his head, repeating an endless delirious loop of,
"Put the hot cocoa back in the cupboard? Put the hot cocoa back in
the cupboard?"

The third elf swirled in and out of the first elf's path, searching for
answers among his repeated rhetoric. "No marshmallows?" he cried,
"No snow, no marshmallows?" Every time the word *marshmallow*
came from his mouth, it was done in a more elaborate fashion than
the time before it. The poor guy was attempting to placate himself
with the very words that would send him further off the deep end.

The elves understood the news, but at the same time, they
couldn't make any sense of it. If you're not totally confused by the
contradiction there, you might be able to grasp a tiny morsel of
the absolute pandemonium which occurred that night inside The
Headquarters of the North Pole.

An elf who was missing from the commotion—Dez, Santa's *Lead
Elf*. Dez would have been able to alleviate some of the ruckus, but
there was a serious coordination issue among five of the in-town
factories. This fell on Dez's shoulders to sort out before the big day.
He didn't have time to worry about whether or not it was going to

snow. Thus, the mayhem continued inside The Headquarters. Lord, if you could only imagine.

One elf cut diagonally across the room, waving both hands in the air, shrieking, "Wire hangers!"

Another elf carried a stack of eighteen advent calendars into the corner. He began ripping the doors off them, pulling the chocolates out, and stuffing them into his pockets. Gracie Elf was usually able to settle down some of Santa's little helpers when they became frazzled. Sensing the need for action, she darted into the corner to save the grief-stricken elf. She was also trying to save eighteen advent calendars from their impending doom. Gracie took the hands of the elf in distress and in a composed nature cried, "WE NEED THEM! WHAT ARE YOU DOOOOING?"

The *advent snatcher* fully ignited. He raked open each of the last calendar doors, and began jamming chocolates anywhere they could fit on his body! In his shirt, in his pants, and in his vest, which happened to be finely decorated with felt hand-sewn gingerbread men.

"WE'VE GOT TO HOLD ON! HOLD ON, GRACIE!" he wailed in desperation.

"Hiding the last chocolates isn't going to hold off Christmas!" Gracie shouted back. Her effort to enlighten the frantic elf had failed. Instead, the frenzied elf dodged Gracie's extended arms, angled his way around a new toy display table, and sprinted down the hallway toward the storage room. Along the way, he jammed every last loose piece of chocolate into his mouth, leaving the shrapnel of destroyed calendars in his wake.

Only one elf remained unfazed. This was mainly because his entire focus rested on the hand he was playing at the Blackjack Table. He may have made the appropriate play for that hand in Blackjack, but it was the wrong call to make in the Community

Room of Santa's Headquarters at that time. Because when he said, "Hit me," the delirious dealer decked him with a thick right cross!

As the card player crawled across the floor, he came across Isaiah Elf, who was kneeling behind the couch in the center of the room, with green hats, chocolates, and shreds of colored paper crisscrossing in the air above him. Isaiah pressed his hands together and prayed, "I could not, would not, on a boat. I will not, will not, with a goat. I will not eat them in the rain. Not in the dark..." Dr. Seuss probably never imagined his *Green Eggs and Ham* would ever be recited in a circus like this, but baby, if it was going to help Isaiah collect himself, then I guess that's what he had to do.

Dani, Daija, and Vicki each raised an eyebrow.

"It is a good book," Vicki conceded. Dani and Daija began to lift a hand in rebuttal, but they quickly retracted those thoughts.

"True," nodded Dani.

"It is," sighed Daija.

Gerald showed up out of nowhere, as he usually did, slithering his smarmy self in front of the three ladies. Gerald is the 2nd Elf In Charge. He *thinks* he's the glue holding The North together. He *is* efficient. That's about it, I guess. He's also snarky...and abrasive. I shouldn't go on like that. I'm a little off track. But Gerald is just so extra. His whole thing that he had goin' on would bother us more if we took him seriously.

Gerald is stockier than the other elves, with a bit more of a belly. He's about five foot three, which doesn't mean much to anyone but himself. Because what it means to him, is that he's taller than the rest of the elves. Think it gives him a better-than-them complex. He knows he's never gettin' away with sayin' a word to me though. I can handle my own when it comes to Gerald. Santa puts up with all of his *energy*, probably out of pity. Givin' him these jobs to keep him out of the way. I have to admit, I do that every once in a while myself.

"I didn't know you ladies could read," Gerald taunted, cynically referencing the *Green Eggs and Ham* discussion. Then he pulled out his trusty notepad and pen, pretending to document his new discovery. "Let's put that in our notes for good ol' Saint Nick."

Vicki lurched at Gerald, but Daija's arm bar prevented the two from tangling. Or in other words, prevented Vicki from beating his—there I go again. Gerald will do it to you, let me tell ya. Whew.

"*Read* a book? I'm surprised you can *reach* a book," Daija ripped back.

The squabble with Gerald continued. He'd never be the first to walk away from a good argument. And those three ladies weren't going to take any disrespect. Rightfully so. I told them not to accept any funny business on day one. Was the *only time* I needed to say that.

Meanwhile, over at the window side nook, two elves decided to soothe themselves by eating cereal. Their cute little bowls had ornaments painted around the rim. Their spoons were shining, smudge free, courtesy of the *Polishing Elves*. Their cereal had more colors than a rainbow.

That could've worked.

"It makes me angry when I see you eat," the friendly elf spouted, utilizing a sincere *I statement*. "The slurping and chomping. You keep making these breathing noises…"

"You don't want me to breathe?" the elf sitting across the table asked in astonishment.

"You don't need to eat and breathe!"

"I don't need to eat and breathe?"

"...and eat. And slurp...and make your face make these weird faces. You chew with your eyes closed!"

"YOU chew with your MOUTH open!"

The two elves raised their milk-dripping spoons. Two warriors about to go to battle!

CLINK! CLANK! CLANK! CLINK! It was a spoon fight for the ages.

Now, if you're multitasking, I need you to take whatever it is you're holding...put it down...switch it off...and listen to this. It all came to a head when a single elf walked over to the new toy display area. He put both hands on one of the display tables and slid a few toys off to the side. Then he pushed himself up, his curly shoes wiggling in the air behind him.

After getting two knees up on the table, he tested it for stability, making surfing motions with his arms as he waved his body back and forth. Satisfied with the *Carpentry Elves* construction of the table, the committed elf stood up straight and turned to face the room. The gold buttons on his green vest lined up perfectly with conviction. The flaps of his vest rolled down over the bottom of his belly with fortitude. He pushed a couple more toys to the side with one of his curly boots, lifted his arms to the sky, and shouted, "THINGS WERE SO MUCH BETTER IN THE '80s!"

"Dani!" Daija called out indignantly.

Dani concurred, "Now, I've *never* heard anybody say that."

Vicki stood up and wagged her finger, "Unh uh. We gotta stop all this." She sashayed across the room to the door of Santa's office with a full battle royale going on behind her.

She opened the door a crack.

Santa could see Vicki's long fingernails wrapping around the inside of the door. But she lost her nerve and shut it right away.

Then she ducked as an advent calendar arced over her head, crossing airspace with a spoon sailing in the opposite direction.

Santa was at his desk, dressed in his casual work attire. Which for Santa, was his plaid tweed sport coat with a beige derby perched atop his head. I know he wore the sport coat to hide some of that belly. I'm always getting on him about eatin' too many cookies. He thinks the coat keeps me from finding out about the days when he makes an extra pit stop or two at The Elf Bakery. *Tuh.* Surely doesn't.

Santa only wears his traditional red and white suit on Christmas Eve. That's the one you're used to seeing him in. The red and white *is* a special suit. I sewed it myself. But he only wears it on extremely special occasions, most notably Christmas Eve and Christmas Day.

There he sat with his fluffy white beard…some pepper mixed in…brown eyes matching the color of his skin. Handsome. I didn't marry him for his brains. We joke about that. So there you have it, yes…I'm Mrs. Claus. Didn't want that to get in the way of the story. *Jane's story.* Soon as I say my name, people get all flustered. Start thinkin' extra thoughts. But I'm just like you, really. I don't expect or accept any special treatment. Treat me the way you treat everyone else. Let that be your own truth, right?

Now, back to my husband and his portly shape. Heh! In all seriousness, he's got a lot more weight on his shoulders than he does on his belly, so when affairs become a bit haphazard or he seems forgetful, it's usually because he's handling ten thousand issues at the same time.

Santa was checking over the wrapping paper numbers, making certain there would be a sufficient amount of paper to cover all of the presents. You'd think creating the toys would be enough, but you have to account for all the man hours and *woman hours* it takes to wrap them, in addition to the quantity of paper itself. He was always saying, '*There's work to be done.*' And sure, he was right.

Santa would have loved to open his door and oversee the Christmas Factory all day. Nothing in the world he enjoyed more than watching those elves in lockstep, carrying out the day's business. '*Three hundred sixty-four for one*' was the elves' motto. Busting their boots for three hundred sixty-four days to provide the maximum Christmas experience for all, on that *one* very special day. But if Santa didn't handle the x's and o's everyday, along with quelling a myriad of other shenanigans, matters would get exponentially worse in a hurry.

And there we were.

Vicki cracked open the door, one more time. And once more, her yellow-polished fingernails revealed themselves to Santa. He glanced upward and adjusted his bifocals. Vicki timidly shut the door and put her back up to it again.

"Eh hem, Vicki," Santa called.

Vicki cowered. "Speaking."

"Come in."

Vicki remained on the other side of the door. "How'd you know it was me?"

"Your nails."

All of Vicki's trepidation washed away. She instantly became herself again. She burst through the door and wiggled herself all the way up to Santa's desk. She threw her nails in his face. "You like 'em? Dani did 'em. She's becomin' *a beast*! 'Cept this little thing happened when she was doin' Daija's.

Santa slid his chair back and gave Vicki his full attention. "Little thing?"

"Real small."

"The last little thing the three of you did, turned my red suit fuchsia. Please tell me my suit is okay," Santa harrumphed.

"Santa, don't be worryin' 'bout that suit, mm-hm. 'Cause after that slight incident you're referencin', Mrs. Claus doesn't let us get anywhere near that thing."

She spoke the truth there, honey. I told the young ladies, the next time they put their hands on that suit they'd lose 'em...their hands, that is. I said it. Can't lie about that.

Santa narrowed his eyes.

Vicki continued unabashedly, "So Daija was like, 'I want one of those aurora borealis patterns that you put on Peaches' nails.' Which I personally didn't think was a good idea, 'cause you know how when you buy an outfit and you're lookin' spicy in it, and other girls start askin', *'Where'd you get that? Oh my god, girl, where'd you get that? How much did it cost?'* And you don't wanna say, but you're so excited you can't hold it in, and you tell 'em anyway, even though you know you shouldn't, and no more than two days later, they come wearin' the same exact outfit you jus' bought, or even they wait about a month or two and you're over their house, and you see it in their closet, 'cause like they're thinkin' *'Pshh, she won't ever see me in this.'* Aww, but you do. You do see it."

Vicki's sassy monologue appeared to come to a close when she pursed her lips and raised her big eyes up at Santa with the presumption she had given him a valuable piece of information.

Santa glazed over in a daze. He wouldn't have been able to follow that conversation in his twenties. My husband can pass for sixty, but most of us know he's a tad older than that. You could figure he didn't have a clue of what Vicki was talking about.

While Santa puzzled over, Vicki had a chance to catch her breath.

Then she carried on. "'Cause they don't know when you're gonna be comin' over…just to check on things. *Mm-hm*."

Vicki put her hand on her hip and lifted the corner of her closed mouth.

"*Vicki*," Santa squared off firmly.

"Oh. So Dani went for the aauuuroooraa booorealis, once again…" Vicki waved both of her hands high across her head, mimicking the path of the Northern Lights phenomenon. "…But Daija was like, '*This looks like a menorah!*' Now you know there's nothin' wrong with a menorah, 'cause like I got lots of Jewish friends celebratin' Hanukkah. Santa, nothing's wrong with that. But then Blake was walkin' by Daija. He seen them nails and called out, '*Shalome!*' Then you know Daija was hot!"

"The nails, the borealis, Hanukkah! I get that story!" Santa interrupted. "Sweetie…" he ushered back with a sleigh full of patience, "…can you get to the–"

"Yeah. So they had a go 'round…Dani and Daija…if you know what I mean." Vicki paused. "But it's cool. They're cool now." She looked into Santa's blank face. Nothing had been gained except for a loss of time.

Vicki continued, with her bright yellow fingernails waving around as she spoke, "Not to make a digression. I know you got a handle on this whole unit up in here. We've never had any problems. But if Janey doesn't get that thing worked out…put the drop on these temperatures…lay some snow down…Psssh…I don't know if *you've* noticed, but these elves are gettin' crazy. If they can't go on and have *snowball* fights out there, they're gonna start havin' *real* fights in here. Truthfully."

Santa surrendered. "Thank you, angel."

"Anytime, Santa, 'cause the elves talk too much, sayin' things like, *'Don't go in there all the time, you're bein' a disruption,'* and I'm like, sayin' in return, he doesn't mind. Who's gonna be pullin' that sleigh after they put all too many presents on it again, anyway? It's not gonna be *them*. It's not pullin' itself either."

"You're always welcome, dear," Santa eased, with a pinch of sarcasm.

Vicki smiled and wiggled herself back to the door.

Then Santa added, "Can you twist the lock on your way out?"

"Sure," Vicki said as she proudly turned the lock on the door-knob. Then it occurred to her that my husband wanted the door locked so she wouldn't come back in. "Hm."

Vicki slinked out, but she shut the door with her head held high. It was important to let the Community Room know, she had been received with open arms and was welcome to return at any time.

XIV

Jane walked toward the podium, which marked the gateway to the Community Room of The North Pole Headquarters. With everyone else sent to pull themselves together and get back to work, Red was left in charge of checking people in. If you had business in The North, this was where you got your clearances. The room was quiet, but the aftermath of the previous day's mass hysteria was still permeating the air. Jane held her hands gently on her waist and glanced up at the corners of the ceiling. She wondered, *Was it a party, or a cyclone?* Jokes aside, she quickly realized what it was.

She turned to Red, who stood next to the podium. Feeling a touch of embarrassment, Red scoped Jane up and down, giving her the *What are you doing here?* vibe. He immediately regretted coming off in such a manner, adding to his uneasiness over the entire situation.

Red wore his restlessness on his sleeve, cringing over the chaos that had befallen their current space just the day before. You see, he felt somewhat responsible. He was Santa's true right-hand man. Gerald would like to think otherwise. As I said earlier, Gerald thinks that without him the North Pole would crumble like a cookie stuffed in Santa's back pocket. But Gerald would fall to a long third behind Red and Dez.

Dez handled a lot of the logistical business in terms of *organizing the elves* and putting that *good feeling* stamp on The North, while Red's duties were more connected to the direction of *the entire North Pole*...everyone included. Nobody embodied my husband's message to The North more than Red. Consequently, there was no one more fitting to pass along my husband's word. The only inconvenience was that Red wasn't at The Pole 24/365 like the others. But he was one of those genuine men. No one better for the job. Could search the world and not find anyone more suitable. In a way...that's kind of what they did...search the world to find him.

Red was *fine*, but extremely humble. His clothes were always classy and fashionable, but unlabeled. One might say, he wore the clothes, they didn't wear him. Form-fitted collared shirt, skinny tie and a crisp sport coat. Worn, new look jeans hitting his dress-style shoes. Yet Red didn't feel especially put together right then. He was already disappointed and self-conscious as to the state of the Community Room, now add onto that, the angst of greeting Ms. Jane in such a way.

Not at a loss for being able to recognize body language, Jane landed what she thought was a necessary counterpunch. "What are you lookin' at?" Then she brushed Red aside and took a few more steps toward the center of the ransacked room.

Gerald busily swept into their presence from behind the nook area, armed with grandeur and self-importance. He noticed Jane and *also* looked her up and down. He seemed surprised to see her. With nothing in the empty room separating the two of them, Jane lined up Gerald with her palm and froze his hand to the toy train he was carrying.

"Hey! Hey! What did you...oww! It's biting me! Jane! Cold!" he cried.

Red laughed to himself.

Gerald tried to shake his hand free without success. He blew on his hands and licked them, trying to melt away the ice by whatever means he could muster. "J-J-Jane, I feel as though I've gotten on your b-b-bad side somehow...after all these years..." he said shivering. "...G-Go ch-check inside the podium, and s-see what I p-p-put on my Christmas List..."

Jane didn't pay him any mind.

Gerald continued, "...A c-c-closer, more congenial r-relationship with dear Ms. Frost!"

Now it was Jane's turn to look Gerald up and down. "You don't need to ask Santa for that..."

Gerald lit up.

"...You need Jesus," Jane finished.

Jane's focus was immediately pulled from Red and Gerald, onto Dez, who had just come out of the Toy Factory.

"Thanks, Red!" Dez called from across the room. Red pointed back at Dez, thankful to be relieved of his post.

Dez usually held down the podium, but he had to go to the factory floor and make sure the elves were operating with clear heads down there. As I previously mentioned, Dez was the Lead Elf. Five feet, two inches tall. He didn't wear the typical elf apparel. He was more of a casual suit type of guy. Never bought into the green hat and curly shoes...or the fancy belt for that matter. His duties extended past The Headquarters, to all of the elf bakeries and workshops across the North Village. But Dez was never too busy to let you know that you were valued and appreciated. He put the *goodtime greeting* on the North Pole. Nobody said, "Happy Holidays," better than Dez.

He welcomed Jane graciously as he made his way to the podium. "Good afternoon, Ms. Frost."

"Dez," Jane responded respectfully with a smile.

"Here to see the big guy?"

"Yep." Under her breath she repeated, "The big guy."

Jane inhaled nervously and wrung her hands.

A few elves entered the room, discussing data on their tablets. They giggled at Gerald walking by with the snow covered train stuck to his hand. Just then, Santa bounced through, wiping his hands with a white cloth. He also came from the factory floor. Dez had gotten the production back in order, but sometimes Santa had to go down there to lend an extra set of eyes...and in some cases an extra hand. There was always another fire to put out at the North Pole.

"Coming at ten o'clock," Dez informed Jane, pointing to Santa, across the room.

"Thanks, Dez," Jane responded.

"Always."

Santa maneuvered through the room, working his way around the busy elves. "From out of her snow globe!" he joked.

Jane laughed quietly, before dropping her head, now feeling a bit embarrassed herself. Santa wrapped his arm around Jane as though she were his niece. They had that kind of relationship.

Jane perked up. "They didn't even have to call you."

"You're always on time," Santa complimented.

"Figured with all you're doing this time of year..."

"...there'd be more of a search party effort to find me?"

Jane nodded.

"I *needed* to see you. You're at the top of *my* list," Santa said with a smile. Then he opened his hand lightly on Jane's back and guided her toward the door he had just entered. "Come on."

Tall, thick floor-to-ceiling glass panels lined one side of the hall-way outside of the Community Room. One look down revealed the entire toy factory in full operation, four levels below. One set of elves was happily building toys using fluorescent green electric drills and screwdrivers. Another group was pouring molds for dolls of all shades. Off into the corner, Jane saw another team weaving countless colored wires into video game consoles.

"Wooow," Jane oozed in awe.

"Never gets old does it?"

"Mm."

"As magical as the first time I ever saw it. That's where it is," Santa said, pointing to Jane's chest. "The heart."

The two allowed themselves to be fascinated. To let go. To release all of their worries from their minds for a minute.

"Amazing…What are those down there?" Jane asked.

"You."

"Me?"

"Yes. Those are *yous*."

"No kid is askin' for me. Can tell you that," Jane shot back.

"They are."

"No."

"Shhhh," Santa whispered, "Watch them."

From high above the Toy Factory, Jane gathered in all of the images her eyes would allow. She witnessed the elves working in unison. How they fired the tools over each other's heads and snatched them out of the air with one hand. How they cheerfully polished brand new bikes as they skipped around them...tossing up their washrags and catching them behind their backs.

She saw elf dolls, reindeer figures, and cute little rabbit figures with adjustable heads. There were toy Father Time characters in white lab coats, as well as Mother Nature dolls in colorful dresses, big-boned and beautiful. In the near corner, Santa dolls rolled by, clothed in rich red velvet outfits with true cotton accents. Jane chuckled when she saw the Dez dolls, complete with fashionable suits. No elf costume for him. Not even on his doll.

To the left, there were tables full of ten different variations of gingerbread figures. They had adjustable arms and legs, decorated with icing that looked so real, you'd think you could lick it off. Jane noticed each gingerbread man had plastic buttons down the middle, mimicking Red Hots to the letter. Made her want to pick one off and give it a taste!

Elves frantically added final touches of paint, tidied clothing, or snapped on accessories, as the toys glided across the factory on the soft beds of conveyor belts. At the end of the line, Jane watched each toy get sealed up into its own glossy mint condition box with clear plastic windows.

"Can you imagine the child who gets to open one of those boxes?" lauded Jane. "To see one of those great people of The North staring back at you through the window...to hold one in your hands...one in a million."

Jane gazed down at the figures of herself until she was distracted by puffy snowmen dolls being accessorized directly below her. Elves were pulling little plastic fedoras out of molds and placing them on the snowmen's heads.

"Rollo! There's Rollo!" Jane exclaimed. "Can I have one?"

"Did you put it on your list?"

Jane was unable to hide the *oops* on her face. She shrugged.

"I'll see what I can do," Santa chuckled. "Might be in the bag already. Sometimes we know, even when you don't ask."

The two of them became young again, watching the conveyor belts transport childhood dreams.

The Santa dolls caught Jane's attention. Something touched her senses. "Looks like they took a few pounds off *you*," she said, giving Santa the side-eye.

"Huah. I may have said something."

The two shared a laugh.

"You're so crazy."

"Am I wrong?" Santa questioned, lowering his fluffy eyebrows toward Jane.

He put his arm around her, and the two began making their way up the ramped hallway. "I want you to meet with somebody."

Alarms went off in Jane's head. She stepped back. "Oooh no."

Santa put out his hand. Jane was reluctant, but she dropped her hand into his, because there existed a trust. And the two confidants continued up the inclined hallway together.

Santa treaded lightly. "You haven't made it easy on the people."

"That's what I was supposed to be doing? We can't all be flyin' in on magic reindeer, givin' presents."

Jane caught herself. She didn't often do that...catch herself. But she had a lot of respect for my husband.

"Sorry. Don't remember it being this way." Jane gathered her thoughts before continuing. "Since when do kids need to be won over...about snow...about how it's magical too. *It is*," Jane finished, trying to convince herself.

"Snow *is* magical. People don't need to fly in on reindeer and give out presents to be *the truth*. It's just what *I* do," Santa said, pointing to himself. Then he leveled his easy brown eyes into Jane's hazels.

Jane began to apologize. "I wasn't saying…"

"What if I pulled back? A half. A quarter. What if I did just a little less? Would they notice?"

"Totally," Jane ensured. "And they'd be comin' to check on you to see if you were okay."

"Who?"

"Everyone."

"Would you?" Santa asked sincerely.

"Of course."

When the two of them reached the top of the ramp, they paused in front of an awe-striking, thirty-foot-high glass wall, which framed a breathtaking view of the North Village.

The North Village was an extensive town, winding deep into the valley. It lay harmoniously among steep purple-hued mountains that helped dress a pink sky every sunset. Splashes of evergreens ran from the backyards of quaint homes, to the banks of wide streams, before tracing hiking paths to the top of gray-stoned cliffs. If you ever get an invitation, jump on it, because you could travel the world and not visit a more fanciful place. *Take your breath away.*

The glow of lights from the small houses and businesses brightened the North Pole's hidden gem of a town, which happened to be a hundred feet below the top of the ramp, where Jane and Santa looked on.

"Woooah," Jane whispered in amazement.

"Over there…the candy shop. Beyond that…the market. To the left, The North Restaurant and The Elf Bakery."

Jane marveled. "Can smell the cookies baking through the glass."

"Over there...Elf Village. On this side...the reindeer stables." Santa shuffled to the left and stretched his big hand out, pointing deeper into the valley, "Right down–"

"The Runway!" Jane exclaimed.

Santa nodded silently.

"I've never seen it like this...from up here." It was as though Jane were a child again, standing in front of her first snowman. *"Reindeer Runway."*

She covered her mouth with her hand.

Santa broke the moment. "What's missing?"

Jane faced Santa. Torn. Her childlike wonder melted away. As she fixed her attention on the slate-tiled roofs of the houses in the North Village, she couldn't deny the answer to Santa's question. *Snow.*

Santa shared his thoughts. "Reindeer can get overheated when they're flying around up there on the 24th. It's nice when they have a cool, fluffy spot to land. Eases the wear and tear on 'em...brings their body temperatures down. They like scooping their noses into the fresh snow too." He turned toward the large pane of glass and cast his eyes across the village. Then he chuckled. "I've even been told they'll flip it up on top of their heads and try to roll in it sometimes when I'm in the houses laying out the presents."

Santa was smiling, but Jane's demeanor saw no change.

"You know, the people...they're still in," Santa assured with his deep raspy voice. Then he eased in. "You may have just come a tad too hard for a stretch."

Jane was taken aback. She was at a loss with that one. Santa was about the only one who could levy a critique on Jane. People tiptoed around her for numerous reasons. Not going to go into it now, but one of them was her reception of...we'll say...tidbits of constructive criticism. Telling Jane she may have brought an inch more snow than required? Others might have found themselves frozen to one of those large glass panels with a statement like that. Santa could get away with it, but it made him uncomfortable nonetheless. He wasn't in the business of hurting feelings...conversely, Jane wasn't in the business of preserving them.

Santa shifted his weight from one foot to the other. His bushy beard wriggled. "Snowmageddon. Do you know what that did to Virginia, Maryland, and Delaware? The Blizzard of 2013 in Boston. Twenty-five inches."

"It was twenty-four point nine. And how bad could it have been? They named it after a cute little clownfish."

"How about the blizzard in Texas? Eight-foot-high drifts. In Texas. Not Vermont. Not New Hampshire. Texas. I read eighty-mile-an-hour winds too. Is that how fast you were going?"

"How would I measure?"

"They called it 'Goliath'. Didn't name *that one* after a cute little clownfish. I heard you even sombreroed your way into Mexico," Santa said with a laugh.

"Keep going, you're on a roll," Jane wryly returned.

"Just sayin'. These aren't pumped up stories concocted on the Internet."

"Well, for the record, I don't do tornadoes. So you can put that part of Goliath on someone else. I've stepped it back a little," Jane offered, attempting to work up a better defense.

"How about going back to Chicago in 2015 and laying eleven inches."

"Eleven inches isn't that–"

"In two days."

"I've brought more in one day."

"A week BEFORE *Thanksgiving?*" Santa finished in exasperation.

"The only turkeys that didn't make it through that, were the ones people put on their plates."

"The Blizzard of 2016. Dropping over twenty inches on Philadelphia?"

"Snuggling up with some cheesesteaks in the cold?" Jane offered, grasping at straws.

"You can't get cheesesteaks when there's twenty inches of snow," Santa blew out firmly.

Jane relaxed. It was matter-of-fact to her. Everything Santa said was spot on. She couldn't fight it, and deep down she didn't want to. She really didn't want to listen to Santa bring her all the way up to the present either. "I get bored through the spring, summer, and fall. The winter is *my* time," Jane said, slinging her neck back and forth. "Who do you want me to be...*Hot Jane?*"

Santa peered over his glasses at her as if he were contemplating the idea. Jane playfully shoved him in the arm. Santa's bulky shoulders barely budged.

"Ho, ho, ho...No," he sighed.

"Do you know how low the crime rate was over those stretches? Speaking of the reindeer, who put that snow down in Vegas for them? They'd of been landing on hot sand in the desert."

"Truth...but you're listening. As I was saying, I would like for you to meet someone."

Jane's radar was still going off. "Is this going to be like when you told me I should have dinner with that Lucky Charms lookin' dude?"

"St. Patrick?"

Instantly, Santa and Jane tilted their eyes upward as they remembered the events of that night.

Jane was sitting in a restaurant across the table from Patrick, an enthusiastic fellow, sporting a chromatic green top hat with a black band around it. A long, gold-painted feather peeked out of the side of the band, helping to accent, and at the same time overplay the gold teeth in Patrick's mouth. His dark green tailcoat hung over the edges of his seat while his gold cufflinks blinded the innocent civilians around him. Patrick's bushy black beard held splashes of dark metallic orange, but they didn't take away from his thick eyebrows, which bounced up and down as he talked.

"I'll buy you emeralds. That's your birthstone, right? I know my ladies," Patrick cockily crooned.

To which Jane responded, "I am not your lady. My birthstone is not an emerald. It's a turquoise. But I only wear diamonds."

"Sent him back on the rainbow he rode in on," Jane declared with pride.

"Was one time," Santa defended.

Jane persisted, "How about Jack Orvil Lantern?"

Santa pretended to be surprised. "Jack O' Lantern?"

"There was an entity to Jack," Jane admitted. "Was a nice restaurant, relaxed atmosphere…the date *was* going fine…"

Jack was clean cut. Clean shaven. Down-to-earth. Jane couldn't deny that. Man bun twisted on top of his head. Hairline shaped by an elite barber. *Man, those lines were crisp.* Even his eyebrows were shaped up. Laugh lines…yeah, but he wore them well. His rust-colored leather jacket and green alligator shoes gave that little extra pop to his ensemble. Jack was a focused dude. He listened to Jane's every word…wouldn't take his eyes off her.

"They know who you were?" Jack asked, engaged with curiosity.

"Why he wanted to show out," Jane answered, "But his friends one upped him and asked me to add somethin' extra to the mogul."

"He hit the jump?"

Jack leaned in, eagerly awaiting Jane's response.

"One of his legs hit the jump. The other kept movin' down the mountain!" Jane slapped the table. "His one ski dug, and the other shot straight into the air!"

Jack began to hyperventilate with laughter. "Bet he did a pirouette like a crow in a windstorm!" he cheered. Then Jack gasped for air…unearthing the laugh of a lifetime.

Immediately the image of Jack and his broad smile resurfaced in Jane's mind. Broad smile full of missing teeth, that is.

Jane shook her head. "That's what happens when you eat pillow-cases full of candy."

Santa shrunk a couple more inches. "Two bad dates?"

"Fat Tuesday," Jane shot back.

And with that...she had landed the final blow.

Tuesday had dressed himself up in a three-piece suit for his big date with Jane. He was a large man, consequently the buttons on his vest were begging for a little extra time. His hair was short with classy waves, and he had a face that gave a warmer welcome than a trombone solo on Bourbon Street. Tuesday had a *'make your momma proud'* good-heartedness to him. So, what could've gone wrong?

"Should I ask why they call you Tuesday?" Jane probed with curiosity.

"You should, you should," Tuesday bubbled, wiping his mouth with a cloth napkin from the table. Then he pointed to the sweet potato on Jane's plate. "You going to want all of that?"

"I guess not." Jane tilted her head with a sideways grin. A tiny bell pinged deep in the upper corner of her mind.

"I might be able to eat some of that for ya."

"Ooookay," Jane said, pushing her side of sweet potatoes across the table. "What was that you were askin'?"

"Ah never—"

"Oh...why they call me Tuesday," he said, prior to shoveling a heaping spoonful of good New Orleans mac and cheese into his mouth. "Well, funny is..." Tuesday continued. Then he stopped and swallowed hard. "My real name is Frank."

Jane was trying hard not to laugh. "Frank?"

"Actually…Frankie." He waited a couple of seconds for theatrical effect. "But when I was little, my dad used to say, when I wasn't in school…" Tuesday drew his knife back and forth across his steak, removing himself from the room. Then he pushed the fork into a chunk of meat, swiped it into the sweet potatoes, and stuffed it into his mouth, re-alerting himself to the fact that he was still in mid-sentence. "…and home for the weekend, you know, not being in school for those hours…He used to say to my momma on Thursday, 'You better go to the market tomorrow and get enough food for Frankie to eat…'cause he's gonna eat through the whole weekend.'"

Tuesday proudly pounded more steak. The caramelized sugars glistened over the tender meat and reflected off his dreamy eyes. A man and his steak…and the rest of the food on the table, if we're going to be honest. He didn't need to say more. His story was already told right there. But he did say more…and he ate more.

Tuesday chuckled. Then he tilted his fork down and used it to point to Jane's collard greens. "Going to be able to eat all of that?"

Jane remorsefully stared at her soul-dripping bowl of leafy collards as she slid it across the table. Tuesday used his whole arm to corral the bowl and pull it toward himself. The nuggets of cured pork danced like sugar plums in his eyes.

"'Ventually it became, 'He's gonna eat straight through Monday,'" he unnecessarily carried on. "Then, later it became…"

There was no more vacancy in Tuesday's mouth.

"…later it became…he's going to eat straight through Tuesday," Jane finished, putting herself out of her own misery.

Tuesday happily pointed to his nose, and then back at Jane, as if she were about to win a game of charades. Then he swallowed the last chunk of meat and wiggled his hands in the air, pretending to be a ghost. "Hey, why don't you tell me about the secrets of the Nawth!"

Showing great poise in her highly irritated state, Jane decided to push forward and answer the question, even if she was merely doing it to humor herself. "If you want to know the true secret of The North…" she brightened, "…I think it's that everyone works every day, trying to do something memorable to lift up others…"

"Yes, yesss," Tuesday broke in. "Ya mind if I scoop a bit of those 'shrooms off the side of your plate there?"

"Here." Jane pushed her plate halfway across the table and spun it to give Tuesday proper access to the mushrooms. Without wasting a second, he scooped them all up. Then he pulled back into his chair, grabbed an extra, unused cloth napkin from the table, and wiped the sweat from his forehead.

Exercising full self-control, Jane moved on. "Um…working everyday to find ways to *help* people, instead of finding ways to *take* from them."

"I know. Better to give. Speakin' of. Haven't touched your cornbread. I might do you the favor."

Jane palmed the fresh, warm square of cornbread and placed it in the middle of Tuesday's plate.

"Not to change the subject," he said, before swallowing, "but did you ever hear of a snoother?"

"A snoother?"

"Had 'em in Iceland," Tuesday bantered while breathing heavily. "Cross between a cinnamon bun and a doughnut. Circular, but with the cinnamon overtop and throughout. Real doughy…fried too. Like a doughnut, no?"

Jane couldn't help but ask, "Why were you in Iceland?"

"I wanted…"

Immediately, the answer came to Jane's mind.

"…to get a snoother," she and Tuesday gleefully finished in unison, pointing at their noses and then back toward each other.

A waitress arrived with a dessert plate, carrying two cannoli. They were topped with candied fruit and sprinkled with powdered sugar. Tuesday didn't wait for the desserts to hit the table. He reached up to grab his cannoli off the descending plate.

"I'd be honored to help ya with the other one," he said, motioning toward the second cannoli faster than Jane could lift a finger.

The waitress dropped her hip and spun to face Jane. Upon Jane's direction, the waitress placed the last cannoli in front of Tuesday.

Sure enough, Janey got herself up and walked to the door after that.

"You going to finish your broccoliiii?" Tuesday hollered across the restaurant, "Cause I can take 'em home in a bag for later!"

Santa's face turned bright red. He put his head down and held both of his hands over his large belly.

"But Sadie Hawkins?" Jane added quizzically.

"I was just starting to wonder," Santa replied, trying to justify his final act of indiscretion.

"I didn't have time anyway. As far as this other thing...Santa...I'll do it," Jane agreed out of nowhere. "Don't have anything better to do. But woo." Jane shook her head as she gathered herself.

"I got this one under control," Santa vouched.

Jane changed the subject. "How's the missus...still cookin' up a storm? I told you to send her down to Wildwood for the summers. Could bring in a lot of money, makin' that soul food for the beachgoers!"

"Ha! You know she can't stand bein' out in the sun."

"The only one," Jane followed up despondently.

"You're really serious about this."

Jane sagged.

"Things are going to get right again. Believe what I say," Santa reassured.

The two of them took in the peaceful village below once again.

"Since you brought it up…Mrs. Claus made your favorite the other night. Pulled pork."

"With collards?" Jane gazed upward in a dreamlike state, before laughing out loud. "Mm. Her cookin' makes me wanna slap an elf!"

Santa's smile quickly vanished. "You know they love you."

"I know…" Jane conceded, "…it's just that creepy Gerald keeps starin' at me like I'm a candy cane."

"That's not what it is." Santa put his hand on Jane's shoulder as he faced her. "Where would *they* be…without *you?*"

"*They* would be fine. *Gerald* would find himself huggin' a pine tree," Jane shot back sarcastically.

Santa gave one of his hefty chortles. "Oh, they need you. And Gerald…he's a button pusher, I told you. Didn't want to add this onto your plate, but they're all losing their minds a bit."

"How can you tell the difference?" Jane cracked.

"Seriously. Isaiah was on his knees in the corner reciting a non-stop loop of *'Green Eggs and Ham'.*"

"It is a good book," Jane acknowledged.

Santa was about to give a counterargument. But he didn't have one. "It is," he agreed, before getting back to the subject. "I simmered them down and refocused their spirits…but you know elves," he said, playfully balling his fists, "They're such quirky little things."

XV

From the window of the main kitchen, I noticed Jane leaving the North Pole Headquarters. She pulled up her tight white hood, and slid her hands into the pockets of her puffy white vest. Her slim arms were wrapped up sleek in the white sleeves of a form-fitting top. Streamlined.

Jane took a few steps from the outside door, but then she stopped. Her head dropped. Misty white breaths spread from her nose and mouth. I knew I was witnessing the foundation of ice forming from its initial roots...a frozen mist more pure than you've ever seen. It was *divine* that night. Been a considerable time since I'd witnessed something like that. Made me think of her father.

A rush came over me, then chills...then sorrow. Oh, I could feel for her. Felt like I was standing right next to her. Like I should reach out. A couple of tears welled up beneath my eyelids. They could've been for Jane or her father.

Jane pulled her hands out of her pockets and tilted her head back in my direction. A one-sided smile grazed the lower edge of her cheek. A sparkle of light twinkled in the corner of her eye. She pulled the tip of her hood down a couple inches. Nobody could see in now. One more cloud of misty ice released from Jane's nose and mouth. *White ice.*

She sank back in her stance, then leapt forward with her front foot. In a few mystical strides Jane became a flurry of white flakes. Flakes that rose into the air as if they were in an elevator. I watched with a heavy heart as the night became a cloak for the remainder of the crystals' journey upward.

I put my hands into the sink and finished scrubbing the cooked barbecue sauce off one of the pans. After pulling the pan out of the water, the elf next to me took it, and began to dry it.

"I hope she's going to bring more snow," the elf timidly stated.

I used my apron to wipe my hands. No, I don't wear the red and white suit to do the dishes. And yes, I do my own dishes. Brings closure to the day, I guess. Remember washing dishes as a young girl. Standing on the wooden footstool in order to reach the sink. Simpler times...

"I hope she *cares*," fretted another elf.

"She cares. She loves all of you. She loves The North," I said calmly.

A third elf chimed in, "Sometimes it's hard to tell, Mrs. Claus."

I released a long exhale and turned around to face the elves. The situation *had* gotten deep. As I said, I don't waltz around like a story factory, spreading the new hot takes on the North Village. But our elves are extremely important to us. They're integral to what we do here. They're real people too. And the overflow of Jane's struggles had truly begun to affect their emotional well-being. You know elves can literally make themselves sick with worry...with care... almost with anything. I had to help them put everything into perspective, because I admittedly didn't know if Jane would *ever* find her way through it all. That being the case, I knew they needed to hear it from *me*. Hear how we got here. I could help them in that way at least.

"When Jane was about sixteen…" I started, "… she got herself so upset, she froze herself into a cube, just about. When they talk about *'The Freezing'*…"

The elves gathered closer.

"…*Nobody* could set her free. Peaches summoned all of the resources she could pull. Nothing worked."

"Who's Peaches?" one elf asked.

"Mother Nature."

The elves nodded, and a couple set themselves up on chairs.

"Finally, Peaches found someone. The Source. He saved Jane. Just like he has the power to bring the heat in the summer…he brought *that* same heat to Jane. Melted away the ice. Sadly, as Father Time and Santa predicted, Jane lost almost total memory of her childhood and how she got to that place. Her mother…" I paused.

Hurts me to say. You don't know a mother's pain. Jane's mother. *Whew.* How she did it?

"…She knew she had to give Jane to The North or risk losing her altogether. Accept the fact it was time for her little Snowflake to take on the name that bared her true calling…*Jane of the Frost.*"

I looked to the ceiling. The staggered kitchen lights above my head. The darkness outside the window over the kitchen sink. The red and white checkered drapes reflecting in perfect color off the spotless glass panes. I gathered my thoughts…wrung my hands… and took in the elves once more.

"Autumn brought Jane to a proper place, as advised by Santa and Father Time. Jane fit perfectly…if you can say anything with nature is perfect. In time, she got her own home on the hill…not afraid of being seen every now and then. She's not hiding in those woods all year, I can tell ya that. Still can't find herself all the way through, though…through the mental aspect. Some say she's been lost ever since *The Freezing*. Not what the surface says. But the surface doesn't always tell the whole story."

I lifted my eyes over the heads of the elves to the dark vacant room outside the kitchen. "When you don't remember how you got to a certain place, it becomes relatively…to progress. Not knowing your past and trying to move forward. *Hm.*"

I turned my attention to the three elves gathered closest to me. Then I grabbed a dish towel to wipe my hands, though they were already dry. "Whether it be from the small cabin in the woods or that house on the hill, *Jane has put in work*, miles and miles off the North Wing of Mother Nature's home. But she's still searching."

"For what?" an elf asked from a seat at the table.

"Herself."

I gazed out of the kitchen window with an empty feeling. But I believed in Jane, and there was one last thing that needed to be said.

I faced the elves to be *sure* they'd get it.

"It's true, her hands are like ice…but *her heart*…is as warm as ours."

XVI

Father Time kept the clock ticking on schedule. Green or white, it was December 20th, and nothing was going to change that.

Red knocked on the door to Santa's office at The Headquarters. Rap! Tap! Tap! Everything seemed louder and more urgent when late December hit. Everything had a pulse. The seriousness of getting every gift right, preparing the sleigh, keeping the reindeer out of trouble. The list would stretch from here to next Christmas if I started on it. You could imagine the gravity of lettin' your hand knock on Santa's door just days before the 25th.

"Come in."

Red opened the door. The size of Santa's office was modest. The room itself wasn't particularly a true square. It had four sides, but one side was angled in such a way that the room felt more triangular. Definitely a man space, but there was a warmth to it.

"How are you feelin', Santa?" Red asked.

"Feeling well, son," Santa answered in his hopeful, gruff voice. "Sit down."

Red walked over and sat down in one of the two large chairs, positioned side by side in front of Santa's desk. The maroon leather on the chairs held on favorably, even after fifty years. The cushions were stuffed with horsehair, creating a squelching sound when sat upon. Brass plated upholstery tacks married the leather to solid walnut armrests, which yielded a patina from all of the important people who had sat there before Red. Santa appreciated the craftsmanship of older times. Sometimes I think that's why he still looks at me with a twinkle in his eye. Heh. More than a fair number of pieces throughout my husband's office were simple in appearance. Yet, in reality, they were thoroughly detailed, sturdy, high quality pieces of work. Like Santa himself. "Substance over glamour," he always says.

The elves had to have asked him if he wanted to upgrade the furniture and bookshelves in his office a million times. But in every instance, my husband would give them the same response, *"Don't you dare."* Then he would tell them stories of how their great-grandparents built everything in that office, including the walls. Would tell them if they closed their eyes, they could still hear the hammers banging, and the conversations among all the hardworking elves. The intelligent communication that went into engineering the room, the family stories being passed back and forth...and of course all of the silly jokes too.

There's a picture on the wall of five elves sitting shoulder to shoulder, eating sandwiches on Santa's desk after they had first built it. Decked out in their hats and knickers...sawdust all over them...grins a mile wide. Santa loved those elves. Back then, there were always five or six of them hanging out in his office with him. These days the elves have to make presents for such a large number of children, they don't have time like that anymore. But they were the hardest workers in The North back then too. The *Carpentry Elves* didn't only build. They would scour the forests of the world in order to bring in the appropriate lumber for each specific project. Santa loved the sound the wood made in all the different seasons. He would go into his office and stare at it. Stare at the baseboards, the grain of the wood on his desk...the details of the hand carved bookshelves. Wouldn't always motivate him to pick up a book though. Ha!

My husband felt all those elves were still smiling down on him... sharing the *new* moments with him in that room. Believe me, they were. Like angels. The mister and I are probably the only two people in the world who would use the words *elf* and *angel* in the same sentence. But yes...yes, we do.

Santa hobbled from the mahogany bookshelf over to his desk and sat down. "You're visiting your relatives in Colorado tomorrow?"

"The whole bunch," Red replied.

"Tell them I said, 'Merry Christmas'."

"Mean the world to them, sir."

Then Santa dropped it on the one. "Jane agreed to meet you for dinner."

An anxious relief washed down Red's face. "She know it's me?" he hesitantly asked.

Red didn't really want the answer to that question, and Santa didn't really want to give it to him.

"Does she know she's meeting you, or does she know who you are?" Santa filibustered.

"Either."

"Neither."

Red stood up nervously. He flattened his hands and slid them over his pants. His cheeks filled with air. Then he blew out.

"You can't tell her," Santa reiterated.

"You want her to figure it out," Red rebutted with frustration. "Like a game? Sir, I've been on the receiving end of a lot of games gone wrong. I'm not playing this one anymore. Not on her."

"This is something you steadfastly agreed to. Even as a young boy," Santa countered firmly. "You stood up straight...looked us all in the eye...You had the room. And from that day forward, *they* followed *you*."

Santa rose up from his chair and ran his bold hands over his round belly. "That's how it was supposed to be. And that's how it was."

"I *never* said I would leave her behind. Never agreed to that. I was eight. I was *eight years old*, and I gave myself to this place." Red studied the crown molding lining the perimeter of the ceiling. "Doesn't even sound like...to let this go on. Not as we've been doing."

Red was aghast. He was at a total loss. Nonplussed. And his eyes reconnected with Santa's as if his vision was being thrust through a tunnel at a hundred miles per hour.

"When you get older, you become more aware of the injustices around you. Your heart starts to hurt..." Santa explained while glancing down at his desk, "...for you realize or uncover *many* things need changing. He lifted his head back up, and looked at Red. "*The truth*...can't be changed, Reg. There are no lies here. There are no lies in The North."

It was a point that couldn't be argued. Rite of passage in The North was acknowledging that one actuality. Wrapping paper is made by cutting down trees, *hear?* Your spirit dances when the holiday bells jingle, your eyes dance over the glistening Christmas lights, your feet dance to that holiday music...but you can't dance around the truth. Not even in The North. It's as firm and steady as that glacier just over the North Ridge.

Santa brushed the surface of his desk. He remembered the hands that designed and built it many years ago.

Meanwhile, Red was ransacking the labyrinth of ideas filling his mind, knowing there was another angle to the truth of which Santa spoke. He grabbed onto that angle firmly and brought it to the table with a raised voice. "Her father. We have an obligation to him to protect his daughter."

"That's exactly why you won't say anything. We have the same obligation he had…Father Winter. He *understood* who his daughter was before he sacrificed his life for The North." Santa squared himself to Red. "Without her…he could not have given himself."

"Sir, I feel you. You've done for me." Red's eyes began to fill up. "This…" he said, opening his hand and winding it around his side, "Mrs. Claus, the other reindeer, the elves…I'm whole. I see straight…"

"…and you run straight," Santa affirmed.

"My life is solid. But it *is* unjust." Red paced toward the bookshelf, feeling a fire once more. "As it is *her* now…that could be *me*. *I* could be the lost one. They would look at us, but they couldn't see us. We put our hearts into *everything*. But *nobody* could hear a single beat of ours…"

"We did. That was the beat we followed. It's how we found *you*."

"You did. But take this all in now. Nobody will say a word? I don't understand why we just don't–"

Santa pounded his fist on his desk and thundered, "Because it's The North! It's the way of The North! And nobody has *ever* had any say in it!"

Nothing. The white doves had left the room. The desk, the crown molding, the six-inch baseboards…the books. Nothing. Just two men. Yes, Red was that now. A man. There was no going back.

Santa breathed in heavy as he collected himself. "Yet, not a single soul here, sits up nights crying about it." He pulled the kerchief from the top pocket of his sport coat and wiped the sweat from his forehead.

Red opened up. "I've stayed up nights crying... thinking about *this*."

Excuse me. Just gotta wipe my own eyes here. Can't rock away this memory. Losing your baby boy as you teach him what it is to be a man. You know you have to give up one to get the other. What's best for him and you know it. Let me just reflect for a minute... yes...it's okay, love...it did have to happen at some point. Always comes faster than you think, though, doesn't it?

Santa waited.

"I promised to look out for her. I just don't know what to say," Red continued.

"You're talkin' a lot for someone who doesn't know what to say," Santa mumbled.

"What's that?"

"Nothing," Santa replied sheepishly, before engaging Red with empathy, "Red, we all promised to watch over her. But she needs to come up with the answers. You're going to meet with her. I've done that. You won't tell her. If she can't look into your eyes and see it, then how can it matter what you say? We *all* need her now as much as she needs herself. Lead her there...like reindeer...in the dark of the night."

Santa walked around his desk.

"Sir..." Red began.

"...Mm. Don't. As it was twenty years ago...we are one with you now." Santa put his hand on Red's shoulder. "Godspeed."

Red humbly exited the room with honor.

Santa walked back to his desk. He opened his top left drawer and pulled out a Bible. Then he sat down...and opened it.

XVII

It was December 21st. Jane was peering over the reservations book, resting on the maître d's podium, at a fine restaurant in Fort Collins, Colorado.

"My friend is already here…probably."

"I see a Jenny. Is that your party?" the host asked.

Red popped up from around the corner.

"You?" Jane blurted with candor.

Red admitted with a wink, "We kind of thought you would bail if Santa told you I was the one you were meeting. C'mon," he followed up lightly, "Sure we have a lot in common."

Jane spun her head in the opposite direction. "'Nother hack from the shop."

"You're tough," Red joked.

Jane giggled. "Did I say that out loud?"

The maître d's face lit up when he realized it was Red standing in front of him. "The best table," he directed the host with gusto.

Red felt awkward and a touch embarrassed by the extra courtesy. When the host raised his head, he *also* realized he was in the presence of Red, and the menus began rattling in his hands.

"Absolutely. This way, sir. Not wasting any time," the frenzied host assured.

He led Jane and Red to a more private section of the restaurant.

I guess by now, you've recognized Jane had a bit of hypersensitivity when it came to having interactions with anyone…or *any thing*. So before anybody could get into *her* kitchen, she always put the hot plate on their hands first. Thus she commenced her line of questioning. "What are you doing in Fort Collins?"

"Visiting family."

"And you took time out for me?"

"You're worth it," Red twinkled with charm.

"Why did you pick this place?"

"The people."

"Because they fall all over you?"

"Because they're good. Good people."

"…Who fall all over you."

"Okay."

"Okay, what?"

"Just okay." Red finished.

Jane was temporarily stalemated.

They arrived at the table, which sat on a raised platform in the center of a separate, more secluded dining room. All of the tables were dressed with white linen tablecloths, and set with silverware that twinkled gracefully under the dimmed lights from above. Booths covered in deep brown leather surrounded the elevated seating area where Jane, Red, and the host stood. Around them, darling baby girls were decked out in velvet dresses and shiny black buckle pumps, while the boys wore thick knitted sweaters that rosied their cheeks. The men coolly styled in the freshest suits as the ladies rose above with stylish strapless dresses and heels. Even the teenagers seemed to give in to their parents' wishes and dress up for their family's holiday dinner outing.

"Is this good, ma'am?" the host asked.

Jane deferred to Red.

"Thank you, Victor."

"Your waiter will be out quicker than you can say, 'Merry—"

"Good evening, sir. And good evening to your beautiful company," the waiter interrupted while gliding in front of the host.

Jane cowered with a smile.

"Should we get you in and out, sir?" the waiter tensely offered.

"We have time," Red pacified, trying to lower the frenzy level down to a mild nervousness.

Two waiters scrambled over to pour water into their glasses. The headwaiter's eyes began pinwheeling. His body half jerked to leave, before jerking back to stay. Leave or stay? Stay or Leave? He wanted to say something, but couldn't get his voice to hop between the double-dutch ropes clapping around inside his head.

"Kordell...easy...no hurry," Red calmly reiterated.

"Yes sir," Kordell responded professionally. Then he scurried away.

"All the formality," Jane noted in a subtly impressed tone. "You bring all your dates here?"

Red played along. "So this is a date?"

"Ha."

Jane brushed Red off. But she was blushing.

"My roots are here," Red answered. Then he lifted the white cloth napkin from the table with the tips of his fingers and placed it in his lap.

Jane was perplexed. "Fort Collins?"

Red opened his lanky arms and stated with grandiosity, "The Choice City."

"Why's that?" Jane asked, allowing herself to be walked into the trap.

"It's a place where you can make your own choice," Red stated proudly. "You can make this choice, or you can make that choice. Whatever choice you're going to make...you can make it right here." Red finished off his advertisement with a twinkle in his eye and a half-smile that could knock the charm off a bracelet.

The youthful girl in Jane bubbled out as she attempted to contain her open-mouthed laugh. "'s not why they call it that."

Red studied Jane. He envisioned her wearing a slim corset wedding dress covered in fine beading and pearls that sparkled without her moving an inch...the dress's classic yet modern design finely sharing each of Jane's vulnerable breaths. He imagined the people in the booths surrounding them were their wedding guests... family and friends. While the men were fitted in sharp-looking tuxes, the women wore formal evening gowns and make-up, which accentuated their ethnicities. They all took turns gazing admiringly at the bride...Jane, with her beautiful brown skin...adorned in a pure white, jewel-encrusted gown.

The room spun smoothly for Red, allowing him to see three hundred sixty degrees around it. But he didn't need to look around. Jane's presence. That was all he needed.

Jane appeared sure and at ease. She was without the doubts that other brides might have. Clearly, she had not one. She let herself take in the *fine-ness* of Red in his black bow tie and crisp white shirt. His perfectly black tuxedo dinner jacket–freshly pressed. His eyes...warm and brown as roasted chestnuts. His chiseled jawline with a sprig of five o'clock.

This brother's goofy, Jane thought to herself.

Notice the word, *"thought"*. Not *"said"*. 'Cause absolutely nothing about Red was goofy. Red was so deep he could make you reassess your whole life just to be in the same room with him. Make you feel like you were standing in concrete, all for the purpose of judging yourself before you could move on. Goofy? No. Even the diamond snowflake pendant resting warmly next to Jane's heart knew that. Jane was sitting at a table with her equal, and she felt it. If anything, Red had his stuff more together than she did. She was aware of *that* too.

This is so stupid, Jane rattled in her mind, *I hate this place*. But she didn't. She loved it. Jane was married to white, but on this occasion, she somehow had the feeling casual would be okay. Her brown silk blouse and checkered brown and black leggings worked just fine. No need for protective armor today. When she glanced up at Red, in his burgundy blazer with black acetate lapels, with his ears and those awkward elbows...she was able to breathe through her soft lips...and not worry about a thing.

"Can I tell you about our vegetarian specials, sir?" Kordell interrupted.

"Here we go," sassed Jane.

Red fired back in amusement, "Don't make this be our last date."

"You'll have control over that?"

Red beamed. Then he sighed and wiped his hand down his face. On the note of Red being a vegetarian, no one in the room was eating meat.

Throughout the dinner, patrons of the establishment sporadically expressed appreciation to Red with a tip of the cap, a fist bump, a wave, a point, a thumbs-up, or a dap and a hug. The other waiters made subtle motions of respect to Red as well. It was as though he were some sort of Mafia boss. However, everyone engaged Red in an honorable way, with positive gestures. Not out of fear.

A few tables away, there was a little sweetheart in an adorable red dress with her hair up in afro puffs. She couldn't take her eyes off Red. He put his fingers into the shape of a heart for her. She melted and returned the symbol back to him.

Jane could sense what was happening around her. It was special. This place...felt like The North, but maybe with less responsibility...for her at least.

Wine glasses clinked, creating subtle dreamlike tones in the background. Conversations swirled around them like flower petals being passed along by a gentle spring breeze. And then—

"Miami," Red stated clearly in a deadpan manner.

Jane's face became flush. Her eyes got big. *What in the...?* she thought. But what she said was, "Heard about that?"

"I hear about everything," Red said, holding in his amusement. "What were you doing in Miami?"

Jane hesitated. Was this the time to make up a story? Should she come clean? Now, you have to remember who she was sitting across from.

Red helped her along. "You were looking for..."

Jane wiggled in her seat. "The truth." Her exposed vulnerability made her feel even more uncomfortable than before.

"Find it?"

"I think I found it."

Jane peered down at her glass. With her hands weakening, her focus became diverted to how she was holding the bowl of the glass...as if it was going to tip over from her restless fingers. However, Red provided a comfortability that encouraged Jane to lift her head.

The two of them studied each other.

Red took a deep breath while mutual silence suspended the issue between them. "Jane…you don't need to go searching for the truth…the truth…finds you."

Jane stared through Red hopelessly. She was thinking about what he said. She just didn't have anything to say back.

Red picked up his fork. "People used to put me at the center. Make me the center of attention, only to make fun of me. I'd think I was finally going to get my due…find a trace of acceptance. Then I'd be tricked, teased, or left out of the very game they put me at the center of." He spun the fork in his hand.

Jane became more drawn in.

She closed her eyes as Red continued, "…Laughed at, but you know…I persevered, and fought through it. Here, for me today… things aren't bad. They're good, Jane."

Jane's delicate lashes drew up. "You look good."

"Thanks," Red humbled.

"I mean, you look like…you did it. Like you're there." Jane gave herself away, "I want to be there."

"See," Red said with passion. "I used to be the same way. The place you're trying to get to…I don't know if this sounds bad, but the place you're trying to get to…you're not getting to it, because you don't want to."

Jane fired up. "Don't want to?"

"No, I mean…I *let* them make fun of me, in a way. I put myself there. Then, I woke up one day and decided…*I'm* going to take the lead. I'm not going to walk around trying to find friends, find people to fit in with. I'm going to, for once, be me…do how I do. Now I lead and *they*…follow *me*." Red chuckled lightly as he reflected on

the current. "Funny…But they're not following me to fit in, or 'cause I got the squeeze on 'em. They're following me…"

"…out of respect," Jane finished.

"All I'm saying is, don't let their darkness steal *your* light. You…do what you do," he said, pointing to Jane with conviction.

"Wow." Was all Jane could say. She'd just had it dropped on her.

"I'm not tryin' to–"

"I know, I know."

The waiters arrived with Red's salad and Jane's salmon. Each plate a work of art. Each waiter standing at attention, focused on Red's next call.

"We're good. Thank you."

"Thank you," Jane said politely.

Red began to eat his salad. Jane shook her head.

"What?" Red asked with a shy smile.

Jane wagged her fork at him with a grin she couldn't hold back.

Red finished chewing and swallowed. "When people come at you sideways, it has absolutely nothing to do with who *you* are. It has to do with who *they* are. Most of the greatest people the world has ever seen have been ridiculed and flat out hated by so many. I'm not saying it's right." Red commanded Jane's attention once more. "Listen to me, no great person is loved by everyone."

"Santa," Jane responded timidly.

"All the work he does throughout the year, and there are people out there who don't believe he exists. I mean adults…maybe I can see a few of them if they've had some serious stuff go down in their life. Might cause them to stop trustin' in a lot of things. Third grad-ers, though? Walkin' around sayin' he's some made up hoax?" Our weaknesses can become our strengths." Red worked his fork into his salad. "Dependin' on what you do…it can work the opposite."

"The Choice City, huh?" Jane surrendered lightheartedly.

Red sarcastically concluded his sales pitch, "*Where else would you rather be?*"

Jane and Red enjoyed their dinner like two old friends getting back together. Sharing some stories while avoiding others. Laughing amid the melodic tones of chiming wine glasses. Finding peace in the soothing hum of the friendly conversations surrounding them. Red's time was growing short, but speaking of places one would *rather be*...Red would rather be at a table, sitting across from Jane, than any other place on the planet.

When they finished their meals, a mutual pressure was felt in regard to not stealing away too much of the other's time. Neither Red nor Jane were in a race to leave the restaurant, but eventually, they both felt the need to get going.

Red followed Jane through the seating areas on their way out of the restaurant. When they reached the vestibule, a gathering of people respectfully parted for them, but Red hustled to the door and opened it *himself.* For Jane, of course. And she walked her beautiful figure out of the restaurant, knowing no one had eyes on her. Which was just fine.

Red acknowledged the rest of the patrons with a nod as he and Jane meandered out onto the rocky, uneven parking lot. The dim light, from the lamppost at the opposite end of the lot, reflected off the rainwater resting in the crevasses of the weary blacktop. Drops of rain blanketed the parked cars...hiding their differences. Hiding status. You see how that worked? In that Fort Collins restaurant, even though Red may have garnered a degree of extra attention, the people all entered as equals. As family. And you could tell this by the warm, free flowing spirit inside the place.

Jane shuffled her feet on the way to her car. "Sorry for accidentally shoving you aside the other day at The Headquarters."

"Accidentally?" Red zipped back.

Jane giggled. "On purpose-ally."

"Definitely on purpose-ally."

Jane showed earnest remorse for her actions.

"Forget about it," Red eased, "Remember, I've been treated much worse."

Jane punched him in the arm.

"Ay!"

Jane got close to Red and focused on his face. She checked him over. Red stood like a soldier, nervous, but confident at the same time. He let her work him over in that stare. And she didn't let go. Red was pinned without Jane having moved a muscle.

"I feel a strange familiarity with you. Your face..." she started.

Jane had no intention of letting Red off easy. Deep inside, she was sensing there was more to this meeting. More to this *setup*. Red began to look away, but Jane turned her head right along with his. "I see your face. I know we cross paths around Santa's Headquarters. What do you do there anyway?"

"Work with the reindeer," Red said casually. But he felt cornered.

"You're not one of the elves."

Red shook his head. He began fixating on the lamppost.

"Working with the reindeer is nothing to be ashamed of," Jane consoled. "My gosh, do you know Rudolph? Will you take me to see him one day? *The Spirit of the Night*, isn't he?" Jane gushed, rambling on like she was a kid again. "Makes you believe you have the power to do *whatever*! I mean, I've never seen him up there. He must move like a flash. When you stare into the pitch-black sky on the twenty-fourth…" Jane took an invigorating breath, "…it's like anything is possible…Rudolph…there is one tough–"

"I'll see what I can do," Red interrupted.

Jane doubled back, "Probably get asked that all the time."

They arrived at Jane's car. There was an awkward silence, what with the two of them not knowing how to say goodbye. *Was it a date?* Red knew he was there on business, but he also knew he *wasn't* there on business. And Jane was swept up. She felt a glow. Felt free. Even forgot Red was there for a second. She slid her legs down into her 65 and closed the door. In her giddiness, she zoned out facing straight ahead.

Tap, tap, tap! Jane jumped.

Red was still standing there waiting for her to open the window. Jane pressed the one touch, and the two of them waited…for the glass…to slide down…all the way.

"You're not going to go seal yourself up in an igloo now, are you?" Red asked with a hint of seriousness.

Jane could feel the underlying reality in Red's question. It surged through her like a line of warm blood running down the middle of her chest. She lowered her head to shield him from the tears dotting the corners of her eyes.

Red leaned down…and gently turned his head along with hers. "The *truth*…will find *you*."

"The truth will set you free?" Jane sniffled in an attempt at humor.

"It won't always do that…" Red charmed earnestly, "…but it will find you."

XVIII

Jane was cruising the outskirts of the North Village on an uncharacteristically balmy day. By December 22nd, the ground in The North usually had a cover of snow, and the air would typically have more of a bite to it. But have no fear. For all those concerned, the bite was coming.

Jane's phone buzzed and rattled against the plastic console of her car. The name, "JOKE," came up on the screen of her phone, but she chose to touch the green *Accept* circle anyway.

"Ms. Frost, please," sneered Andre Branch, the sunshine selling realtor.

"You got 'er," Jane coiled.

Andre blasted unabashedly, "You may have destroyed my office, and left all of my important records in disarray, but you'll *never* stop me from meeting with my biggest client ever."

Jane waited indifferently.

"Darryl Richardson."

"Richardson Snow Sports?" Jane cried out, failing to mask her shock and anxiety.

"Ski equipment, winter clothing stores, outlets, lodges, snow hiking adventures, ice fishing treks…"

Andre paused for effect, before continuing with an air of braggadociousness. "Richardson knows those days of cold winter snow are gone. That winter mystique. He knows it's over. And when I get Richardson, the *whole world* will be knocking each other over to live in a balmy place with lots of sun! One more thing, Ms. Frost…I wouldn't do anything low-down. Remember…Santa's watching."

Jane hung up on Andre, but that didn't diminish his full satisfaction. Andre was the cat who had just swallowed a canary. He was absolutely certain there was nothing Jane could do to get in his way this time. The paperwork was already in his briefcase. All it needed was a signature. Andre smiled at his bag as he put his phone down and gathered the keys to his SUV.

Jane pulled over to the side of the road. She opened up the map app on her phone and started entering addresses. She intensely scrolled up and down with nerves growing like a blazing fire in her stomach. One swipe took her out of the maps, and a quick tap put her into her *Contacts*. Another exaggerated swipe landed her on the Rs. She tapped on the name *Rollo*, to call him. He answered on the first ring.

"Snowman!" Jane shouted in relief.

"What choo need?" Rollo belted out with open arms.

"Am I on speaker?"

"No."

"You sure?"

Rollo's seven sidekicks edged closer to his phone, sensing *a happening*.

"Rollo, you sure I'm not on speaker?" she repeated.

"As sure as I am white."

Jane pulled the phone from her ear and inspected it, temporarily confused. Then she proceeded. "You asked me for a favor earlier... The snow."

"I'm listening."

"I need a favor from you, first."

Like a shot, Rollo's right-hand sidekick blurted out, "CODE BLUE!", triggering the rest of the cavalry to join in, "CODE BLUE! CODE BLUE! CODE BLUE!"

The sidekicks began boomeranging around the room hysterically. They jumped off the back of the sofa, put each other into headlocks, and ran full speed at each other, doing a great imitation of a steel cage wrestling match.

"CLOTHESLIIIIINE!"

Rollo's recreation room was transformed into an all-out mosh pit. Playful strangling put the cherry on top of an otherwise low-key afternoon. Rollo pressed a finger to his opposite ear so he could at least *hear Jane*, because he certainly couldn't hear himself think.

"Thought you had me off speaker!"

"I did!"

Pillows started firing across the room. "CODE BLUE! CODE BLUE!"

Rollo gave an exasperated apology. "Sorry, Jane! They're driving me crazy!"

"Good," Jane said feeling appeased, "'Cause I can use a little crazy right now."

XIX

Andre Branch had just left his realty office in northern Saskatchewan. His gospel music comforted him as he guided his SUV through a series of small towns, en route to closing the biggest business deal of his life. From the street he was on, he could see the highlands on which winter mogul Darryl Richardson lived. The house was in the distance, but there was nothing blocking Andre from a view of his destiny.

HONK! HONK! BEEP! BEEP! ERRREACH! An all-white Hummer came swerving behind Andre's SUV. It was Rollo, with his right-hand man riding shotgun. Two of the other sidekicks were sitting in the back seat with their feet knocking around several inches from the floor.

ERREEAACH! Behind Rollo's Hummer, a second white Hummer from his squad approached. Inside it, one sidekick handled the wheel. The other scrunched up on the floor below the driver seat, manipulating the gas and brake pedals with his hands. ERRRRR! They veered to the left, overlapping Rollo's Hummer on their way to try and pass Andre on the wing.

On Andre's stereo, the gospel singer called for Jesus on cue, belting out, *"Jesus! Jesus! I need you!"*

"Mercy heavens, Mercy heavens! Help me Lord!" Andre squealed.

I don't know if Andre was on Jesus's radar that day, so take his plea for help with a slice of Black Forest Cake.

"Jesus! I'm waiting for a sign…" the song continued.

BRRRRRM! THWAP! THWAP! THWAP! A third white Hummer from Rollo's team came tearing up the road with flames shooting from its exhaust. It slid over to tail Rollo. RRRRRRMMM! The sidekicks inside the third Hummer were using the same wheel and pedal system as the 'kicks in the second Hummer. But the third Hummer had more juice to it. ERRRRRR! They wove out and passed Rollo, before wiggling up tight to the second Hummer's rear bumper. BRM-RM-RM. However, both Hummers had to gear down and fall back to avoid oncoming traffic. RAEERN! RAEERN!

Diagonally parked cars squeezed the road even further, helping Andre maintain his lead. The windows of mom-and-pop stores vibrated dramatically as the caravan charged through, forcing the stores' patrons to lower their knickknacks, step back from the sidewalk, and take notice of the wild pursuit blowing by.

Andre gunned it as soon as his car grasped daylight at the opposite end of the strip. ERRRMMMMM! *"Glory! Glory!"* his radio celebrated. "Holy Mary! Holy Mary!" Andre howled.

The Hummers tucked together, single file, in order to make it through the center of town, allowing Andre to open up a two-block advantage. HUMMMMM! MMMMM! Suddenly, a sparkling, Polar White SL 65 popped out from a side street, cutting Andre's lead in half.

"JANE?" Andre questioned in despair. "HOW?"

ERRRRR! Andre ripped his steering wheel to the right and knifed down a one-way backstreet. He thought the shortcut to Darryl Richardson's estate would pinch off the pack on his trail, but the three Hummers and high-powered Mercedes shuttled through the old-time town like a pack of IndyCar drivers. Andre's lead was dwindling by the second. While he was preoccupied with Jane, the road widened. Rollo managed to get his front bumper within a couple feet of Andre's rear gate.

Jane swerved back behind Rollo, reached her hand out of the window, and sprayed ice on both sides of Andre's SUV.

"NOW!" the sidekicks blurted in unison.

They jumped out of the back doors of Rollo's Hummer. "Woooooah!"

The 'kicks surfed on Jane's ice path, and latched onto the rear door handles of Andre's ride. Andre began slapping and smacking at his lock switches.

"Aoww!" Smack! "Ugh!" Smack, smack!

Instead of locking the doors, Andre accidentally unlocked them. They flung open! The two sidekicks hung on for dear life. But they were able to use the momentum of Andre's gear shifts and turns to wrap their legs around the inside of the doors, and swing themselves into his back seat. With the wind furiously whipping through the car, the 'kicks still managed to slam the doors shut and seal themselves in, while Andre's SUV barreled down the tight streets of northern Saskatchewan.

Andre upped the ante by driving more erratically. It was working. Jane couldn't pass him and the sidekicks became disoriented from all the swerving. The 'kicks tried to pull themselves together. They reached up, grabbed their seatbelts, and buckled themselves in.

CLICK! CLICK! Then one of them leaned forward and reached for Andre's arm.

"What are you doing?" the other 'kick hollered.

"I'm stoppin' him from drivin'! I'm gonna get 'im!"

THWAP! THWAP! THWAP! THWAP! Andre's SUV zipped passed the parked cars in front of a small town market area.

"How you gonna do that?"

"How do you think? I'm gonna grab his arm!"

ERREEACH! MMMM! Andre whipped his vehicle around another corner, with Jane hot on his tail.

"You grab his arm, he's gonna crash!"

"Isn't that the point?" the inspired sidekick shouted over the noise of the chase.

"WE'RE IN THE CAR! IF HE CRASHES, WE'LL CRASH TOO!"

"YES, WE'LL CRASH TOO!" Andre agreed, somehow keeping up with their conversation.

Andre sensed he was only three miles from the elongated driveway leading to Darryl Richardson's home. *I did it!*, he thought to himself. He opened his window and shouted in grand euphoria,"… AS FAST AS YOU CAN, YOU CAN'T CATCH MEEEE! YOU KNOW WHO I AM! YOU KNOW WHO I AMMMM!"

The two sidekicks sat back in their seats, shrunken like two children on a ride to their grandparent's house. There was a tranquil pause. Then one of the sidekicks grabbed a newspaper from the floor, rolled it up, and whapped the other one with it. Whap! Swat! WHAP! The second sidekick used his arm to shield himself as he was barraged again. Whap! SWAT!

"Come on!"

"You come on!"

WHAP!

Eventually, the sidekick in duress spotted a roll of rubber-banded pamphlets below his seat. He stretched his arm down, scooped up the roll, and cranked his elbow wide. But then he hesitated. Having a brief glimpse of clarity, Rollo's warriors set in motion an attack on Andre...swatting *him* instead of each other. WHAP! SWAT! SMACK! SMACK!

"Aah! Stop! Santa's watching!"

Andre ducked and tried to block the onslaught with his arm while weaving his SUV back and forth. GRRREEEACH! "Ooh! Uh! SANTA'S WAAAATCHING!"

WHOOSH! The third Hummer roared forward. The 'kick on gas and brake duty grabbed the hockey stick that was lying between the front seats, and handed it to the driver.

"For the pedals!" he shouted.

Then he hopped up, hit the sunroof button, and began climbing out of the top of the Hummer. The driver jammed the end of the hockey stick onto the gas pedal to keep the speed.

The sidekick on the roof jumped...

And landed on top of Andre's SUV!

Rollo's fearless friend tried to pry off Andre's sunroof like he had seen it done in the movies...but this was no movie.

He gasped, "Why is this not...?"

ERRREEE! ERROOO! Andre snaked back and forth. Rollo's little trooper was sent flying! Thinking fast, the airborne sidekick pulled a cord on his waist, which opened a parachute from the back of his jacket. It swallowed a gust of wind and shot him straight into the air. He rose above the power lines and floated over the stores until he found a safe place to land, in a park at the center of town.

Meanwhile, Rollo had made a sharp right and then a left, putting him on a street parallel to Andre.

Rollo's wingman panicked, "That's not the…"

"We only have four blocks to pass him!"

"C'mon then!"

"We got 'em…we got 'em."

Andre thought he was in the clear, because he was about to enter the semi-circle opening to Darryl Richardson's driveway. However, Rollo and his right-hand 'kick could see they had gained a few car lengths on him. As Andre slowed to navigate the entry to the driveway, Rollo flew in full speed, rode the curb, and roared his Hummer into the mouth of the driveway ahead of him. He still needed to stop, though.

"HOLD ON!" he shouted.

Rollo pulled his wheel hard, spinning his Hummer into a three-quarter turn. ERREEEE-EEEE-EEEACH! Burned rubber smoked into the air. Andre swiftly maneuvered his SUV to try and cut around Rollo's roadblock. But Rollo's sixth sidekick was able to recklessly bolt over the opposite curb ahead of Andre even though he was now operating the third Hummer on his own. With no one to work the brake pedal, the sixth 'kick *also* had to find a way to stop. The hockey stick trick would not suffice as a braking method with the high level stunt he was about to perform.

He spoke to his Hummer, "Don't roll, don't roll…"

With only one hand on the wheel, he desperately threw the gearshift into park, gripped the steering wheel with both hands, and yanked down. VROOOO…RU-REEEEECH!

Andre jerked his wheel to the left, ERRRR, and avoided clipping the tail of the *Fire Hummer* by inches. But he lost his angle on Richardson's driveway.

Seizing the opportunity, Jane knifed inside the path of Andre's SUV, and nosedived her Mercedes into the small opening between Rollos' two Hummers. She was through!

Within milliseconds, Rollo's sixth sidekick completed his Hummer's one-hundred-eighty-degree spin, matching Rollo's Hummer front bumper to front bumper, as they teamed up to close out Andre's SUV like two pinball flippers. Andre slammed on his brakes. SHRRRRRRAH-RAH-RAH-RAH! The last Hummer came in hot and ripped another one-eighty behind him. ROOOAR-EEE-EEE-EAACH!

Andre was boxed in.

Dense particles of burned rubber floated down from the air in slow motion. Smoke rose up in the opposite direction. However, when the gray dissipated, the temperature of the event did not cool.

The heavy white doors of Rollo's vehicles opened, and the last standing sidekicks began hopping out. The first group lined up alongside the two Hummers centered in front of Andre's SUV. The sidekicks in the backseat of Andre's vehicle stepped out next. They brushed themselves off and broadened their chests.

Andre slowly emerged in disbelief.

It was a pretty big scene, but the custom, all-white interior of Rollo's Hummer demanded Andre's attention the second Rollo casually opened his door. Each stitch of the diamond-quilted leather said *BOSS*. The floor mats, the headliner, the steering wheel...white as snow.

Rollo stepped down, sauntered to the middle of the roadblock, crossed his arms, and gloated, "Thumpity thump, thump, my good man."

Andre was dripping with sweat.

He exhaled in delirium, "What happened to the jolly, happy soul?"

Jane was already out of sight. She jammed her foot on the gas coming out of each turn. Leaves kicked up from the back wheels of her Benz as she fired her way up the steep meandering driveway of Richardson's compound. Zzzzrmmm! She almost forgot she wasn't in a race anymore. Jane rose higher and higher onto the hill. Eventually a sense of peace grew within her.

She arrived at the roundabout in front of Richardson's house.

Jane hadn't planned what to say, but she gave no pause. She parked her car and marched herself straight up to the stone porch of the world's most renowned winter mogul. Knock, knock, knock!

Didn't take but a minute for a brawny, six-foot-five, flannel-shirt-wearing mountain man to open the door. His dark brown hands were mighty. His knuckles harbored white ash, as did every other crevice and scar lying across his hands. About fifty years old, with a touch of gray hair and an unapologetic round belly. Overall straps hung from his broad shoulders, attaching themselves to a bib, which led down to worn, faded pant legs. Pale brown, steel-toed leather work boots corralled his tremendous feet. And there he was…examining Jane on his doorstep.

"Mr. Richardson," Jane pushed out with trepidation.

"Hey."

Jane didn't know how she was going to get through to this sizable man. Didn't know if she should pull on his heartstrings, talk *man talk* to him, or stumble around and hope for the best. She *was* conscious of the fact of how close she was to him, and how she might never get this close again.

"Wanted to speak to you about some developments."

"I'm actually supposed to be meeting with somebody right now… but they're not–"

"It will only take a second."

Darryl squinted…waited a beat…then opened his large wooden door all the way. He moved aside without speaking. Then he began walking back into his house.

An open door from Darryl Richardson was about as big a welcome as anyone was ever going to get. Aware of this, Jane entered behind him, and followed the mogul inside.

"If ya don't mind kickin' off those leaves. Keep from slippin'."

Darryl walked through the living room. "I get ya a drink?"

This meant one thing. Jane was invited to stay. Couldn't tell how long. But she was in.

Rollo and his seven sidekicks had come through on the highest level. A frantic bunch they were, but good friends to have. You know, the kind you don't get to hang out with all that often, but even still, you find yourself thinking about 'em all the time. There's always somethin' happens in a day to make them pop into your mind, whether you have an event to celebrate or you're feeling a little down. When the whole gang gets together all sorts of craziness breaks out…for bad or good. The authenticity of a reciprocal friendship. *Yeah,* Janey was lucky to have Rollo and the seven. They were *real* tight. In a way, they all came from the same place.

"Powdery snow will be gracing your resort for a long time," Jane initiated, sensing she better move forward.

Darryl's cell alerted him of an incoming call. He picked up his phone, glanced at it, and then dropped it back into his top pocket.

"Wish I could get that in writing," Mr. Richardson said in his gruff voice. "To be perfectly blunt, I don't know why I *should* continue to hold these properties."

Jane was sitting on the edge of her seat on the couch, leaning over, with her elbows on her knees. She wasn't used to being the one making the sales pitch. "Your ice festival *always* makes the headlines. You're going to turn down all that business?"

"Ice Fest, the Snowmobile Finals, the slopes, the lodge…we could both go on and on. But did you see? It's a few days to Christmas, and my grass is as green as it was on the first of May. Those days you're remembering…that magic…it's gone." Darryl's bold, deep brown hands rubbed the bottom of his chin.

Jane realized she was going to have to open Darryl's mind back up with her own two hands. With her own will.

"That's why I came to you," she said with conviction. "Heard you were thinking of shutting down. Didn't want you to give all this up…" She directed Darryl's attention toward the two-hundred-seventy-degree view beyond his expansive living room windows. "…give it up…and regret it later."

"Regret?" Richardson pounded back as he rose up in his chair.

Jane recognized her stay could be coming to an abrupt end. She grasped for a lifeline.

"Eighty-five and sunny?"

Darryl grunted.

"Flat land and smog. Is that a good time? There's nothing *close* to the nature here." Jane was gaining wind, and the big burly man was now eager to listen to Jane's next thought. "The sparkle of the ice on the edges of the creeks and rivers. The way the snow glistens at seven in the morning when the sun first hits it. How the wind sweeps up the powder and brushes it across your face. It's as though you're inhaling the first air that's ever been."

This was no longer a sales pitch. Janey could talk about snow for days. The glamour of the cold winter was attractive to her. She forgot Darryl was in the room as she gazed out past the windows. The glass was gone. The wind was coming through. She could hear it.

She could feel it against her warm brown skin…against her pitch-black hair. Yes…and when she talked, she spoke not from her lips, but from her core. "The clear slate the new snow brings. White," she whispered.

Jane noticed Mr. Richardson once more, but now he and Jane were staring out into the mountains with the same set of eyes.

She didn't let up. "…Your sweat freezes to your face after chopping wood into the evening. Mr. Richardson, I bet you even drink a cold one on a fifteen-degree day."

Darryl nodded.

They both let the breeze flow unto them…around them…past them. Darryl closed his eyes. His mind cleared.

This was Jane's poetry. This was why she persevered to climb that hill. I know Jane. We've had a lot of one-on-one time. I've shared my thoughts with her in the past as she's sat and stared out of a window. She *is* listening. Don't often get much back, though. I know her from her works. From *the artist*. There, it all comes out, whether she wants it to or not. The cold, the snow, the wind… these things were her poem…her song…her painting. *Yes*. Breathe it in, child. I'm talking to you, now. Breathe in The North. You feel something you didn't feel before. Why I needed to tell this story… why you're reading it. There's more to it.

And the artist had just signed another masterpiece… from her soul.

"So I'd be crazy to think I'd be happy drinking a hot latte while renting out jet skis to a bunch of pansies, who think the only time they can eat ice cream is in the summer."

"Pssh, right?" Jane answered, sounding like a teenager.

Darryl blustered out a short laugh of content, "Pfuf." Then his phone rang again. This time he tapped the red *Decline* circle.

"There was a day when you decided to buy this land, start your business, and raise your family here," Jane continued.

Darryl's excitement gradually intensified. He pointed directly to where Jane was sitting on the sofa. "Where you're at, was the top of our Glistening Snow Ski Mountain. Lift would drop off skiers right there. My father and I built each chair…one by one. Rented the crane…ran the cables all the way up here." His eyes opened wide as he pointed outside the window to a massive mountain, rising up behind the high peaks in the foreground. A gondola with the name *Snow Dreams* cruised on cables toward the mountain's summit. "The new one," he stated proudly.

"It's everything," Jane whispered in awe.

"Snow Dream Mountain. Two thousand feet higher than where we're standing now."

"Did you build that too?"

"Heck no!"

Darryl and Jane burst out laughing.

"I'm not crazy…" Darryl stood up and took a drink from his big coffee mug. Then he winked. "…not easily convinced either."

"I didn't convince you."

"You didn't. But you reminded me of a lot." Darryl turned his back to Jane, and faced the great landscape on the other side of the windows. Then he pointed to a framed black and white photograph hanging on the wall. It was nine-year-old Darryl Richardson standing with his father on a frozen lake. There was an ice hut to the left of them and an ice-fishing hole in the background. "It's a picture of me with my dad."

Jane studied it.

"You see where I was looking?"

"At the fish?" Jane responded, taking a stab.

"No. My dad's hands."

Jane was puzzled.

"I dropped my gloves in the ice water, so he gave me his. I kept wondering how he was surviving. Thinking his hands might freeze off at any minute."

They laughed again.

"Was as if he were an *ice man*, carved out of one of them glaciers. Heh...I wear gloves," Darryl admitted. Then he gently patted Jane's back with one of his mighty, bear-paw-sized hands. "But I'm an ice man too," he said, looking Jane in the eye, "...Wear it like a badge of honor."

Darryl took a few steps toward the living room when his phone rang a third time. This time he accepted the call and listened, before responding, "...No, sir. Come to the conclusion I'm happy right here where I am. But you have a good day, Mr. Branch."

"Thank you, Mr. Richardson," Jane said with appreciation.

"Don't thank me...you're spot on, *Ms. Frost*."

Jane's chin pulled back into her neck and her eyes saucered. She couldn't hide her surprise...or the feeling that maybe she had been caught.

Darryl tilted his head with a warm smile. "You don't think I'd let just anybody into my house? If I'm caretaker of the biggest snow entertainment corporation on the planet...how could I not know just a little something about frost?" Then he showed Jane a text from Andre, which read,

> "I'M GOING TO TAKE EVERY
> LAST PERSON FROM AROUND
> YOU! YOUR SNOW RESORTS
> WILL BE EMPTY! YOU'LL BE
> LOST WITHOUT ME! WE

COULD HAVE BEEN GREAT
TOGETHER!..."

The text was abnormally long. Darryl gave his phone several swipes, scrolling down to show Jane its absurd length.

"Oooh. All caps too," Jane interjected with feigned worry.

Darryl chuckled. "And no moji thingies?"

The heads of Darryl's two children were pressed against the spindles of the railing on the upstairs landing. They swallowed up every piece of conversation, every image, as though they were in the presence of St. Nick, himself. And now, for the first time, Darryl found *himself* on the other end of the bargaining table.

"Ur, uh, Jane?" he pushed out timidly.

Jane paused, fully aware of the audience above.

"When you're done with your work, my kids would love to meet you...if you do that sort of thing."

Jane nodded and smiled while giving a wave to the children.

"Oh wait," Richardson called out excitedly. "Only take a second... think you can appreciate..."

Darryl led Jane to his mammoth garage. To Jane, it more resembled an airplane hangar. He hit a button to open the large garage doors. Then he walked over to one of the walls and picked up a heavy extension cord. "Give me a hand with this guy?"

Jane helped Darryl drag the thick extension cord over to a generator. Then she plugged it in for him. Jane could anticipate what was coming and she couldn't wait.

There was a large red power lever on top of the generator. "Can I?" she asked eagerly.

Mr. Richardson gave the okay. "We're ready."

When Jane pulled the lever, white Christmas lights sparkled across the entire property.

Jane marvelled, "Spectacular, Mr. Richardson."

"Darryl."

"Darryl," Jane repeated, turning up a smile.

Jane walked toward the magical display. She put her hands in her pockets, taking a moment to absorb the clarity of each shining bulb. While she was admiring Darryl's accomplishment, she was also contemplating her next course of action. Jane knew she had to push on. She took a few steps in the direction of her car, but her train of thought was interrupted.

"Hey, Jane!" Darryl called out.

A blast of wind pulled itself up from the hill below and roared across Richardson's estate. Jane let the gust pass, before glancing back.

Darryl lifted his chin and pumped his husky fist. "Go get 'em!"

XX

THE GERMAN ALPS

Jane stood on a small plot of grassy land, seven thousand one hundred fifty-four feet up, on the side of a mountain in the German Alps. Before her, sprawled the isolated, yet cozy, compound of Father Time. The bright sandstone of the central building contrasted with dark evergreens that spread over the tightest and steepest curves of a stretch of hills, which snaked downward from the mountain's tallest peak. Not far away, smaller mountains surrounded a voluminous lake that lay without a wrinkle, in the center.

Tucked a few thousand feet below the highest peak in the German Alps, Father Time's compound was a place one would only travel to, if they desperately needed an answer...or some help. *Was it worth the climb?* I like to say. No bridges or gondolas to get you up there. You wanted to meet with Father Time, you better have two things: a bag full of supplies and a mind full of patience. Janey had neither. But, by now you've probably noticed, she didn't quite do things by the book. Jane made it up there on will. Guess you could add that to the list of things you need to make it up to Father Time. *Will.* And child, they ain't sellin' that at the corner store.

Jane's white boots pressed careful steps into fallen ferns and needles, which covered a soft dirt path leading toward the main entry of Father Time's compound. She inhaled the serene scent of the evergreens, but the powdery dirt beneath her feet made it clear she was not on stable ground. As she ventured on, she found that the true path to the front of the building was clouded under the dark shadows of the giant trees surrounding her. Littered branches and needles obscured the walkway all the more. This left Jane doubting which direction to take. Furthermore, she began to grasp the fact that there were more than a couple of entryways.

One side of the building showed signs of being either a stable or a sunroom. It was hard for Jane to tell. On the opposite end there was a withering greenhouse, with glass panes so foggy, the plant life inside had to be growing entirely on its own.

Jane brushed away some of the plant debris with her boot, unveiling stones cut into oversized squares. Her focus was then drawn to aged, life-sized marble chess pieces trapped under fallen branches. When she spun around, she noticed the chess pieces were sporadically arranged around her.

The haphazard greenery forced Jane to meander through the chessboard, guessing which entrance was the correct one to approach. She tentatively moved ahead, not knowing what type of mess she might fall into if she set down a foot in the wrong place. However, as she twisted her way around a low branch, two giant, arched redwood doors revealed themselves, dropping her uncertainty into the chaotic plant life behind her.

Jane stepped deliberately toward the grand entry. She knocked on the door several times, but there was no answer. She inhaled deeply and reached for the large black wrought iron door handle. Although the handle was made of a cold metal, it felt warm to her palm, encouraging Jane to give the heavy iron handle a pull. The door creaked open as if no one had touched it for a century, but its wood smelled freshly carved. The door's patina carried the reflection of a flame dancing on the wick of a candle as it sat on an entry table just inside the foyer.

"Hello?" Jane called out, "Hello?" Her voice echoed through the entrance hall. She breathed in. It smelled like an old castle. Jane hedged, reflecting on her position…high on a mountain…alone… inside a building that was large enough for a king, yet bared no riches. She wondered, *Is anyone here?*

"Hello?" Jane leaned forward and called out again. Except for the sound of her own voice travelling back to her, she was met with only silence.

She decided to walk down the hallway. The sound of her boots clicked off the stone walls with each step she took. As Jane cautiously proceeded, she became aware of evenly spaced side tables along the hallway, holding a variety of chess boards, all appearing to be in mid-game. In addition, she noticed names scribbled in black ink on cards peeking out from under them.

Jane passed the corner, and there, for the first time, she saw a shadow move. When she looked down at the opposite end of the hall, she could see light spilling into the hallway from under large wooden doors. The shadow rippled again. Jane approached tentatively. She allowed herself to be drawn right up to the door where she caught her first glimpse of a movement. But she would not proceed farther.

There was a subtle sound. Tick, tick, tick.

"Are you going to stand out there all day? Or are you going to come in?" an African-accented voice called from deep inside the room.

Jane was startled, but she felt compelled to follow instructions. This was a new feeling for Jane. Nonetheless, she went up to the door, opened it, and scooted herself a few steps inside the room. Father Time sat facing away from her. Only the top of his head was visible from his high-back chair. He would not remove his intense focus from the huge clock hanging high on the wall behind his desk. But he did speak.

"Two roads diverged in a wood...and I took the one less travelled by..."

Tick, tick, tick.

"...and that has made all the difference," Jane finished. She unclasped her hands. "Robert Frost."

Father Time spun his chair around, baring a sly smile, which no one could embody as fully as he. Appearing to be sixty-five years old, the Father of all time could make you feel welcome and uneasy at the same moment. Like you were disturbing him, but he was happy you did...if that makes any sense. He always wore a dress shirt and tie...like a doctor...and he was *always* at work. Even when it looked like he was resting, his mind was churning like the gears of his clocks. As a result, if you went to him, you could be certain you were disturbing him, but you could also be certain you weren't interrupting his sleep. Because he didn't do that.

Time ran his hand back through his rich gray hair. He stared at Jane, who was waiting for an invite. An invite that wasn't going to come. Jane's mind wandered. The air in the room was thick, but pure, like that of an old church. Then there were the clocks. There were *so many* clocks.

"Your visit here is based on a need for something, or you just dropped in to say, 'Hi?'" the African bantered with a sarcastic grin.

There wasn't a wide range of ways for Jane to phrase the purpose for her visit. Moreover, she had begun to hone the art of being direct with her requests. So she refocused herself and went for it. "I need to buy some time," she said, clasping her hands at her waist again.

"To buy time, you need money. Did you bring money?" Father Time replied while sternly looking Jane over. "How about giving me that diamond bracelet?"

"No."

Father Time blitzed Jane with his eyes, but flattened quickly. He sighed in resignation. Then he opened the bottom-right drawer of his desk, reached down deep, and pulled out a tiny bag. After gently tugging the purple drawstring at the top, Time poured three beans out into his hand.

"Here then. You can have these. Three magic beans...one... two...three."

Jane was confused *and* irritated. "Magic beans? Magic beans aren't going to help me." Her light brown eyes began to hazel.

"No?" Father Time answered dryly.

"You're wasting my time," Jane returned, losing patience.

"You are wasting mine. Although I do seem to have much more of it than you do," Time replied calmly with swagger. Then he perused the close to seventy timepieces arranged around his office.

"I'm not going to make it from Kilimanjaro to the Black Forest, across the ocean to Hokkaido Island, past the Rockies, and in and out of every neighborhood in between, unless you can make time stand still for me..." Jane began to sweat. "...for everyone. I don't even have enough time to *name* all the places—"

"For everyone? Stop time? You're asking me to *stop* time?" Father Time was indignant. "Do you know how hard that is? Jane, I only do that on the twenty-fourth. Which won't be long enough for *you* to travel the globe. Unless you have a team of flying reindeer, that is." He turned his attention toward his desk and started sliding papers into folders. Then he rambled on, "You *could* just poof yourself into flakes and fly the skies on the wishes of the winds. Might take a little longer, but you'd cover the globe...eventually. May not meet your deadline..."

"You're right. I can't work fast enough to cover–"

"Then here," Father Time interrupted as he gathered Jane's hand, trying to release the beans into it.

Jane pulled her hand away before the first bean could drop. Then she reached under her wrist, unclasped her bracelet, and handed it to Father Time. He accepted the bracelet, dropped it into the inside pocket of his sport coat, and smiled at Jane.

"I'd also like some of Mrs. Claus's ribs...ur, no, uh...was it the..."

"Pulled pork?"

"No...uh..."

"I don't have all the time in the world!" Jane snapped impatiently.

Father Time tilted his head to the side as if triggered. He felt no pressure. He looked toward the stunning eight-foot-tall antique grandfather clock in the corner of his office. He absorbed, one by one...its ornate golden moon dial...detailed hands...perfectly cylindrical weights...and finally, its massive pendulum, showing nary a scratch. Then he brazenly stepped back from his desk in order to study all of the other timepieces in the room. The sundials and hourglasses covering the long side tables...the wristwatches and pocket watches strewn across his desk...

Their hands practically put him in a self-hypnotic state.

Tick...tick...tick.

"Where was I?" he continued with charm. "The beef briskets."

"Done," Jane promptly conceded, hoping to intercept any further requests.

"Follow me," Father Time said in an obliging fashion.

Just before they reached the large redwood double doors of his office, Time opened a tall closet and pulled out a white lab coat. He slid in one arm at a time. *Want one?* he motioned to Jane. She declined.

Then he hastily shuffled up to Jane's side and put his hand on the door to block her from opening it.

"As I said, I'm not going to *stop* time until the twenty-fourth. That will be in accordance with the big guy's schedule," he reiterated.

Jane squinted.

Then Time winked as he added, "...but I should be able to assist you with your little identity crisis."

160

XXI

Father Time led Jane down a series of long hallways to his work-shops. There was a cold, modern industrial feel to the corridors. It seemed the whole place was empty. Almost like a shell. Room after room of closed, heavy-duty steel doors with small windows at the top. Lights off in every one of them.

Finally, after traversing much of the facility, Jane was able to catch a glimpse of scientists working inside one of the rooms. She peered through the thick glass at the top of the door. Time obliged Jane's curiosities by turning the metal doorknob and opening.

Inside, there were four scientists, all in their early twenties, wearing white lab coats matching Father Time's. They sat on industrial swivel stools at a rectangular metal table. Each of them were working on individual projects, with small tools. The studious group went on about their business without acknowledging the new company.

Father Time beamed with pride. "See how hard *my* elves are working."

"Ha!" Jane blurted.

Time took a few steps forward, but Jane's *You can't be serious?* tone caused him to hesitate for a second. He eyeballed her with displeasure.

Jane pressed her pointer finger over her lips to shush herself, but she could neither contain nor conceal the grand smirk on her face.

"Shh. Sorry," she whispered, trying to hold in a giggle.

Ticked off at the mockery Jane had made of his prideful operation, Father Time promptly halted his tour. He stood at the corner of the worktable and peered at her over the top of his glasses.

Jane carried on with feigned obliviousness. "What is she making?"

Time answered with some trepidation. "A modern sundial. I know it sounds like a bit of an oxymoron…"

"What are you making?" Jane interrupted, directing her question toward the next scientist.

"A grandfather clock," the worker answered without lifting his head.

Jane briskly moved around the table and fired off the same question to the third scientist. "What's this going to be?"

Father Time tried to interject, but as he raised his finger to deflect the answer, the young scientist blurted out, "A pocket watch."

Jane turned to Father Time, unable to repress the spilling of more sarcasm. "Setting the world on fire, are we?"

Time was on his heels. Flustered. And an uneasiness was spreading through his body. Jane never missed an opportunity to *go there*. So *there* she went, casually strolling in the direction of the fourth scientist until she was standing over his shoulder. "Let me guess…a coo coo clock?"

"A high-powered doughnut maker," Father Time jumped in and answered, desperately trying to halt the interrogation. "In case…"

Jane was visibly perplexed.

Time couldn't finish his own sentence. He didn't have a good explanation. Finally, he humbly conceded, "We all have our vices, Ms. Frost."

He led Jane out of the scientists' workshop, down another corridor. In his flustered state, Father Time forgot to close the door to the workshop behind him. As they passed other rooms, Jane peeked through the windows. She noticed an assortment of unfinished projects, but she couldn't make heads nor tails of any of them. *At least all the rooms aren't empty,* she concluded.

"Concerning the bracelet, forgive me. Can't exactly sell this stuff online," Time said, referencing the slew of gadgets within the compound. "Gotta fund this operation," he mumbled uncomfortably as he shuffled along.

"How is a bracelet going to help pay for all of this? " Jane swiped back.

"Not just *any* bracelet. The bracelet of *Jane Frost,* whom I've heard…only wears diamonds."

Jane shrugged, feeling a touch awkward. Yet she offered no objection to Father Time's statement.

They arrived at massive, thick steel double doors. Time punched a code into a keypad on the side of the wall, and they slowly opened. For safety purposes, he never shut or locked the doors once he was inside. It was the only way to exit that end of the facility.

Once inside, Time casually walked forward onto a landing. Then he stepped forth more deliberately until he reached the ledge, which was seventy-five feet above the floor, with no railing. Jane followed him to the perch and peered over, taking in a full view of what appeared to be an enormous gymnasium.

As she tilted her head to glance up at the ceiling, one hundred fifty feet above the landing, Father Time moved behind her. He paused. Then he continued walking across the platform to a steel hanging tool cabinet on the sidewall. When Time swung the doors open, deep shelves full of modern, high-tech devices were revealed. Jane was impressed. And impressing Jane wasn't easy.

Attempting not to openly display his joy in Jane's approval, Time grabbed a launcher from the cabinet, tilted it to make it vertical, and stuck it firmly into Jane's chest. Jane gripped it tightly without blinking. She immediately recognized the device's sturdy, sophisticated design.

Father Time pushed forward without hesitation. "Aim the launcher at your desired target. Then press this button."

"Do you want to put on your goggles?" Jane asked.

Time shook his head, *no.*

Jane aimed and fired. The kick popped her hard in the shoulder. Thud! A shiny chrome spear drew a zip line cable high across the gym at bullet speed, before penetrating the wall at the opposite side of the facility. A booming, smashing sound of twisted metal and hammered cinder block tore through the expansive test area. Dust rose from the point of penetration, exposing damage to the wall. However, the cable itself was as tight and straight as an arrow.

"Now ice the line," Father Time directed.

Jane leaned back with the launcher still tucked to her shoulder. Then she put her free hand over the top of the cord, and sent a sleeve of solid ice from one side of the line to the other. Swooooosh!

Time swatted the top of the zip cord launcher. Pat! Pat! "You'll detach this end of the rope from here. Secure it to a tree or something stable. I have a rope cinch and a spring link to throw in your bag. You'll have two spear cords..." Then he took out a shiny chrome V-shaped object, turned it upside down, and handed it to Jane. A rubber grip was wrapped around each end of the open sides of the V.

"Hold it like so. You'll put one hand on each grip...put the chrome over top of the line...and go."

Jane nodded.

Time became more serious. "We won't do that here. Because whenever or wherever you use this, you'll need to hang on tight. Depending on the degree of the slope, you may be cruising through the air faster than an SR-71." He yanked the launcher out of Jane's hand and swung a weighty white pleather bag into her stomach. Whap!

Jane's distaste for the way Father Time was handing her the items was deflected by her familiarity with the bag. She thought, *I feel like I've seen this before.* But Father Time was moving affairs along too quickly for her to entertain the idea.

"Put this on."

He helped Jane slide her arms into the straps of the backpack. Then he grabbed a belt strap that was dangling down the side of Jane's thigh, and put it in her hand. She pulled the other side of the strap and connected the two ends of the belt buckle at her waist. Click!

Time shuffled back six or seven steps.

"Now, push the button," he said, pointing to a plastic sapphire-blue circle clipped to the belt.

When Jane pressed the button, bright white hang glider wings popped out violently from behind her. FWAP! She tried to get a proper view of the wings by peering over her shoulder. It was hard for her to see. The wings stretched nine feet across, but even Jane's neck craning wouldn't give her the full picture. Time took a small mirror out of his pocket and handed it to her. With a shift to the left and then to the right, Jane was able to take in the angles she was searching for. She gave her consent.

"Can soar through the sky, covering about one hundred fifty miles per hour. Aluminum alloy. Typical synthetic sailcloth. The twist on this…" he said pointing to a section of the glider, "…these handles. Tubes run from the handles, out here…to the edges of the wings." Jane listened studiously. "You won't have to worry about convergence or mountain waves. And you won't have to rely on ridge lift, because of your *own talents*."

"That's good," Jane confirmed professionally. But what she actually thought was, *What the heck is all that stuff?* Knowing better, she made her question audible. "Now, explain convergence, mountain waves, and ridge lift?"

"Basically, it's the way wind and air naturally affect your glide… as it does with a bird. However, you can remove some of that, I'll say *interference*, by shooting your ice or snow through the tubes and tilting your wings. This way, you'll be able to achieve the *exact* path you wish. If you want to…"

Jane stepped off the seventy-five-foot-high platform.

Father Time gasped in shock.

Jane soared in a circular path, forcing her snow through the tubes to power and direct the glider, while taking advantage of the full span of the indoor test area.

Time regathered himself. "Glad that worked," he voiced under his breath in relief.

Jane dipped and swirled with incredible precision. Snow shot out of the ends of her wings, helping her to steer, as she flew around the open space in elongated figure eights. Father Time became entranced by her flight, marveling at what his creations could do in the hands of *true talent*.

Jane tilted the wings to a forty-five-degree angle, glided past Time on the ledge, and made a steep descent. Then she swooped up into a vertical position, smacked her hip to pop the skate blades out of her boots, and sprayed snow out of the bottom of the wings as she softly eased her way down to the floor of the gymnasium.

Jane shouted up to Father Time, "How do you feel about miracles?" Her euphoric voice echoed through the cavernous test site.

"I believe in miracles...and science!" Father Time whooped with his arms raised in celebration.

Jane powered herself back up to the overhang, this time rising on the formation of two snowy ice columns, which she shot out from the bottom of the glider wings. Then she cut free from the ice and sailed upwards even farther, before lowering herself down in a snow-blown landing next to Father Time.

"WATCH!" he yelled.

But it was too late.

Snow shot under Time's lab coat and between his legs, causing him to lose his balance. He was about to go down, but Jane skated up to him, hockey stopped, and grabbed his arm before he dropped. In the same motion, she swung him erratically to a dry patch of floor near the hanging tool cabinet, but Time's momentum forced his midsection against the table. Boof! Fortunately, he was able to get his hands up in time to lessen the impact.

After corralling his slip-sliding feet, Time steadied himself. He stood upright. Then he gave the metal table a couple of open-handed pats. Although Time had just seen his life flash before him, he did no more than grit his teeth and shake his head. He straightened his lab coat and stepped away from the table.

Jane walked over to meet him on a dry patch of floor in the middle of the platform.

Time got back to business.

"When you press this button, the wings will relock. Wait until–"

Jane hit the button, and the sturdy nine-foot wings fiercely snapped back into place, whizzing a half inch past Time's nose. He put his hands on his hips as he angrily mumbled to himself, "*Don't know how anybody...*" Then he stormed toward the door, appearing to call it a day, miraculously losing his shuffle in the midst.

Jane, however, never budged.

Time figured Jane would come rushing after him to beg for his mercy. But he heard no footsteps. There was no pleading. No beg for mercy. And no sign of a whimper.

He took a deep breath as he faced the door. Time could sense Jane was still waiting. She wasn't going *anywhere*. Hence, he rotated slowly with arms crossed, and waddled his way back to Jane...ever more disturbed than before. The urge for him to see the rest of his gadgets in Jane's hands drove him to expeditiously turn the page and ignore the dings to his ego. "Now press this button."

Once again Jane's response was instantaneous. This time, Father Time quickly pulled his foot out of the way, before the entire hang glider disengaged from the backpack and dropped to the floor. Clank, bang, rangalang!

"I wouldn't. But if you wanted to lose the weight...it's an option. Now pull here."

Jane obliged, causing a light, bunched-up white fabric to slide out from a hard plastic compartment on the underside of the backpack.

"It's a paraglider," Father Time stated professionally. Then he removed a remote control from a sleeve inside the tool cabinet, and pointed it up to the wall. A video screen slid down. With another tap of a button, a cross-section image of a paraglider came up on the monitor. Father Time gushed over its cutting-edge craftsmanship.

"The wing shape is controlled by suspension lines. Ripstop polyester. There are over fifty baffled cells." He edged closer to the screen, pointing to the fabric portion of the paraglider's image. "Those cells allow for flight, which can last for hours and cover *hundreds* of miles."

"What's the twist on this?" Jane asked.

"No twist. Could've bought this yourself online through RichardsonSnowSports.com." An extra thought tapped Time's mind. "Actually…there is one difference. Not a good one. We took off the bar. So there's nothing to sit on."

"No place to sit?"

"We were kind of worried it would get tangled with all the other apparatuses. Basically, you'll just be hanging on…"

"Hundreds of feet in the air…" Jane emphasized for the purpose of clarity.

"…so don't let go. Or else, I guess you'll have to poof yourself into snow as you fall, and land wherever you decide to land."

Jane shook her head, thinking, *Whatever*. Then she removed the backpack and attempted to stuff the paraglider back into the plastic tube at the bottom of it.

"Oh, here." Father Time reached onto the underside of the container and pressed a switch.

Woooooo. The sound of a vacuum came from the plastic tube. Jane could immediately feel the suction.

"There you go," Father Time said, helping Jane gather up the paraglider.

Jane angled the glider toward the mouth of the cylindrical compartment until it was vacuumed tightly inside. Then she snapped the lid shut. Click. "Alright."

Jane paused…wondering…

"How you're going to morph into snow and carry the backpack with all the devices?" Father Time completed her thought for her.

He wasn't a mind reader. But you didn't have to be a mind reader to raise that question.

Jane nodded.

"I don't know either," Father Time admitted, "But I'm sure you'll figure something out."

Jane was slightly unsettled. But she refrained from making a comment.

"Saved the best for last," Time informed Jane on his way back to the cabinet. He retrieved five identical metal disks, and lined them up on a black-cloth-covered side table. The discs resembled flying saucers, but they were compact in size. Each one was a bit smaller than a dinner plate. He picked up one of the discs and led Jane to an adjacent platform, overlooking a pseudo shooting range.

"These discs will fly farther than any Frisbee *you* ever saw."

Jane pulled her stomach back and dodged to the left, expecting Father Time to wallop her with the disc as he had so enjoyed doing with the other items. Pretending he didn't know what the fuss was about, he placed the disc in his open hand and waited for Jane to take it…which she did, while exercising caution. Then he handed her a pair of white-rimmed protective goggles. Jane put them on as she listened to Time direct her through the process.

"Put your hand on," he instructed. Then he gently guided Jane's palm on top of the disc. Time drew in Jane's attention further. "Force your snow through the disc. It has microscopic pores. The snow will keep breaking down into liquid from the pressure inside. The *outside* of the disc must cool to minus ten degrees Celsius. It will ice over. This will de-ionize the magnets on the *inside*."

Time flipped a switch, which sent a large black drape across a steel rod curving over the space behind them. They were now, for the most part, sealed in.

Fifty yards down the hallway, mounted, caged, blue industrial lights lit up in the four young scientists' room. Without missing a beat, they casually slid on anti-noise earmuffs and returned to work.

Father Time tentatively tapped the back of Jane's hand as it rested on top of the metal disc. "When thrown, the frozen disc will warm due to friction with the air...thus prompting immediate precipitation and the reaction of snow. Will help you hit those hard to reach places...and *save time*, of course," he finished with a wink. Time's mind was lost in the glory of his joke. He only refocused himself when he realized Jane hadn't offered his witty remark so much as a sideways grin.

"If you *forget* to freeze the disc, and throw it, you'll have a *flaming disc* with electronic charges blitzing around inside. Then we could say, you'll have an explosion the size of which, would make Mt. Vesuvius seem like a campfire." He took a moment to let that important piece of information sink in. "Freeze first."

Jane could not contain her giddiness. "Freeze first," she repeated with great anticipation. Her eyes were almost as big as the discs themselves.

Jane's childlike reaction gave Time rising anxiety. However, he couldn't wait to see his crown jewel matched with her crafts. Although he tried to conceal it, he was one hundred percent as eager as she was.

Jane inhaled. Her mouth was preserved in an open smile. Yet, she still had her doubts. "This is going to fly far enough?" she questioned aloud.

Jane was imagining the grandness of what was about to happen. All things being equal, the idea of it going south didn't quell her juices from flowing either. In fact, it may have even heightened her exhilaration. The two of them stood there like little kids. Yes...

171

Time had it in him too. This wasn't only about Jane finding Time, believe me.

"Each disc is made of the world's lightest metal. Almost lighter than air. It's a microlattice...much like our bones," he said pointing to Jane's forearm. "Solid on the outside for durability, but porous on the inside...keeping it lightweight. Made of ninety-nine point nine-nine percent air. *One hundred times lighter than Styrofoam,*" he finished with his bold African accent rising to fully embrace the essence of each word he spoke.

"Your clockmakers made this?" Jane asked in disbelief.

Father Time's agitation was reawakened. He peered over his glasses at Jane with discontent. "...Fantastically lighter than aluminum, but entirely as strong." Then he changed his tone to a casual one, "I love it here on Earth, but if anyone is going to go to other planets on the regular, it's going to be done with a rocket made of this material."

Jane stared past Time, absorbing all of the information she felt worth remembering while eagerly waiting for him to finish.

"Therefore, in regard to your questions...yes, the discs *will* fly far enough...and yes, my *scientists* made these." Time was clearly offended, but he was quickly distracted by the experiment in progress.

He tapped Jane's hand. "Whew...chilly, Miss Frost." Time shivered and stood back. "Let's give her a toss."

Jane wasted no time. She coiled her arm, ran forward, and released the metal disk into the air. It passed the two hundred-foot marker in less than a second and exploded! A wave of white ripples blew out in every direction, leaving no time for a reaction. A snow tsunami rumbled and roared toward Jane and Father Time. It blasted through the two of them on its way to mangling the drape divider. The drapes' clanking echoes were entrapped in the rolling wave of white, which ripped into the facility and blew through the corridors, before bursting into the scientists' workshop.

Jane and Father Time remained upright, but they *were* covered in snow.

Time removed his goggles and wiped the snowflakes from his eyes. Then he tracked his way across the terrace in somewhat of a shock. By the time he was standing in front of the master control panel, the ringing in his ears had subsided. He opened the panel and reached in. Click! The traumatized curtains screeched as they obeyed the switch's command...gradually opening...to reveal four unhappy snow-covered scientists standing side by side behind it.

Time turned to Jane and noted aloud, "Worked even better than I had thought it would."

Jane slipped off her goggles and whipped her hair back in agreement, ignoring the wrinkled faces of the perturbed scientists.

In his infinite wisdom, Father Time subtly retreated toward the table and covertly pushed the extra discs off to the side. "I think she'll only need one."

Although Jane could not make out Father Time's mumble, it wasn't hard for her to guess what he was saying. She shrugged, conveying her sentiment that, *I just did what you told me to do.* Though, as you could figure, the scientists received her gesture with little consolation.

"You folks carry on," Time prompted the young scientists as he brushed the snow off the bottom of his lab coat. When he hit the switch again, the beleaguered drape crossed the ceiling once more. The scientists hadn't moved. They continued to stare lifelessly through the gaping holes in the fabric of the curtain...even after it had closed in front of them.

Time ignored the temporary audience as he and Jane pulled together all of her new devices. There was a lot of double-checking, zipping, and clicking, what with the two of them working together to make sure Jane was fully equipped and ready to go. While Time was preoccupied with locking up the tool cabinet, Jane stuffed the remaining discs into her bag and zipped it shut. She was all set.

As Father Time guided Jane back through the corridors, they passed the room of scientists, who were now holding snow shovels instead of tools. The scientists peered up at Jane in a disgruntled fashion, before returning their attention to shoveling heaps of snow into large plastic bins. Clearly, it was not going to melt on its own.

Jane could detect their negative energy. She spun around to make a *Nyeah, nyeah!* face at them when she walked by. "If you all weren't so preoccupied with those clocks, you could've shut the door," she said quietly to herself, so they could hear it. Time hurried her along. He wasn't going to get roped into a conversation about the clocks again.

Jane walked with Time, through the long hallways, past the chess boards on the side tables, to the entrance of the compound. They each pushed open one of the front doors and exited side by side. Once more, Jane could smell the fresh foliage. Normally, the attributes of greenery wouldn't hit her radar, but somehow at this extreme elevation Jane was invigorated by the life of its scent.

She followed Father Time, past the life-sized chess pieces, and across the front lawn. Eventually, they reached a plateau overlooking a steep incline covered with trees. Although the ground just before her took a drastic drop downward, Jane focused straight ahead across the air suspended above the Alps. Time stood behind her, feeling he should say something...but he didn't.

Once again Jane didn't move. Her chest rose and eased down with careful breaths. She stood with her back to the man who had given her everything she needed, without personally connecting to her in any way. He didn't wait for a thanks…didn't seem to want one. He got the bracelet out of her, but as she stood there, she wasn't convinced he needed it in the first place. Didn't offer a good-bye… didn't seem to care if she left. Not a good luck…not a nothing. The emptiness permeating the entire setting was what caused Jane to wheel around and tap the white pleather backpack.

"Who was all this going to be for?"

Jane didn't expect a response, but she got one.

"Since day one, I've been enamored by your gifts. You have the ability to preserve things in such a way that *time* can't even wear them down. To freeze-frame life…history…perfectly…with a coating as pretty as diamonds. Suspending time in a way that no one else on Earth *can*…or in my humble opinion, ever has."

Jane lifted her head and looked at Father Time. Her brown eyes washed sadly to hazel, and then paled to a clear blue. With whatever distractions were ever running through Jane's mind, she always had an inner strength. And it took every morsel of that strength for her to go to *this place*, a place she hadn't gone with anyone before… at least not to her memory.

"My father?" she offered quietly.

And Father Time…*mh*…he just slowly walked away.

For Jane, these powers so great, could not have been born to her in isolation. She knew enough to know there was more to know. Knew enough to know she should ask the man sharing that high plateau with her. But Time continued to walk away from Jane, creating an ever-widening void between them. Her heart was being pulled toward him. And it was burning. Yet he shuffled away from her…one step at a time…until he stopped.

Time pulled a glossy, white and blue snowboard from behind a tree. Then he shuffled back in Jane's direction.

Jane reached up to the back of her neck and opened the clasp of her necklace. She carefully gathered the necklace in her hands and slid it into the right pocket of her vest. She made sure it was secure, because she anticipated her *next journey* would most definitely have a few extra bumps.

All of Time's humble steps brought him face to face with Jane again. She could see his soul now. His depth. A connection. This time, instead of whapping her with the snowboard or holding it in front of her indifferently, he gently placed it against her hand. He wrapped her fingers around the board and held them there. The drops filling his eyes could have been from tears or from the wind… but in either case, they revealed their age to her. His once steady hands shook, drawing Jane's attention to each one of the wrinkles crossing them.

"Your father…that's a story you don't have time for right now… but your questions…" Time turned. He moved with purposeful steps toward the front door. There was a great pause between his phrases, as though he needed to gather himself to push each one out. "…there are answers…"

He blanketed his next thoughts in a mumble reserved for himself. "Answers, crystal clear, like the ice, which enveloped the North…in the coldest winter ever."

A frigid wind shuttled between Jane and Time. A wind almost identical to the event Time had just recounted. The whirling ice and snow forced him to lift his forearm to shield his face from the sideways-whipping sleet. The glacial chill remained, but the snow dissipated. And when Father Time turned back toward the edge of that high plateau…Jane was gone. The bags under his eyes felt full. But he didn't move. Instead, he finished a soliloquy, which it seemed he'd begun many years before.

"…and she took the road less travelled. Good luck, Snowflake."

XXII

A vivid white streak thundered ahead aggressively, down fifteen-foot-high drop-offs, through a harrowing minefield of trees, in an urgent plight to reach the base of the tallest mountain of the German Alps in negative time. I could picture it well. Jane had a fearlessness to her, for sure. With her palm extended in front of her, she created a path of icy snow, which she carved into using the high performance snowboard from Father Time.

Jane rode the board hard, not caring if it was left in splinters by the time she reached the bottom. At times, a crack or a bang would fire off through the woods, lending to the sentiment that it was about to be snapped in half. The icy snow path that Jane created didn't always cover the narrow, eight-inch-wide stumps scattered across the terrain, but she kept her palm forward, knees bent, and eyes trained hundreds of feet below on the most vertical descent possible. A broad stroke of white etching the dark canvas of the mountain in a jagged onrush of fury.

Jane reached down to grab the edge of the board as she sailed off a thirty-foot-high shelf, not knowing if the opposite side of it was still attached. In the air, she thrust a thick forceful stream of white flakes to her intended point of landing. Poof! She landed with precision, blasting powdery snow in all directions, while maintaining full momentum on her temerarious, high-velocity, seven-thousand-foot crusade to the bottom of the mountain. BANG! No amount of friction would slow her...it was her mountain now. Janey was a force, *know that.* Finally, after going to war with the mighty Alps, after dodging every tree and landing every jump...the forest opened up, turning the landscape over from a steep incline to a more welcoming gentle slope.

Jane swung her hand out slowly in an arc around her body while making a nice heelside turn and a smooth stop at the base of the mountain. A whirlwind of flakes blew at her back, pushing her hair over her shoulders. In a position of settle, Jane unbuckled her boots from the snowboard and stepped into the snow. While sliding the cellphone out of her back pocket with one hand, she slid her hand against her neck and tossed her hair back with the other. She pressed her fingers onto the inside of her wrist to warm them, because Jane's cool fingertips would often fail to register on the face of her phone.

It was time to make a call to Air Traffic Control.

"State your purpose, please," traffic controller 5731 responded.

Jane spoke into the base of her phone, "I'm going to need you to hold all flights and ground all planes."

"Ms. Frost!" the controller sparked with surprise, breaking from protocol. "Copy that Ms. Frost!" Cshh. "We're grounding all planes and suspending all flights." Cshh. "Anything else?"

Jane's heart filled with happiness. "Merry Christmas."

"Merry Christmas to you too, Ms. Frost." Cshh. "Welcome back."

And at that, ATC 5731 initiated a chain...an extremely necessary chain, for an *All Jane Event*. "Command Center One, we just got an alert from Ms. Frost to ground all planes and postpone all flights."

The traffic supervisor pushed the message to the higher-ups with urgency. "Captain Howard, we just got an alert from Ms. Frost."

The top commander of the control center solicited further confirmation. "Thee Ms. Frost?"

"Affirmative, sir."

Captain Howard flipped an alert switch to the left of his control board. Phones vibrated in all of the traffic controllers' pockets, accompanied by a medley of alert tones. After all the ATCs had quieted their phones, they zeroed in on Captain Howard, who stood behind a thick, round steel railing, on his special deck, elevated over the floor of the tightly protected control room.

"Giving strict orders to ground, divert, and/or postpone any and all flights immediately," the Captain's voice powered through the room.

The workers calmly sat down, put on their headsets, and began contacting all of the airports across the world.

The Head Floor Supervisor shouted up from the middle of the ATCs, "Santa starting early?"

The room paused.

"No..." the Captain matter-of-factly stated, "...Ms. Frost."

With those simple words, all bedlam ensued. Headsets went from straight to crooked, papers flew, coffee spilled, and air traffic personnel scattered in all directions. When it came to Janey, people understood, once she gave that warning...she wasn't going to need to give another one.

Captain Howard surrendered. "Since there's no going back..." He reached to the right of his control board and pressed a large blue button with a white snowflake on it. Immediately, the control center was aglow with turquoise lights.

The Floor Supervisor repeated Captain Howard's message, raising her voice over the sound of the ruckus, "That *is* a directive from Ms. Frost. I repeat, we are clearing ALL airspace for Ms. Frost! As you are aware of the date, this is NOT a drill! I repeat, this is NOT a drill! We will get these birds back in the air later. Everyone *will* make it to their destinations before Christmas, but as of now, all flights must be grounded, diverted or postponed. All flights must be grounded, diverted, or postponed!"

Captain Howard's assistant wandered in beside him. "Captain, did I ever tell you the story of the time I saw mama kissing Santa Claus?"

Captain Howard razored his eyes at the assistant...but then he broke. The corner of his mouth snuck upward. "Go ahead, Briggs... let's hear it."

Cshh. "Air United 416, we're going to need to divert you to Des Moines," Traffic Controller 5008 instructed the pilot.

ATC 5000 was on another frequency. "Terry, we're going to need you to postpone Luftansi flight 628 until further notice."

"Southward Sky 261, change course to 121 West Longitude," ATC 4521 directed.

"This is Captain Parker, America Flight 54, requesting permission to return to Orange County."

Cshh. "This is Flight control six-five-eight-zero, in Long Beach, Captain Parker...twenty-one miles from...you're welcome here, sir."

"Invitation accepted, six-five-eight-zero. Officially requesting permission to land in Long Beach."

"Permission granted, Captain Parker...there's a chill in the air!"

"Finally!" celebrated the captain. "What's your name, six-five-eight-zero?"

"Keisha. Keisha Rogers, sir."

"Keisha, Merry Christmas to you and your family."

"Merry Christmas to you too, Captain. Let us give thanks and praise…It's gonna be a white Christmas!"

The Air Traffic Controllers were uplifted. However, back at the Community Room of Santa's Headquarters, things were about to boil over again. Lyndsey, a delicate packing elf, had her mitts locked onto the collar of an unsuspecting elf from electronics. The jolt of her grip knocked his glasses diagonally across his face.

"What did Lyndsey do?" she pleaded to the startled elf. "What did Lyndsey do to deserve this?"

At the opposite end of the Community Room, four extremely athletic men played on a giant-sized, five-by-eight-foot ice hockey table. In The North, those tables don't use air like common air hockey tables. They use real ice.

The fellas would get into it back there, every now and then. A few hot heads in the bunch, much the same as any competitive young men you may know in their twenties.

Kade was one of those competitive fellas. Smallest of the group. At first glimpse, you'd see your average man. But he was rock solid and incredibly handy. Blue-collar vibe…but nothing blue about him. A cool brown. Make you feel like…you had a problem, he could fix it.

Don was another one of the young men. He was bigger than Kade. He had a thick build, but was more streamlined than your basic bodybuilder. Over six feet tall. The lamp above the table would crown his bulging ebony biceps. Bump into him by accident, and it would throw your whole shoulder out of whack.

Right next to Don, stood Blake. He was a track star clone. Not an ounce of fat on him. Dark and lovely. Pleasant as the day too… when it came to the women at least.

Then there was Prince. His build was comparable to that of a professional basketball star…fashion to match. Skin the color of caramel. The young ladies would always say how dreamy he was.

So yes, they were complete gentlemen. But every once in a while, the competitive spirit of those fellas would get out of hand. Would happen most often when they were deep in the throes of their ice hockey games. In this case, the puck had just rattled into Kade and Prince's goal. Apparently, one side suspected the other of bending the rules a bit. *Men.* Give them too much free time…

"Thunder and Lightning!" Don shouted as he fist-bumped Blake.

"Cheap and Cheater," Prince hammered back.

At first Don agreed, "Yeah!" And then he disagreed, "Wait…I ain't cheap."

"And who's a cheater?" Blake followed up indignantly.

But Prince was more than happy to double down, "Y'all cheap cheaters!"

"*What are you sayin*?" Don asked while puffing out his chest.

Kade moved halfway around the table and pointed at Don and Blake's goal. "Every time we shoot at your goal, Blake lays his arm down in front of it."

Don was perplexed. "Lays his arm down?"

"Yeah," Kade snapped.

Blake acted confused. He may have indeed been, but with Blake it was hard to tell. "In front of the goal?" he questioned in a high-pitched voice.

Prince backed away from the table, waving his arms up and down. "You know what you're doing! *He knows what he's doing!*"

Blake saw Q walk in and reached out for him, as if he were trying to pull him into a life raft from the middle of the ocean.

"Yo, Q! You wanna weigh in on this?"

"No," Q answered as he strolled by.

Q often hung with the boys, but he avoided all the nonsense. He didn't have the athletic build of the other men. Though that didn't make a difference, because he was five foot nine, and fine. Heavenly brown skin. Sharp dresser too...but not conceited, you know. Yet, he wasn't going to get dirtied or waste his time on any foolishness. He didn't need to.

"Q!" Blake pleaded. But Q was out of there.

Don dredged up the argument once more. "He's not puttin' his arm in front of the goal! Okay, how?"

Blake gave himself away by pressing his forearm over the mouth of the goal. "Like this?"

"Yeah! Yeah!" Prince and Kade celebrated in righteousness while hopping up and down.

"Didn't it look real regular when he did that?" Kade animatedly cheered.

"Your face looks regular!" Blake yelled back.

This is why Q kept walkin'. He could've easily predicted how the fellas' little disagreement would turn out.

Kade jumped onto the ice table and tried to run across the top of it with the intent of launching himself at Don and Blake. The only problem...it was an *ice* table. Kade spun his wheels and belly-flopped onto the ice. Then he got up and tried again...and he spun his wheels again...and he fell on his face *again*.

"Kade," Prince calmly interjected, "Go around, Kade..."

At that instant, a four-foot-wide, neon-blue snowflake light brightened high on the wall at the back of the room. The men immediately stopped their quibbling and turned to face the sign.

Jane had just texted her alert to the North Pole's Headquarters. There was going to be snow! To the elves...and everyone else in The North, this was the only present they cared about receiving.

It only took seconds for the whole place to break out into a scene of jubilation most closely resembling a championship celebration at a sporting event. I swear there was even confetti! Hands went up in the air. Everyone jumped up and down. Fisticuffs swirled into hugs and grimaces lifted away into laughter.

Gerald tried to maximize the opportunity by prancing over to Vicki, holding up a mistletoe. Vicki gave Gerald a glare of *Not a snowball's chance*, before spinning around and laying a gigantic smooch on a random elf behind her. The elf fainted blissfully by her side. Gerald was left holding a piece of plant. He spun in the opposite direction to try his luck with Daija and Dani, but they were already over with the boys practicing their boxing techniques.

Daija was dealing body blows to Don's rock-hard stomach, while a couple feet away, Dani was on her tippy-toes launching left hooks into Prince's arms. Tears of joy filled Don's and Prince's eyes as they absorbed the ladies' mock fury. Kade hopped in from behind and playfully put Prince and Don into headlocks. The ice hockey melee had washed away. The score of *that game* couldn't have mattered less to them now.

Q hung out at the corner of the room, shaking his head, flashing his million-dollar smile. He approved. This time, when Blake pointed over to get his attention, Q pointed back with great pleasure. And the two of them would laugh and laugh, along with the rest of the North Village, deep into the night.

Close to three thousand miles away, Jane had secured the snowboard to her backpack. She resumed her tear across the Alps on foot, sprinting through densely wooded hills, and over broad clearings, until she reached the edge of a cliff. Her next step, if she had taken it, would have descended into air.

That's where Jane stood.

She lifted her chin high, but peered downward to take in the valley below. She tightened her belt and her backpack. Metal buckles, dangling from the excess straps, scraped and clinked together, echoing their isolated tones into the cold white air. A long strand of Jane's black hair caressed the side of her face. Her chest rose and rested calmly once more.

Then she directed a message through that icy air...with a purpose...and a warning..."It's time to deliver the mail."

XXIII

It was the night of December 23rd. While most of the world was sleeping, Jane was performing a miracle you couldn't stuff into a box and wrap with paper. In the air, pilots were able to sit back and take in the beginning of the show as sparkling snowflakes decorated their 747s.

"Air United Flight 513. Up here, we're seeing it first! The most beautiful flakes I've ever seen," Pilot Captain Perry applauded.

ATC 320 seconded, "I know that's right! Now get that thing down here and take a break."

"Thank you three-twenty. Almost there! Can you do me a favor?" Cshh.

"Sure!"

"I'd like you to thank the artist of this masterpiece for me."

"Confirmed, Captain Perry. We'll do just that. Enjoy the time with your family."

At the main air traffic center, one of the controllers leaned over to the other and brought them to church.

"The angel said to them, don't be afraid, for behold, I bring you good news of great joy which will be to *all the people*!"

"Luke 2:10!" the other controller cheered.

Jane made her way in and out of every neighborhood, working the snow like a crew member on a sailboat. She pulled down forcefully, arm over arm, dropping lines of thick snow over each home. In other instances, she pulled down and swung her arms in a circle as she struggled with the weight of heavy flakes, before driving them over every yard. Moving from position to position, across streets, and throughout the tight nooks and crannies of every city, Jane whirled powder with finesse, as though she were putting together a showcase of her finest works.

She made a calculated pitstop in the St. Louis suburbs next. When she arrived at a house marked with the last name Hensford, she unhooked her snowboard and took it in her hand. Then she ran hard and spun into flakes. The board rotated over her snow squall like a helicopter while Jane moved over the delivery truck in the driveway. She descended in front of the garage, condensed back into human form, and rested the snowboard up against the garage door.

"It's a little banged-up..." she admitted. "But considering who made it..."

Jane *knew* it was a prize.

She exited the driveway and got back on the streets. Jane picked up speed, spreading flakes recklessly from her rapid twirls like it was sawdust firing off from an electric saw blade. When she swept down the neighborhood roads, Christmas lights illuminated houses on each side of the street, two by two, as if lit by the beat of music.

Inside daycares, shaving cream snowmen seemed to look out of the windows and smile their approval while reindeer of traced hands and feet hinted of more grandeur to come.

In town, white flakes rested in perfect form on the winter coats of customers, who happily left stores with all of the Christmas trinkets they had been searching for. Passersby cradled poinsettias, which complimented Jane's windy white with festive splashes of red, and midnight green boughs of holly peeked out from the snow along their paths, fully bringing to life the spirit of the holiday season.

Lines wrapped around the corners of packed bakeries and honey ham stores, but an aura of togetherness made the wait feel worth it. The conversations among those in the lines filled each person with a sense that *unity* truly was an element of *their* community. Time spent with strangers, reinforced for folks that, yes, there still were people who cared. And still young people around who didn't mind linking arms with an elder to get them to their car safely.

Beyond the stores, Jane's snow encouraged the strengthening of family bonds.

Nestled inside toasty apartments, Grandmothers guided their grandchildren through the process of liberally adorning bell and angel-shaped cookies with red and green sprinkles. The love from the grandmothers and the smell of freshly baked cookies blended together with the graceful snowfall outside, filling everyone inside with a blessed warmth.

Farther out, families were greeted at the garland-lined doors of their aunties' homes with a "Merry Christmas!" and a "God Bless," while the soft bass and smooth violin of soulful vintage Christmas songs played in the background. Aluminum foil pans, with majestically rising steam, passed from person to person, as cousins, uncles, aunts, sisters, and brothers ushered themselves into loved ones' homes, putting all conflicts aside. Packing together into kitchens and living rooms helped *all* to remember...the winds of the good times, the depth of their family's roots, and loved ones who were greatly missed. Although the flames of the fire in the living room and the eruption of laughter from the uncles provided an instant thaw, the children purposely lagged behind in order to scoop up some flakes and shove them into their mouths before their parents would notice.

Then there was quiet. Breathe in. Breathe out. Wush, wush, woo. Wush, wush, woo. Jane heard only the silence. Only the stillness. Only the night and the sound of her flakes as she powered on to the next town. Whu, whu.

Soon, the muffled rumble of rap music arose from beyond the next hill. It increased in volume with each stride Jane took. She sprinted across the field, showering the entire area with snow as she ran. Suddenly, a massive lodge appeared, its windows aglow from a bouquet of lights on the inside. The bass of the rap music got louder...

Jane circled the lodge, blasting a blizzard across it from every angle, before turning the corner and entering through its open doors. Once inside, her focus became so extreme, she no longer heard the music. She only felt its vibrations pulse through her body as she put in work.

Jane took snapshots of the room while she moved across the dance floor, seemingly in slow motion. It was Darryl Richardson's Club Lodge. And its founder, architect and builder, was standing with his family on a private balcony overlooking the partiers below.

The grin on Darryl's face and the large glass mug in his rugged hands told the story of a celebration that was a long time coming. His children smashed into his legs while playfully swiping at each other in a game of tag. They were giddy with giggles from eating too much sugar, and of course, fully hyped due to the sheet of white on the other side of the towering crosshatch windows.

The dance floor was packed. *Ohh*, the passion of the people, as they swung to the beat of the DJ and the rhythm of the rapper. You would've been right on in there with them! Pulsing royal blue lights illuminated jewelry, which reflected across the room. Raised hands cradled colliding cups over the middle of the round. Clothes swished back and forth, in and out, and up and down, like the liquid riding within the plastic cups elevated over the heads of the people on the dance floor. It was a full on club scene.

Jane heard the muffled beat once more, followed by the full bass lining the track. Finally, the precisely chosen lyrics bouncing off the rapper's inspirational voice amped back up within her. A vitality burst from Jane's soul as the rap artist's flows provided a platform she could synchronize her work to. When she breezed by, the royal blue lights phased to turquoise. Cascading light reflected off the peoples' jewelry, sending sparkles across the club! Jane's snow illuminated the border of the dance floor and brightened the ceiling in a way that words could never fully describe. When people sit down in Richardson's Club Lodge today, they still recount the splendor of that night.

Jane swung her arm and iced the entire bar from one end to the other. On cue, the bartender proceeded to slide drinks to those folks stretched along that massive slab of finished cherry wood. The gorgeous ladies, the handsome gentlemen...baby, there was a party goin' on! Jane almost appeared to be a comic strip character, the way her body was able to maneuver through the lodge with such extraordinary agility. *It was phenomenal.*

Then there was quiet. A *hush* flowed over Jane's inner spirit. Once again, she was accompanied solely by the sound of her *own* swift, free-flowing movements. When she reached the opposite end of Richardson's Lodge, Jane found the reality in herself once more. And she dashed out of the exit, leaving the turned-out club in her wake...to enter the pitch black again.

XXIV

Jane was running out of time. It was already midnight, less than twenty-four hours from Christmas Eve, and there remained countless miles to cover. After jogging about three hundred feet from Richardson's Club Lodge, Jane pulled the paraglider from her bag and spread it out in the shape of an arc. Then she grabbed the handles, which were connected to the cords, and pushed a swirling gust of snow into the fabric's baffled cells. When the glider lifted off the ground, she angled it to the side. She pivoted away from the high end of the steep, grass-covered incline, and allowed herself to be pulled into the air. In short time, Richardson's Club Lodge was only a speck in the distance.

Hours later, Jane had covered the mountains and valleys with an unblemished fluffy powder. Floating through the air with her palm tilted outward, she blasted snow over acres of land. She had pushed the paraglider to its limits, and it began dipping drastically. Jane decided to land the paraglider, before *it* could bring her down. With no seat to support her, she gripped on tight to the handles, as the arched fabric overhead assisted her gradual approach to the ground.

Eventually, she touched down with a hop and several skips, before jogging to a stop.

"Okay," Jane exhaled, talking to her equipment, "Get you…and you…pretty good there."

Dragging the glider to a nearby tree was more difficult than Jane had thought it would be, but her self-talk kept things moving in the right direction. She unwrapped the cords from her hands, and shook her wrists to loosen them. Then she hit the switch on the underside of her backpack. Woooooo. Within seconds, the paraglider was back in its compartment. Jane snapped the cylinder shut. Click!

"Set."

She jogged forward a few paces, but then broke stride. Jane realized, by scientifically working the time zones, she had bought herself more time. This gave her a moment to contemplate which territory was the best one to cover next. She used the back of her hand to wipe the sweat from her forehead and the drip from her nose. Then she took a breath. Her body didn't need to rest. When Jane made up her mind, her body was going to follow. She just needed to figure things out.

After scanning the landscape, Jane sprayed a sheet of ice in front of herself. Then she smacked her hip, popped out her skates, and darted toward a steep-dropping forest on the nose of her blades. She hopped just before she reached the trees…and disappeared over the edge! Jane skated downhill at full speed, finding security in the very things that most would consider terrifying.

When she came out of the woods, a cliff moved up on her quickly. She came to a hard stop. Shhhhhk! Jane could see that the cliff dropped off vertically, setting forth a divide between the wilderness and the more densely populated neighborhoods below. She had to make a choice. BANG! She popped out her hang glider wings, skated toward the precipice, and jumped off. As Jane soared through the air, she reflected on her process. She would not let the pressure or urgency of the mission compromise the quality of her work. The idea of cutting corners would not find a safe haven on her blueprint.

She angled herself over large towns, dropping soft white powder in volume, with care. Farther inward, Jane blanketed each metropolis with snow more cozy than the white comforters dressing the beds of their five star hotels. She would not miss a crevice. The flurry of white made it so that her skin was the only serene brown shade gracing the landscape under the moon's spotlight. The marvel of her hands appeared to brush ebony in swirls over her self-created canvas. This performance was one for the elite.

Using the hang glider, Jane commanded the sky for most of the night, but the clouds began to pass in front of the moon, making it difficult for her to see the details of her ground cover. She decided to check things out on foot.

Jane questioned her decision before she had even acted on it.

"Don't know if this is a good idea."

She landed softly and snapped her wings in. CLANK! She maneuvered over rocky crevices and trekked through small towns. So far, Jane was pleased with her coverage.

"All checks out. That's what I was going for. Now…" She looked around. "…to get out of here."

It was dark.

"Of all the gadgets…" Jane remarked as she patted herself down, "…no flashlight."

She knifed out of the small village she was in, and raced down a boulder-filled track on her way to the next town. But before Jane knew it, she had descended much farther than she had imagined. She couldn't see any sign of a city, a barn, or a house for that matter.

"Where in the world?"

She had to get back into the air. But when Jane edged forward, she realized she was standing at the foot of a cliff. A quick survey of her surroundings revealed gray stone inclines walling her in on three sides. Backtracking would take hours. Trees were pushed up tight to the boulders at the base of the cliff. There wasn't enough room for her to snap out the nine-foot hang glider wings. Jane looked up.

"Could use those magic beans now," she admitted.

After carefully retreating between the trees, Jane pulled her sleeves down tight and spun herself around on the balls of her feet. Then she ran a full sprint, straight toward the stone wall, sharply shifting between the trees on her way. When she cleared through a hole between the last set of trunks and branches, Jane spun hard. But she slammed into one of the immovable rock faces just before changing over to a swirling snow. Her backpack clanked and rattled among her twists and turns, yet it still rose upward from the thrust of her sweeping gust. After rising to the top of the cliff as recklessly weaving flakes, Jane used all of her power to morph back into human form and snatch the bag out the air before it could crash to the ground.

The damage of the impact had caught Jane square. Serious pain dropped her to one knee. The compounded fatigue of the night began to wrap itself around her. A thought flashed through Jane's mind. Was this it? Had she run into *the final wall?* She refused to put her other knee down, but she did not have the power to stand. The pain in her shoulder was growing stronger...swelling ensued... and the pressure began moving down her arm. A burning feeling spread to her wrist and hand. They both began throbbing intensely.

"Uhhhg," Jane writhed in pain.

Ice began streaking through her body. This was good. Her internal defense system was setting forth in generating a freeze to restore her strength.

She put one hand down on the ground to prop herself up, but between the streaks of cold, Jane was blacking out. Blue lights fired off in her mind, though they were cut short by waves of total black. She fought to maintain consciousness. To help herself ignore the blackouts, Jane closed her eyes and concentrated on one thing… trying to stand. Now blinded by the intense pain and swelling, she wouldn't be able to see if she did open her eyes.

Jane's free run…was now restricted. Her breaths became short. With each one, it seemed she paid a price…a wince…a brief loss of consciousness..a piercing shot of pain. There had to be something she could grasp onto. But at this point, she could barely stay alert, let alone think. The clouds passed for a brief moment…but the moon, a spotlight on her earlier magic, now cast a shadow of doubt. Truth is, doubt and Jane had tangled more than once. But what Jane would teach herself on that night…was that she could beat doubt with one hand tied behind her back.

XXV

The way Jane told it to me, she was going to cut her arm off if she needed to. It was with that kind of inner toughness, she opened her visionless eyes and forced herself up onto her feet. Like a boxer staggering to avoid the TKO, she raised her chin. But would she be able to continue to fight?

Her blue eyes faded. They grew more pale with each passing second...yet Jane *was* upright. She swung her left hand hard against her right shoulder. Her eyes flickered to sapphire, before quickly fading again. The glow in Jane's eyes returned to deep blue when she gave her shoulder one more whack. However, her sight only reawakened intermittently. She would not be able to make headway in her current state.

The brown terrain in front of Jane filled her with urgency, as she was able to absorb, once again, the unfinished job that lay ahead. *Things done in halves are never done right.* The words ran through her head. She would not accept this from herself. She swung her arms through her backpack. Then she wrapped her hand over her shoulder and bicep to cool them down.

Jane's eyes worked their way back to hazel. She was finally able to draw lung-filling breaths, in spite of the sharp pain that continued to shoot through her arm. She pressed her thumb into the palm of her weak hand to alleviate the throbbing. Jane would not wait for a full recovery. She trudged on while continuing to use all of her power to relieve the swelling.

After several acres of merely managing to put one foot in front of the other...spraying snow with her free hand whenever she could muster the strength...Jane's focus began to return. She pulled her eyes from her feet. She could see the moonlight reflecting off her glossy white pants and the creases wrapping across her pleather sleeves. When Jane lifted her eyes further to see what was up ahead...she could finally do so with full clarity.

"There you are," she said, as if she had found an old friend.

With steady brown eyes and regained vision, Jane gave her arm one last hearty slug. Then she shook her head, pounded her chest, and ran straight at the world.

Jane's ground coverage was so rapid, *so precise*, it appeared she was following natural instincts. Upon her arrival at each new territory, there were posted signs to assist her in identifying the location, whether it was *Mount Kilimanjaro, London, The Colosseum,* or *Howard University.* But Jane didn't care where she was. If it was green, she was going to make it white. There would be no unfinished business.

With one arm tucked close to her body, and the other straight out in front of her as she ran, Jane blitzed the ground with inches upon inches of snow. Her use of time zones proved essential, but the night hours were quickly dwindling. It was time for her to use the best-saved trick in her bag. She unzipped her backpack, reached in, and pulled out one of Father Time's discs. Jane aimed her free hand far ahead, and slid her palm slowly from the left to the right, until she had iced a thirty-foot runway.

She positioned her body sideways. Then she dug her skates in hard and powered forward. Shuck, shuck, shuck! Suddenly, Jane gritted her skates to a hard stop. Shhhhhk!

"Freeze first," she nervously reminded herself.

Jane could envision the bullet that had been dodged. Father Time *had* warned her. Yet there was no time to sit back and fully calculate what could have happened if she had actually cast a flaming Frisbee into the night. Without a second thought, Jane glided back to her original position. She placed her hand on top of the disc and held it there for a few extra counts.

"Force the snow through the pores...extreme freeze..."

Jane spirited herself forward a second time.

In an instant, Jane was twenty feet from where she started. She carved in deep, cradled the metal saucer, raised her knee in a dynamic spin, and released. The disc rose levels like a Frisbee while streaming through the air at the velocity of a jet. Then POOF! Five miles away, ice and snow snapped out across the sky, resembling fireworks under the light of the moon. Yes, the skies were clear again!

A polar bear was lying in wait on the other side of a great snowdrift, but it was instantly exposed by the reflection of the brightened flakes. The imposing fur-covered beast swung its head from side to side, spraying slobber in every direction. It gallantly romped in a circle, leaping and pounding its mighty paws into the deep snow, as if applauding the splendor of Jane's creation.

Counter to Father Time's advice, Jane used the rest of the discs too. You thought she wouldn't? The white spread farther than she could see.

Jane ripped herself into a snowy whirlwind again and floated as flakes for miles. Eventually, she was able to fully realize the capabilities of her gifts matched with Father Time's tools, because everywhere she looked there was deep powdery snow...accompanied by peace. When Jane twisted herself back into human form and landed in snow time after time, she was sure she would cover the world by the morning of Christmas Eve. And she was also sure, with the help of Father Time, the people could take her check of a white Christmas to the bank of the North Village...and cash it.

XXVI

Janey could have stopped there...but did she ever? She had pulled an all-nighter, and created a winter wonderland of a lifetime. Yet she still circled back around on the morning of the 24th and delivered round two. Her new flakes drifted charmingly over Rollo's property, further decorating the fifteen inches of snow she had dropped there the previous night.

When Rollo awoke, he could feel a genuine love in his heart... and in his belly. After pounding his bed, he let out one of his bold laughs. Then he pushed himself up and joyfully lumbered down the hallway. His sidekicks raced out of their bedrooms, down the stairs, and around the living room. But, what the sidekicks didn't do...was go outside. Instead, the swirling bolts of energy circled throughout the house in a holding pattern.

By the time Rollo reached the bottom of the steps, his delirious comrades had lined his path to the front door as if he were the Queen of England. Except Rollo didn't keep a straight face. He cheerfully smiled at his exhilarated assortment of allies, locking arms with number four, as number three patted him on the back. He grabbed his fedora from the hat rack, turned the doorknob, and pushed the door open a crack. A sliver of sunlight kindly blinded Rollo and his 'kicks in the way that it reflected off the pure white snow.

By now, all of the sidekicks had jostled in behind their jovial ringleader. Then, Rollo opened the door fully...to reveal the untouched snow gracing his property.

Yes, open your eyes and take it all in. A view of eternity. The powder snow, full of fresh new ice crystals, just sitting there, waiting for someone to make the first mark in it.

That's exactly what Rollo did.

He lifted his foot and stomped into the fluffy white. And then he hopped...not like you and I hop...but like more of a bouncy big man hop...maybe even a gallop.

"That's what's up! That's what's up!" Rollo repeated with increasing bravado as he pranced and thumped to the center of his yard. *He was in his element.*

His sidekicks were hanging over one another in the doorway, watching the big fella leave wide oval-shaped tracks in the deep snow behind him. Then they began pushing and jockeying to catch a glimpse of what was to come. Rollo's world. Yes, this was his *true calling.*

"Yes it is!" Rollo cried, "Yes it is! Ha ha ha ha!"

Rollo took a breath of life, and released a frozen mist in his exhale. He removed his fedora and raised his free fist to the sky in celebration.

The sidekicks watched in awe as swirls of snow wrapped around Rollo's feet, up his calves, and around his thighs. He turned to face them, with a smile a mile wide, while the snow circled his torso and moved down his arms and wrists. As if powered by remote control, the snow rapidly spiralled back up his arms and chest, before swirling up over his head like whipped cream topping a sundae. Rollo had fully transformed into a *living snowman*! Now, the air reaching his lungs was more crystal clear, more sweet than ever. He placed the fedora back on his head with his large snow hands, and threw both of his snowy fists to the sky.

"Woooo hooo! Wooo hoo hoo hoo! Ooh hoo hoo!" he shouted with glee. "BAM!"

That was enough for the sidekicks. They charged out of the doorway, full steam ahead! Then they hopped…not like you and I would hop…but like…well…rabbits, as they darted in, out, and around Rollo at Mach speed. One by one, they began diving into the powder, losing themselves, and popping out again. When they leapt from under the snow, they emerged as *soft cuddly rabbits* with tender beige-colored noses! White, furry long-eared bunnies, pouncing in and out of the snow, weaving through each other's paths, while circling the big snowman with infinite energy. The transformation was complete! The snowman and his rabbits were alive!

Rollo galloped between his rabbit friends and pumped his puffy fist alongside his powdery white hip. "Yeah! Wooo hoo hooo! BOOM! Ha ha ha ha!"

Jane had kept her word. She had turned Rollo's yard into a playground fit for a snowman and his arctic friends. The sidekicks were always poised for pandemonium… sprinkle a little snow on top of 'em and you got the works. The powder was poppin', the ice festivities were in full effect, and it was only 10 a.m.! Janey could set things off for sure. Trust me, she definitely was aware of that. I get a laugh, thinkin' of the whole scene…it was *alright*. You can't look at Rollo the Snowman without losing yourself in his happiness.

Early noon had arrived. By then, Jane was fulfilling her goal of dropping a bonus four inches on a few chosen cities. She was floating around a skyscraper when she came upon a man and woman sharing a delicate moment on a quiet street corner. Jane couldn't let it go. She circled back, morphed from a spiraling blizzard back into human form, and touched down. When her backpack fell from out of her snowsquall, she allowed the straps to drop down through her raised arms without ever turning behind to look. She worked up a windy blast and blew the woman into the man's arms. Then she circled the two of them in pure white flakes as they nestled together sharing Eskimo kisses. The young lady snuggled up against her man's jacket, giggling, while Jane playfully lifted up a wall of white, and blew away in a gust.

When Jane reached the suburbs, the snow play continued. This time, she blew all the snow off an old man's driveway when he went to grab his shovel. She moved throughout the neighborhoods, taking time to feed off the people reveling in her creation. Her whirlwind of white provided a synergy that stretched across the globe.

Amped-up elves danced and joked as they built toys to fulfill the requests of late-arriving lists.

"You da man!"

"No, YOU da man!"

They cheered each other on as they wrapped and organized presents in perfect synch, making sure the details of all the last-minute lists were obliged. In a variety of cases, children were flipped from the Naughty List to the Nice List in late-time decisions, riding on the wings of a few, "*Pleases, thank yous, and sorrys.*"

Back in Saskatchewan, Andre Branch cynically sauntered from his realty office. He paused just outside the door. A glance upward gave him a view of Jane's glistening flakes floating down in front of the gas lamps lining the street. The snow feathered onto his hat and jacket, where they rested in perfect form. He didn't raise an eyebrow, but he did raise his head, and yes, it's been told...that even Andre Branch couldn't refrain from sticking out his tongue to catch a flake or two.

Meanwhile, Jane had positioned herself on top of a gorge with the zip line launcher resting on her shoulder. She aimed at her target... an office building in a town center, down below. Steady and fire!

Pfffffffshhhhh-CRASH-CRAMALANGALANG!

"Hit somethin'," Jane observed aloud with a shrug. Her face reddened. Not from anyone watching on her end, but from who might be standing at the other. She could hear the spear make its impact from where she was...however, it was hard to see its exact placement among the buildings.

"The day of Christmas Eve. Nobody's gonna be in there...wherever it hit," Jane said to herself, trying to extract the uneasiness from her stomach. She disengaged the cord from the launcher and stuck them both back into her bag. Then she used the spring link to secure the cord to a tree, before whacking her hand over the top of the zip line a few times.

"Tight," she confirmed.

After laying her hand over the line to ice it, Jane pulled the V-shaped chrome hanger from her backpack. Then she threw the hanger on top of the cable and sailed down the line at an unsafe speed, spraying hearty flakes from the river below all the way to the houses on the outskirts of town. She had just layered the inner borough with another three inches when she noticed a large office building coming straight at her!

"You're kiddin–"

Jane quickly released her weak hand from the hanger and hung on sideways, barely ducking her head enough to clear the window that the spear had broken open. She couldn't dodge every partition, desk, and chair along the way, but all of the smacks and bangs helped slow Jane to a stop before she hit the wall at the opposite end of the office. She may have knocked over a few files, but nothing to the extent of what she had done to Mr. Branch's office a week earlier.

"Yep, nobody here," Jane shrugged.

After hustling over to the elevator, she pushed the hair from her face with her forearm. "Sixth floor?"

The down arrow was in plain sight, but Jane wouldn't reach for it.

"Don't have time for that," she uttered.

Broken glass and pieces of drywall littered the floor at the foot of the wall where the spear was lodged. Behind Jane, glass fragments covered the desks and chairs where she had crashed into the office.

"Could do some cleanup..."

Jane spotted a broom and dustpan in the corner. But she decided not.

"I'll have someone take care of that," she reassured the phantom people in the room. Then she locked back in on the window through which she had entered. It wasn't exactly an open door.

"It'll do," she convinced herself.

Without a forward thought, Jane ran full speed at the window and launched herself out of it. Her boot clipped glass on her way through the frame, knocking her feet and body recklessly out of form. In the air, amid freefall, Jane spun herself hard and morphed into a snowy whirl, avoiding the fast-approaching asphalt by inches. Her backpack clanked off the ground as she twisted out of control, but it became wrapped in Jane's spiraling snow and was swept up right along with her. Not knowing up from down, Jane thought fast and gusted herself horizontal to the ground until she was able to rotate herself and the backpack smoothly into the air.

Jane floated freely with the wind once again. She opened her mind and allowed herself to be whisked away into the twilight, lifted high into the sky, where nothing could touch her. Finally, Jane could rest feeling satisfied...or could she?

XXVII

Santa was sliding his fingers into his white gloves, twenty feet from the landing area of Reindeer Runway. He stood decked out in his special suit. Yes, his *famous suit*...glowing bright in red and white. Its hand-woven fabrics absorbed the floodlights shining down from the pitched, wooden roof of the reindeer stable. The vibrancy of his whole ensemble was centerpiece material, right down to his boots, sharp and black. Bold. There was no turn back in those things. He took a step forward. Solo.

As Santa slid his palm down his mouth and beard, you could see him. The real him. Not the one who had to lead, but the one who was born a leader. Not the one who had to learn to care, but the one who was born caring. *A saint.*

His beard resembled polished marble, in the way that specks of black glistened like precious jewels from within the bristly white waves flowing down his face. His eyebrows feathered perfectly above his sparkling eyes, and his puffy cheeks rosied as content filled his belly. He was called to this place. He knew it. And *I* knew it. When I say *this place*, pay attention, because I'm talking about more than just an exact position on the Earth.

Glowing, he was…more than his suit. Even his breath came out in ample white puffs, enhanced by the luminous lights above. These were Santa's last moments to himself, before the big ride.

It was December 24th. The sky was perfectly clear, as it was every Christmas Eve. But when Santa glanced back, he noticed an isolated blizzard of snow descend close to the entry of his Headquarters, about a hundred yards away.

He watched as the flakes condensed into human form.

Jane's white pleather gear intensified under The Headquarters' spotlights. Her smooth brown skin glowed in contrast. She peered inconspicuously from left to right, searching for something…until she settled on Santa, who was casually walking in her direction.

"How was your dinner?" Santa shouted across the field.

Jane took several strides forward, closing the gap between Santa and herself. She was hoping to avoid broadcasting her feelings over the entire complex.

"Not bad," she called out, trying to conceal her giddiness. But her gratified voice gave her away as it echoed clearly across the stables, to the big man in the bright red suit, now fifty yards away.

"Ho, ho, ho!" Santa gloated, allowing his playful voice to resonate back to Jane. He would not succumb to using the actual words, *I told you so.*

The two of them continued toward each other until they were almost in the dark, as they had outdistanced the reach of the floodlights shining from opposite sides. They could only make out each other's silhouettes, but on this night, that was enough. Jane only had one question…and she didn't need to ask it.

Santa pointed to the slope running down from the side door of The Headquarters. "Over there," he offered stoutly.

Jane tried to control her smile. She thanked Santa with a wave, hooked her thumbs into her pockets, and began walking toward the back of The Headquarters. There were no lights on the backside of the building, but Jane was still able to make out a lone set of tracks as she worked her way down the hill.

"Look who had a change of heart," Red called out when he saw Jane's ebony form emerge against the snowy backdrop.

"Pshh," Jane deflected while continuing toward Red as if she planned to march right through him.

Jane kept Red in place with strong eye contact until she could get within arm's reach to deliver a stern shove to his shoulder. "What are *you* doing over here by yourself?"

"Thinking."

Red gave the short answer. But Jane was looking for the *complete* answer.

"About..." she guided softly.

Red didn't speak. He just pointed up into the sky at the aurora borealis. The splendor of Earth's most dramatic light exhibition decorated the dark sky above them. Fluorescent green and purple lights appeared to be frozen high in the air, mid-swirl, like cotton candy being pulled from its paper cone. Jane looked up at the divine display in the Earth's magnetosphere. As she took in the beauty of the sky, the beauty of the sky took in Jane, outlining her silhouette while shimmering off her black, wavy hair. Even the whites of her eyes remained clear and pure, unfazed by the close to twenty-four hour whirlwind tour she had just made.

"You matched it with your snow," Red said as he gently slid his hand behind Jane's upper arm.

"Tried to frame the picture a little," Jane returned in jest.

Red turned to her, and spoke with sincerity, "It all blends together…the way it's supposed to."

Jane noticed she was staring at her feet. She lifted her head and relocked eyes with the gentle man who stood before her. The man who had invested such care in their meeting, had accepted her without judgment, and was as handsome as he was sweet. And for only the second time in her life, she experienced an emotional sensation strong enough to fill her whole heart.

"You have to promise not to laugh at me when I say this…" Jane levied nervously.

Red took Jane's hands and sheltered them in his. "I'd be the last, remember. I'm not going to…"

Jane wasn't listening to Red's reassurances anymore. It didn't matter what he said. She was going to open up, and *nothing* was going to change that. She glanced over Red's shoulder at the northern lights once more, took a deep breath…and could not get anything to come out. Her eyes leveled down from brown to hazel, and then to green. When she looked back up at Red, a solid blue had emerged. Blue like sapphires…cold like them too. And empty. Jane said nothing, but she was feeling everything.

It was clear to Red, *he* had to say something. But he choked on every sentence, on every word, and every letter that tried to make its way from his heart to Jane. All he could offer was silence, which at that particular time, was the equivalent of not being there with her at all. Without a sound emitting from his lips, he let go of her hands. Then he slid his arms under Jane's, and embraced her, as if he had been waiting his whole life to do it.

The icy mist of Red's and Jane's breaths clouded their figures on that crisp night, but their tender souls still met…still connected… bringing a clarity that seemed to need not for words. Jane's quivering began to subside, yet it didn't leave her. Although her eyes began to level up again, they would not progress past bluish green. Her heart weakened. The ice tear clinging to the corner of her eye... it was clinging for a reason. And when *that* tear fell, more tears formed behind it. She rested her head on Red's shoulder.

Red could feel the ice of Jane's tears against his neck. This wasn't how he had imagined this embrace would be...you know, when he was imagining it forever. You can't predict emotions. Though, I do know *this dream* ran through Red's mind more than a million times. As he wrapped his head around everything which had led to this moment, he finally found a voice.

"Isn't it funny how sometimes...when you're looking for one thing...you find something else?"

He sniffled, but I can tell you, it wasn't from the cold.

Red could feel Jane's chin bumping against his shoulder. She was nodding in agreement. The two couldn't have been closer if they had melted together. Jane exhaled a frigid breath of air across Red's chest, as though she had been holding it in for a lifetime. A breath like that would've frozen common, everyday folk solid. But Red... let's just say, he wasn't your everyday fella.

"Ruuu!" Santa shouted into the night.

Red separated himself from his hug with Jane, yet he reached out to gather her hands. "Jane, it's Christmas Eve."

Not totally grasping what was going on, Jane wiped the frozen tears from her face. She tried to pull herself together. Red appeared ready to up and leave, but he tilted his head toward Jane instead. The two of them closed their eyes and allowed their foreheads to gently touch.

Still, Jane could sense *this was it*. She just couldn't understand why. She questioned aloud, "Now? Thought the work would be done and we—"

"RUUUUU!" Santa blasted down the hill.

Jane glanced down at Red's hand holding hers. Then she lifted her focus back up to his childlike face.

His breaths were short. "I missed you too."

Jane struggled to make sense of Red's short phrases...to try and fill in the moment with some semblance of answers.

"RUUUUUUUUU!"

Jane was jostled to the side by what seemed to be an invisible force. But this force was not invisible. As she regained her balance, she could see Red was changing.

White and light brown fur began billowing from his skin. He dropped to all fours to support the weight of his expanding ribcage. Red's head elongated while light beige antlers extended from the top of his head. Simultaneously, his nose enlarged and blackened. Even his brown eyes grew in size, with thick lashes slowly rising up over them. *Red was morphing into a reindeer!*

Hooves busted through the bottom of his boots. Soon after, his arms tore through his sleeves and his legs burst free of his pants, on their way to becoming four sturdy legs, each growing longer by the second. Red's head was now nine feet in the air and his body stretched ten feet long. Thick white fur flowed out from his neck and hung down like the underside of a mane. When Red's ears grew to their full length of seven inches, he began twitching them, as though he were starting to rev his engine.

Jane didn't backtrack. In reality, after the original push, she moved closer to Red. She watched him draw in the crisp, pure air through his wide black nose while his antlers grew outward and upward. Jane knew this was something *anyone* would give up *anything* to see. But it was just her. With Red. *A performance for one.*

Red gave his wide white tail a quick wiggle. Then he lifted up his rear hooves one at a time, before placing them back into the deep snow. His antlers now spanned five feet wide and rose seven feet above his head.

Red was majestic. His big brown eye drew Jane in, letting her know that, *yes*…this was still him. She was sure of that. She could see it in the confidence of his stare and the way he raised up proud, knowing he had an important job to do. Red always had an important job to do. Yet Jane would not be remiss in sending him one of her candid, *you got me* looks, conceding at the time, this was a piece of information he had never let her in on. In acknowledgment, Red whipped his long head away from Jane, before twisting it back in her direction. He lowered his forehead toward her face.

Jane reached out her open hand…and slowly ran it down his nose. Red rose up again.

From his ample nostrils, he blew out a foggy steam that evaporated into Jane's crisp night. Like an old vaudeville show gassing up its lights for another go, Red's antlers began blinking a vibrant blue. Simultaneously, his hooves did the same. The glow extended through every point of his antlers, but flickered on and off as it went. Eventually, Red's hooves filled completely with such a cerulean shade of blue, it lit up the snow all around them. Shortly after, his antlers fully illuminated with the same blue light, brightening the ground as far as a hundred feet ahead.

Red was poised and confident. With his fluorescent antlers glowing above his head, he put a sincere eye onto Jane to reassure her that *he was okay*. Here, as Red faced Jane for the first time as a reindeer, he could only hope that she would be okay too. Jane placed her hand gently on Red's upper leg...solemnly...and then took it away.

Red looked down at Jane respectfully.

She returned a nod.

Jane knew this was not a matter of choosing. It was just something that had to be done. If you lived in The North, you understood that for better or worse, things stayed moving. Guess it's the same everywhere...can't control everything, can we, baby? No doubt, Jane was reminded of that when Red gave her one last glance, took two huge gallops, and powered himself up the hill, out of sight.

Now, where did Jane stand? *Where?* I don't know. But hollow. No place to go. *Hm.* Rest? Careful what you wish for. No, truth is, Jane never wished for this...not even in her deepest moment of darkness.

XXVIII

Jane's cold air continued to provide a halo for the North Pole. In fact, the chill became ever more biting with each passing minute. Outside Santa's Headquarters, floodlights beamed to their full capabilities. It would blind you to look into them, but they were hardly a match for the darkness of Christmas Eve at the Earth's most northern point.

The elves were scurrying in all directions. Yet make no mistake, each elf knew exactly where they were supposed to be, and the protocol they needed to follow when they got there. Their hands operated with such speed, you could barely see what they were doing under the cloak of the night. Two details did stand out, however. The elves' Kelly green suits dazzling under the high-powered lamps, and the misty white puffs coming from their noses and mouths as they hustled to make everything perfect.

Leatherworking Elves ambitiously dipped cloths inside metal tins. They shined up the reindeer harnesses with their eyes pressed inches from the leather straps. The smell of their oils wafted up and down the harness line while the sounds of their work gave the ambiance of a well-run factory.

"Number 6!"

"We got ya!"

"Tin!"

"Heads up!"

"Down here!"

"We got a fray on 8…"

"We'll get the Double E's on that!"

"All set?"

"All set!"

"Out everybody!"

They hastily slapped the leather harnesses into the hands of the awaiting *Coordinator Elves*, who transported them to the landing of Reindeer Runway. As the *Coordinator Elves* trotted toward the landing with the extra weight, the *Leatherworking Elves* had a chance to celebrate. They bounced around with special hand slaps and spins, demonstrating the close-knit camaraderie of the team. They bustled over to their next job, but not before the last elf gave a trailing elf one big celebratory swat on his behind!

Santa's shiny red sleigh sat a short distance from the reindeer stables. Elves ran around it with toolboxes, tightening screws by hand. No part of the sleigh was ever created, fabricated, assembled, or fixed with a power tool. It was always my husband's notion that it should be a work of hand craftsmanship. Used to joke around and say, if something went wrong while he was thousands of feet in the air, he wanted to know which hand to blame. On a serious note, that was why only the most elite *Craftsmen Elves* and *Technician Elves* ever got to put their hands on that thing.

To be honest, the sleigh itself doesn't exactly sound like a luxury jet. There's a lot of rattling goes on with it. My husband says it gives him comfort, because when he hears the parts rattling, at least he knows they're still there. Don't even talk to me about it. He's his own person. You can't tell him *anything* for his own safety. Hehe! I'm not saying the sleigh was a piece of junk, because nothing could be further from the truth. No, those elves had brilliant minds... skilled with their hands just the same.

The sleigh was seven feet wide and fifteen feet long. Bright red... cushioned black leather seats...sharp black runners underneath. I'm not the only one to feel this way, but of all the items we have lying around here at the North Pole, my husband's sleigh is the most magnificent. Sure, I've ridden in it, child. But you can be clear, I remind those reindeer who feeds 'em before we take off. None of that *thousands of feet in the air* stuff. One modest lap above the complex is enough for me.

Once the *Tool Box Elves* tightened all the nuts and bolts, *Polishing Elves* filed in to buff out any remaining smudges.

"Get it, men!"

"Need two of you on this side!"

"Easy there..."

"What do you think?"

"Let's see...step back a little..."

When they were finished, you could walk over to that sleigh and take in an exact reflection of yourself, no lie.

"All clean!"

"Go, go, go!"

"On to Red!"

"Grab a bucket! Grab a bucket!"

While all of the reindeer prep was going on, Jane ventured just far enough up the slope to observe the production without being noticed. For real, she was only focused on one thing. And that was Red. From where she stood, she could see a group of *Preparation*

Elves moving around him as though he were royalty. When he was strapped into his harness, Red's head remained high. His blue-brightened hooves held to the ground firmly, and his body braced like steel...as Santa's hardest workers prepared him for flight.

Next, The *Polishing Elves* moved onto Red, wearing their white gloves. They worked over all the silver bells on his harness until each one embodied the most perfect state of precious metal a human has ever seen.

After the bells were polished, The *Musician Elves* strode up with all their supplies. They held headphones up to their ears and placed small microphones up to each individual bell, measuring every one of them for perfect pitch and tune. Ping! Ring-a-ling-a-ling!

"We need a replace for 11!"

"...And 19!"

"I got your 19."

"We got a 4 here too!"

"Is that it?"

"That's it!"

As the *Musician Elves* took over the bells, the *Polishing Elves* moved down to Red's hooves. They swished long white towels over and back, across each hoof. Rhythmically. Fluidly. And artistically. The cloths danced and swirled, but there were no smiles here. These were the four blocks that were going to lead Santa's sleigh into the air. One tiny crack in a hoof...one imperfection...could lead to a kink that would disrupt the flight the whole night through.

"Look here!"

"What do we got?"

"Naah, we're all good...all good. Sorry."

"No sorries. That's what we gotta do!"

The *Enhancement Elves* rushed in last. They were also known as the *Double E's*. They made sure Red had received the full treatment, and that no bell had gone unpolished. They smoothed down the leather straps to remove any slack, took care of sewing up any frays, and meticulously inspected Red's hair and fur. If there were an issue as minute as a piece of fur lying in the wrong direction, the *Double E's* handled it. There were different brushes and combs for every part of Red's body...for his tail, his legs, and for the fur flowing from his neck and chest.

"Left hind!"

"Check!"

"Right ear passes!"

"Right ear, check!"

Two elves positioned themselves over a case full of brushes and fired them up to the elves doing the grooming. It was all about speed and precision. Wasn't an operation you'd want to get in the middle of, because The *Double E's* didn't mess around for nothin'. You wouldn't want to get caught by a flying brush. Heh. I laugh... but it's true.

When *The Double E's* finished the job, not a drop of sweat appeared on their foreheads. Their suits were still pressed fine. You'd find not so much as a sideways tilt to one of their hats. Cuffs straight and white too. These were the *"Marines"* of the elf conglomerates.

"What do we have on the front-right hoof?"

"She's ready, sir!"

"Final confirmation!"

"Grooming confirmed, sir! Good to go!"

The leader of the *Double E's* shouted across the landing, "Ready for flight!"

Then, something you'd be lucky to ever see. To me…this is where Christmas Eve truly begins each year…

Dez made his way up a nearby slope and entered the landing area.

Each one of the *Double E's* reached out and put a hand on the side of Red. The lamps shone down, catching the elves' radiant green suits and hardworking ebony skin. All the elf teams involved in Red's preparation, and the fine-tuning of Santa's sleigh, also gathered in tight to Red. They knew what it was…the last step before the ride. More elves came up to the landing and put a hand on the shoulder of a brother or sister while others dropped a knee into the snow, waiting for *the message*.

The *Double E*, whose hand rested on the side of Red's neck, spoke first. "Remove your hats."

The elves gathered their hats in their hands.

Dez stood to the front right of Red and began. "Bow your heads, men….women."

There was a shuffle or two, but then the landing quieted. In the still of the night, one couldn't even see the elves' breaths rising up anymore. Undeniably, the *whole Headquarters* came to a stop, and all of the North Village paused right after in the same manner. There was a sense across the North Pole. Never this moment was missed. Those chosen elves surrounding Red…and a message to be delivered before the night's journey.

Dez led the group in prayer, "*Dear Lord,* help us to understand, we should never cut what we can untie…"

"Yes sir," elves vocalized from different places among the circle.

"…Yet help us to remember that the best way out…*is* often through."

"Praise Jesus," an elf on one knee offered with depth.

Other elves nodded and bowed their heads in unity.

Dez continued his prayer, "*Lord,* please keep all of the children safe on *this* of *all* holy nights. Watch over them as their parents tuck them into bed to sleep. In addition, Lord, we ask you to watch over our children in the morning, as they open their eyes to *your gift...* the breath of a new day."

"*Praise God,*" the elves chimed in.

Dez turned to Red with conviction. He let his voice spread across The North. "Jesus spoke to them, saying, '*I am the light of the world! He who follows me will not walk in darkness, but will have the light of life!*'" Dez was aware this was Red's favorite verse.

"Eight-twelve," one of the elves lauded proudly.

Dez lowered his head. "In Jesus' name, amen."

"Amen," the elves resounded.

One by one the elves went up to Red, placed a hand on his side, and walked away. Dez moved in front of him after all of the elves had cleared out. Red closed his eyes and bowed his head, lowering his grand, dangerously sharp antlers on each side of Santa's Lead Elf.

"God bless," Dez said with respect. He patted Red's nose. "In peace."

The two of them shared in the quiet focus of that moment like two brothers who had been through wars together. Red's head rose once more. He took in the runway before him. His eyes wouldn't close again until Christmas morning.

XXIX

"Donner! Blitzen! Cupid! Where are you...*yooooou* little Vixen?" Santa shouted in mounting frustration. This was his second attempt to pull the rest of the team together. Daija's own prayer and pregame hype session had run a little long, so she was just bringing everyone home.

"...All in *love*..." she finished.

"LOVE IS ALL!" the team responded.

"Donner. Blitzen. Cupid!" Santa called out in a staccato fashion.

The boys were ready. Inside the community room, Don, Blake, and Q transformed into reindeer one by one.

At the sound of the name, *Donner,* Don began his changeover. He was a hulk. Don's antlers were glossy brown like polished oak. Pointed sharp as daggers too. They'd say his chest was a brick wall. His back and belly covered in brown fur, and a wide strip of white emerged across the side of his body. Don lifted his head high and gave his body a shake.

When Santa hollered, *"Blitzen!",* Blake morphed. White and gray fur poured from his skin. *Gray clouds and white lightning*! His coat emulated that of a white jaguar. But his whole look received a shot of spice when tan antlers rose from his reindeer head. He rotated his antlers fifteen degrees to the left, before swinging them, full turn, back to the right.

At the call of *Cupid*, it was Q who elongated and rose into a large, coarse-furred white reindeer. A hazelnut brown, diamond-shaped patch of fur marked the top of his nose, between his eyes. Light brown eyebrows feathered in, as toasty brown pelage brushed out gently from the sides of his face. Pristine antlers and a shiny coat. Power suit...all business and dressed to the nines. He gestured to Don and Blake. Then the three steeds bounded through the traffic of elf personnel on their way to the landing.

"Comet! Dasher! Prancer! Viiiiiixen!" Santa hollered forcefully.

Kade morphed into a reindeer at the cry for *Comet*. Shiny coffee-colored hair draped over his body as white fur adorned his neck. Kade's legs covered in deep mahogany-colored fur while his hooves became insulated with thick white hair. He gave his wide white tail a twitch, clip-clapped across the community room, and powered out of the front doorway.

"*Prancer!*" Santa called out again.

This time, Prince heeded the shout-out. His extremely thick, short fur was a bronzy-wheat shade. His legs were black coffee, very similar to Kade's, but they were muscular like an ox. His antlers spanned out wider than his outstretched arms when he was in his human state, and small spears jutted out from them, drawing attention to the already wide setting of his rack. Those who got a glimpse of Prince in his reindeer form always had the same response...and that was simply, "*Wow.*"

Elves monitored the doors to make sure they were open for any reindeer leaving the community room. But there was always a gust of wind that would happen at the wrong time, which would put them in the precarious position of risking their lives to save the doors from being obliterated by a stampede.

Whoosh! Bang! On cue, the doors slammed shut, just before Prince reached them. They were fortunate it was *only* one reindeer coming through...although they were unfortunate that the one reindeer was Prince.

"PULLLLLLLL!" all of the elves shouted in panic.

The elves on door watch lifted their feet and contorted their bodies to whip the doors back open in a blur of Kelly green! Mid-swing, the elves each threw a hand out to reach for one of the wrought iron brackets welded to the face of the building. They were able to latch on. With the gust still whipping, they closed their eyes and braced themselves, heels swinging in the air.

"HOLD IT!" the armchair elves yelled from the wings, offering no assistance.

Prince charged through. The elves hanging from the doors air-walked their legs out of the way in time to dodge his antlers. They wouldn't want to be grazed by one of those things. Especially not Prince's. He'd barely clear the doorway, even when he ducked his head. On that day, Prince did catch the tip of one of his large antlers on the upper frame. Come to think of it...I guess that's why the Carpentry Elves were up there every New Year's Day, sanding and repainting the top of the entryway. Probably happened more than once.

"*Dasherrrrrrrr!*" Santa blasted once more. We used to get a chuckle at the way my husband stretched out the second syllable of Daija's code name whenever he got flustered. Wait now, don't judge. If a spouse can't laugh at the other. He does it to me too. And no, I'm not opening that up now. Let you see it for yourself when it happens. Ha!

Daija has such a free-flowing name. Sounds like a song when you say it. And she rose into reindeer form just as divine. Her eyes spoke from knowledge. As a deer, she could tell you everything she needed to say with only a glance. Her pure white fur was brushed with silver and black hues on her back and lower shoulders. Thin white antlers rose outward from her reindeer head at twenty-degree angles, before tilting inward at the top points. Dark gray rounded her ears while white hairs swept in between to soften the lines. I'd say she most resembled Q. *Graceful Daija.*

"Dasherrrrrrrr!"

She stood still. Daija wouldn't move until she was ready. But when she *was* ready, she was gone, without the sound of a single hoof tap on the floor.

At this point, Santa's voice had to compete with the frantic communication of the elves loading presents into the sleigh. From the landing of the runway, Santa sounded off, "Dancer! Vixen!"

Dani had those long legs. When she heard the name, *Dancer*, and decided to ride, her legs covered with burgundy-brown, mahogany-colored hair. As for Dani's big brown eyes and beautiful lashes, they only appeared *more* captivating in her reindeer form. Of the whole group, Dani's reindeer state most closely resembled her human self. Pale beige fur dressed her sturdy body while brown fur eased over her long face. She peered back. And there was Vicki, sitting crossed-legged on the couch, lounging in pink workout gear.

The repeated calling of *Vixen* had no effect on Vicki. She continued to flirt with a fun bunch of Toy Making Elves, who were basking in her crumbs of attention, however small. To be close to her, to sit on the same couch, to wait on Vicki…that was enough to spin them. Wrap them around her finger. But *she* wasn't distracted, oh no, sir.

"Save the best for last," Vicki enlightened her audience, letting them know she was staying put for no other reason.

Dani was always entertained by Vicki, but she wasn't going to be the last one to the lineup. She wheeled around and trotted out to the landing.

Now, Vicki was *officially* the last reindeer left.

The elves couldn't wait for *the one and only* to get out there and get the party started.

"VIIIIIIIXENNNNNNN!!!" Santa shouted. He was about to lose his mind.

Vicki stood up.

She swung to the left, looked back at her human self one last time, flipped her hair, and went savage. She arched her back and leaned forward. Her arms extended as reindeer legs and her hands morphed into hooves before they reached the floor. Dark walnut fur flowed from Vicki's legs as white fur spread from the middle of her head, down her neck, and across the side of her body. The top of her back and hindquarters floated out a pear wood shade...the same as her face. Antlers extended from her head in a slow, fluent motion, weaving upward, until they reached their highest point. Hints of reddish cinnamon snuck out across Vicki's body, while her tail bloomed, dark brown down the middle and fluffy white on the outside. She gave it a twitch.

"VIIIIIIIXENNNNNNN!!! FOR THE LAST TIME!!!" Santa blasted *for the last time*.

Vicki leapt diagonally forward, leaving her hooves at a bad angle. Her hind legs slipped out from under her, and she bounced off the ground. She kicked out, launching a side table across the room, into the wall. With pieces of broken table ricocheting in all directions, Vicki popped up, jumped to the left to re-right herself, and barreled toward the exit. The Toy Making Elves hooted and hollered in the background as Vicki recklessly bounded through the double doors. Santa's last reindeer was on her way to the landing!

The last minute setup...the packing of the sleigh, pulling the reindeer together...it's not from a lack of forethought and planning. Those things *can't* be done until it's close to takeoff time. Could anyone plan ahead for *each toy* on the late arriving Christmas lists? Could you polish the silver bells and line up the reindeer a week in advance? There was a special timing for everything when it came to the 24th. As for Reindeer Runway, it had been dressed and waiting for a full day. And now, the curtains were raised, the spotlights were on, and the evening's star-studded cast had taken the stage!

XXX

There was a peace within. Eight of Santa's reindeer stood harnessed, lined up, and focused on the trip ahead. Until, of course, Vicki came bouncing and skidding in on an earmarked path toward Red's backside! She avoided clipping Red's rear leg by inches, somehow finding a way to shuffle her hooves backwards and recklessly moonwalk herself into proper position before contact.

Red stomped his left hoof down with thunder, tilted his head sideways, and blew out a forceful snort of impatience. Vicki was on thin ice. Not literally…but you know what I mean. She dipped her head, cowered down, and slinked her legs out in front of herself. Blake straightened up tall in his position next to Vicki to remind her of the necessary pre-flight stance, which didn't involve bowing and haphazardly flinging hooves around.

The only time you'd see humility in Vicki was when she bashed her way into the lineup every year. Once she got the stare down from Red and the glare down from Blake, let's say she'd *tell herself* she would never be late again…even though three hundred and sixty-five days later, she would barrel in, last minute, just the same as the year before.

Red tilted his head to the other side and slammed down his right hoof this time. A vibration was sent across the ground, rattling the runners of Santa's sleigh more than fifty feet behind. Red had to shut down all of the nonsense in a hurry, because, trust me, the takeoff ritual for Santa and the reindeer didn't involve all the delays that tend to occur with commercial flights. The team more resembled racehorses entering a starting gate. Once those reindeer were latched in, it was go time.

One of the Double E's anxiously sprinted through the center of the reindeer to hook up Vicki's harness on the right side. On his way, he ducked under and swung from all of the harness straps connecting the other pairs of reindeer. Another one of the Double E's ran a parallel line on the outside of the team and latched up Vicki on the left. Click! Cinch!

"Out!"

"Go!"

At the same time, Santa climbed into the sleigh with a few of the elves. He chose different elves each year depending on the tasks at hand. Being selected was the ultimate honor, and this highly respected duty was never promised to anyone ahead of time.

With Vicki finally secured, Santa raised a white glove into the night. All of the lights shining down on The Headquarters cut off in an instant. Next, Red's antlers and hooves dimmed, as though lowered by a switch.

Marshall Elves waved blue light sticks into the air at the other end of Reindeer Runway, some two hundred yards away. A pair of Double E's took a knee on either side of Red and bowed their heads, while two Technician Elves knelt down on opposite sides of Santa's sleigh. A long, ice-cold breath of wind moved across the landing. There was no more sound...there was no more activity...

save for the blue lights of the Marshalls, waving up and down at the opposite end of the runway, as if in slow motion.

"DASH AWAY, DASH AWAY, DASH AWAY ALL!" Santa boomed from the sleigh.

Red straightened up and blew an icy mist from his nostrils. Then he slammed his right hoof down. Powdery snow exploded into the air. By the time the flakes landed, Red's hooves were glowing and his antlers were raised to full illumination, beaming across the first hundred yards of the snow-covered runway.

Red tilted his top points down like a bull.

Both of the Marshall Elves looked at each other with a mutual fear running down their faces. They fully grasped what was coming, but they couldn't fold now. They had to hold their positions until Red reached them at the other end of the runway.

At a signal from one of the Double E's, a Polishing Elf shot in from the side and ran straight at Red. She did a baseball slide, popped up, and polished one last silver bell on his harness. Then she spun out of harm's way as Red rose up on his hind legs, elevating his front hooves fifteen feet into the air. With the power of a machine, Red threw his body forward. The sleigh gave a lurch at first, but after his second tug, the harnesses and reins became taut. With one more thrust, the rest of the reindeer and the sleigh were launched into a steady path behind him.

The last two elves ran in from opposite sides, grabbed a guard rail, and hopped into the sleigh. At the same time, the other reindeer picked up their pace, following Red's lead in a synchronized full-throttle race toward the Marshalls.

With puffy cheeks jiggling and eyes watering, Santa and the elves tightly grasped the sides of the sleigh to keep from flying off. The team of reindeer tore ahead, their hooves sending vibrations throughout the grounds of the entire North Village. All the while, the sleigh rattled and clanked behind the Earth's largest and most powerful reindeer as they moved like a freight train toward the terrified holders of the blue wands, now only a hundred yards away! RUMBLE, RUMBLE, RUMBLE!

Red began to lift into the air and land in ten-yard spans. Boom! Poof! Boom! Poof! Rattle, clank, rattle! The sleigh seemed like it was going to burst into a thousand pieces. The elves glanced over at Santa with trepidation. Rattle, CLANK! RUMBLE, RUMBLE, RUMBLE, RUMBLE!

"Men," Santa bellowed over the clamor, sending back a deep-voiced nod of reassurance.

Red hit top speed, then pulled with all his might. But the extra burst caused his antlers to short out. Next, his hooves blinked out. The last fifty yards of the runway were now totally black, leaving the brave Marshall Elves as sitting targets. They were the only ones who could light the path for a runaway train, which was gaining momentum with each stride of all nine reindeer. The only thing the Marshalls could see was a cerulean blue flicker here and there. However, the sound of galloping, from what seemed like a stampede of a thousand horses, became more amplified by the second.

Suddenly, all of Red's blue lights flashed on to their highest luminosity. The Marshalls quickly became aware that the stampede was only fifteen yards away. RUMBLE, RUMBLE, RUMBLE, RUMBLE! The Marshalls were virtually blinded by the light, but they *could* catch a glimpse of each other's unified decision to toss their light sticks into the air and dive out of the way.

CRACK! CRUNCH! Red trampled over the wands on his way to lifting his front hooves into the air. His hind legs immediately followed. WHOOSH! Red's full body had left the ground!

Vicki and Blake followed Red's path over the Marshall's abandoned light sticks. CRACK! CRUNCH! CRACK! In an instant, they powered up with their rear legs and elevated behind Red. Without breaking stride, Kade and Dani galloped off the ground, with Q and Daija rising next.

For Don and Prince, each stride was a heave. Each leap took a toll on their bodies. The duo used every muscle in their shoulders, every ounce of brawn they had, to lift themselves into the air...pushing forward with only flight on their minds. Up and up, they continued to drive, though the sleigh itself had yet to leave the ground. Upon their next thrust, they were finally able to yank the large red carriage past the Marshall Elves...and the back edge of its runners gave one last kiss to the snowy runway.

"HO! HO! HO!" Santa bellowed with glee.

The sleigh's weight became lighter by the second. In no time, the team was a hundred feet in the air...then two hundred...then four.

"HO! HO! HO!" Santa celebrated again.

The elves next to him clapped, before linking arms. People might say they were lucky. But they weren't lucky. *They were deserving.* They had earned the right to be on that trip.

Red's electrifying blue lights led the team into a hard veer to the left and another elevation as they tore the vibrant red sleigh off into the dark night.

The Double E's, once kneeling beside Red, now took to their feet alongside the Technician Elves. They gazed in awe at Red and his team of reindeer pulling Santa's magnificent sleigh. Farther back, the rest of the elves watched. From the stables. From outside of The Headquarters. From the lawns of their village homes, and the windows of their workshops and bakeries. *The ride.* That's what they called it. Their focus didn't break from the sky. The elves watched until only a collection of blue dots and a dash of red remained.

In an instant, those dotted glimmers vanished, but the eyes of The North stayed trained on the place of that last vision. A stream of brilliant colors materialized in their minds. A stream holding the dream…a dream they were gifting to all of the world's children. This was *their* promise. This was *their* bond.

I watched from the side of The Headquarters, just outside the creaky wooden screen door to the kitchen. Large flakes blew up and then slanted down from the roof, throwing blurred impressionistic strokes over the colorful images before me. Like the elves, I'd seen the event of the twenty-fourth a million times. But each time was as wondrous as the first. Each time there was a new wrinkle. A uniqueness. Something to bring out the *oohs* and *aahs* in all of us.

On that night, Jane's swirling snow turned upward from the ground, blending the lines of red, brown, and green across the image of the alluring sleigh high up in the distance. The cerulean blue shine of Red's antlers vividly cut the darkness. The pristine fur of each reindeer, the variation of colors crossing them, flowing up and down in gentle waves…

It was a painting. More than that…it was *a movement.*

I reached my hand in front of me and ran my fingers over the ridges of each paint stroke on the canvas. The air was so clean to breathe in. And I spoke into it, yes I did.

"Jane Frost, *The Voice Of The North,*" I said, " You brought more than snow…you brought hope…without you…*Hm.*"

I shook my head. Closed my eyes. And raised a palm to our Lord Jesus.

XXXI

Specks of gold glitter floated down onto the forest green bench as Reggie shifted his weight to put a shiny gift box back into his pocket. He took the contents of the box and pressed them into Jenny's hand. Then he helped Jenny close her hand, before sliding his palm over the top of it, to serve as a lid, which might keep the youth and innocence from escaping.

In her grasp, Jenny held a necklace dripping with flawless diamonds. A snowflake pendant pinched at her fingers, yet it sparkled with blue and white flashes when she loosened her grip. Reggie pulled his hand away when he was sure Jenny had the necklace firmly in her clutch. Jenny paused for a second. Then she began to open her hand while moving the gift back in Reggie's direction.

"No. Hold it," Reggie let out softly.

Jenny spun toward Reggie. Her knee touched his.

"What's this?" she asked.

"I want you to remember me. That I'm coming back…"

"You don't even know when…or how…" Jenny calmly replied.

She spoke in a way that was meant to bring Reggie down to some form of reason. To dial him back a little. To turn his absolutes into something less rigid. But for Reggie's sake, she decided to play along for a little. Given their long-standing relationship, she felt it was the least she could do.

Jenny opened her hand fully. Unblemished platinum prongs carefully held carat after carat of diamond after diamond. Together, they formed a chain, which appeared to have no end. A chain, whose stones shimmered in Jenny's hand, even on that cloudy day. The gray sky, if anything, accentuated the one-of-a-kind craftsmanship, which sent bursts of light in all directions with the tiniest flinch of one of her fingers. As if created by a team of the world's greatest jewelers, the diamonds, each of perfect clarity, seemed to cascade down a platinum river, before melting and refreezing into the shape of a stunning snowflake at the bottom of a valley. Truth be told, it captured Jenny's attention. She was lost for a second, without a doubt. Then she snapped alert.

"Where'd you—"

"I found it," Reggie interrupted with attempted assurance.

Jenny joked, "In your mother's jewelry box?"

But Reggie was serious. And he sweetly continued, "We'll always be workin' together, Jenny."

Jenny hung her head. Then she turned to Reggie and cracked a smile, "Fightin' crime?"

Reggie nodded tentatively, yet he would not totally surrender to Jenny's diversion. He sat silently, waiting for her to take him more seriously.

Well, if he wanted to stick to a script, Jenny was all ready to step onto a page of that script with him. Her frustration became more visible. "How are we gonna do that, when we won't even see each other…with you just up and leaving?"

Reggie studied his fingers while flares of light from the necklace took repeated shots at the corner of his eye. He spoke quietly, but chose words that would reinforce his message.

"I'll still be with you," he said. "We'll always be workin' together… even when we're apart."

It seemed as though a cyclone had whirled away the reindeer, the sleigh, and everything around it. But when the lights were cut back on, a lone figure remained. Down the gentle incline, behind The Headquarters, Jane stood tall against a cross-blowing wind. With swirls of snowy gusts taking turns ripping against her, ripping against the emptiness she felt inside…she would not waver. She didn't tilt. Her skin, still smooth…still had that ebony glow to it. She didn't change her stance. Yet Jane grew *lonelier* with each one of her soft breaths.

Surrounded by only that little flashback in her mind, Jane reached into the pocket of her white winter vest. She closed her hand tightly around the only thing she could feel inside it. Sharp points dug into her palm as a soft, cold stream slid between her fingers. She raised her head and exhaled. When Jane pulled her hand from her pocket, she was holding a flawless diamond necklace with a stunning snow-flake pendant.

A priceless memento to anyone else…at that instant, meant nothing to Jane. The logistics of how it made its way to her hand. Her gifter. He was not with her now. The ones who clamored for her snow were not with her. Her family. The North. Who stood beside her at that moment? Herself. The same *self* that worked so hard in order to end up at the place where she began. You can imagine that. This emptiness sits in a part of you too, I know. Work so hard to end up where you started. You wanted that fairy tale? I told you this was the wrong story for you. Because this was real life. This is the *true story* of Jane Frost, and I had to tell it so nobody would try and tell it different. Why this book will never be found in the children's section of the library, you can best believe.

Jane had reached out to the people around her. She had reconnected. She *gave* the people what they wanted. And yet, there she stood...alone. How could that be? As if she had travelled a full circle. The dream where you exhaust yourself...working to complete a task that you can never finish. *Mmh.*

As for me, I took to heart Jane's hollowness. I feel almost *every* whispered emotion that flows through The North. I feel the empty souls. I feel the fulfilled hearts. I feel the *happiness* and the *despair.* I feel the togetherness...and unfortunately, yes, the shadowed moments of solitude. I feel the warmth...and *I feel the ice.* I've felt strength, even within God's most *humble* creations, but one thing I've never felt...is weakness. I am the matriarch of The North. I *am* the struggle. But weakness? No child, I've never been about that. And when I let that screen door bang shut, I did it to wake up Jane, to remind her she ain't about that weakness either. You know, you'd be right to start movin' on too. Dreams don't come true just for opening your eyes...as you can be sure they don't come true for closing them.

But the screen door didn't wake Janey. *If it were that easy.* Instead, her brown eyes sank to hazel...and then to blue. The *hollow within* began to extend through her body. Jane searched for a substance deep inside herself, but even her head became void of thoughts. The reindeer were far away. Her mind was no place.

She stared *far* into the open.

The screen door banged shut once more. This time, it was Gerald...coming out.

The deep snow was hard for him to clump his way through. His steps were awkward and side-to-side, set even further off balance by the mid-sized, velvet burgundy sack he carried. He switched it from one hand to the other in order to help him maintain his balance as he navigated his way down the incline on his path to Jane. A gust of wind blew rising steam from the sack into Gerald's face, before throwing falling snow across his body. He staggered for a second... then steadied himself. But when he picked his head up, Jane's tracks were gone.

The same driven snow that had stolen Gerald's balance, had smoothed over all the imprints Jane's boots left behind. The only thing he could follow was Jane's image. Was as though he were walking toward a ghost. How Gerald explained it. Jane standing there as if she wasn't. White enveloped in white.

Still, Gerald plodded forward, eventually closing the distance between Jane and himself...until she sensed his presence. Gerald didn't need to lift his head before the placement of his next step to recognize that. *He knew it.* And for the first time ever...he stopped dead in his tracks. Dead. In. His. Tracks.

"Miss...Ms. Frost?" he called out timidly from behind.

Jane swirled her head around to face him. Her eyes exhibited the coldest, iciest color you've never seen. Such a *fine* pale blue, they were almost white. Like ice over ice.

Gerald could feel cold sharp pins shooting through his body. But I sent him. He understood he wasn't there for personal reasons. Therefore, he was also aware there wasn't an avenue or choice of retreat. With his heart in his throat and his stomach churning with fear, Gerald stayed put and bowed his head. He lifted his arm and extended the velvet sack toward Jane. His hand had become clammy and the sack began sliding through his grip, but Jane reached under his palm to firmly secure the bag in her clutch.

She turned her back on Gerald and centered the sack in front of her ribcage. Then she loosened the gold rope tied around it, with the diamond snowflake necklace still wrapped between the fingers of her left hand. Jane peered inside. She didn't need to examine the contents too closely, because the steaming smell of the soulful meal I had prepared rose up to her face the instant she wiggled at the knot.

Gerald nodded. "For Father Time." Then, with his hands shaking, amid his flustered state, he found a way to reach inside the pocket of his vest and pull out a small piece of folded paper. "And this…for you."

Jane would not fully face Gerald. But she shifted the sack to her hand which held the necklace, and reached out with her free hand to take the paper from him. She unfolded it close to her chest. It was a note from me. Jane read it to herself. "*God loves all his children. In faith – Mrs. Claus.*"

Jane peered over her shoulder and gave Gerald a flirty little smirk of *thanks*. She carefully tucked the note into her pocket, before slowly zipping it shut. Then she unwrapped the diamond snowflake necklace from around her fingers.

Gerald watched as Jane lifted her hair and clasped the necklace behind her neck. She held her position, but continued to stare off into the distance. Jane's subtle look of confusion was not hidden *or lost* on the experienced elf.

"The blue glow?"

Gerald gave Jane pause. She turned halfway.

The wind picked up, prompting Gerald to elevate his voice over the howling snow. "Giving him the nickname, *Red*…our little joke!" The storm pulled back for a moment as it mustered up the power for another heavy surge. Gerald seized the opportunity to add, "And another thing…You can't believe everything you read in books!"

Jane relinquished a light smile. She gave him that.

Gerald felt a bit more at ease.

He sidestepped and shuffled his feet in the deep snow, before trudging back toward The Headquarters.

Jane scanned the night, noticing the darkness and how far it stretched. Her posture resembled that of one who had fulfilled a mission…but inside…she still felt lost and alone.

Gerald stopped. And exhaled. The internal struggle, which many had endured when dealing with Jane, arose within him too. He rotated slowly to face her once more. He took off his green cone-shaped hat and held it tightly with both hands. Jane was locked in, thirsty for any other morsel he could offer. In turn, Gerald laid his next set of words on top of the wind, letting the swirling gust decide whether she should receive them or not.

"Jenny…it's okay," he said, "This is the truth you've been lookin' for…" Raising his voice over the roar of the blizzard he finished, "There are no lies in the North!"

Gerald said all he was going to say. In The North, you be careful not to overstep your bounds. If he *had* tried to add more, his next set of thoughts wouldn't have had a prayer of reaching Jane any-way. She had already swung her head around, with a synchronized motion of her arm, and blown an escalator of powdery snow up Gerald's back and into the air above him. The large flakes clung to his clothes without mercy, as he fought his way up the slope, and vanished behind the wall of white.

Jenny stuffed the snowflake necklace into the front pocket of her white pleather schoolbag.

Reggie uttered shyly, "You want me to–"

Jenny burst out, "You can't go away. I don't have anyone! I *won't* have ANYONE!"

"You really jus' going to be mad at me for going someplace where they'll understand me…understand *us*? *Where they get us*? Do you think you're like any of these people? Can you relate to *anyone* here? We're not the same as them. Can't you see?"

For an eight-year-old, Reggie spoke with amazing wisdom. Then he finished, "This isn't your life, Jane...you're not like them."

Reggie flinched as if he had stepped on a hot coal.

Jenny was on fire. Her eyes filled with tears, and a desperate flush filled her face. She spoke from her throat as she fought for air between words, "Jane? Jane! Who is *Jane*? Who is *SHE*?"

Reggie turned around slowly with a cringe that he was somehow able to conceal. Tears were streaming down Jenny's sweet brown face, but her sadness came out as rage. Probably Reggie's only saving grace was that his reaction was blurred behind Jenny's frantic, inconsolable fury.

"Who is she?" she screamed. "WHO IS JANE, Reggie? WHO IS JANE?"

Jane lifted her head...her eyes a *cold blue*. A stream of icy tears clung to her face. She walked down the snow-covered slope to the frozen lake. Upon reaching the bank, she put down the velvet sack and dropped to one knee. Then she dabbed her middle and index fingers onto her tongue to moisten them, before signing her name in cursive across the ice of the snow-dusted lake.

Jane Frost

Yes, she was. She surely was, child, mm-hm. Take a few breaths on that.

Jane stood up straight with a chest full of air. She put the burgundy sack over her shoulder. Then she used her knuckles to wipe the frozen tears from her face. After taking a few hard strides from the lake, Jane ripped herself into a hard twist, and rose as beautiful flakes, into the icy wind. Her sweeping flow of white camouflaged the sack and her backpack...snow was all that could be seen. Just snow.

Jane rode wind, maintaining the structure of each of her flakes...preserving their infinite facets...and more importantly, their unique differences...as her past crystalized within her mind, like frost interlocking over a pane of glass.

XXXII

Not in a race toward the future. Not in a race from the previously spoken past. But just to run in the present. And when that little girl from St. Louis, Missouri put her track shoes on, there was nobody on the planet who could catch her. As Jane hit an opening at the other end of the forest, large white and gray wolves emerged on her sides. They had been tracking her for miles. With each pump of her arms, Jane's past became ever clearer.

"Nobody fits in everywhere," Reggie's voice arose in her mind, *"Even Santa had to leave his hometown to go find his place."*

Trees lit up with luminous turquoise beads as Jane passed. Her ice dotted the branches in such a way, they were able to capture the moonlight and propel a mystical glow across the woods. THWAP! She extended her hang glider wings and soared off a cliff. The wolves followed her to the edge of the overhanging rocks, craned their necks upward, and howled into the cold air with a passion, "Owooooooooo!"

Jane swooped down and slung the burgundy sack in front of Father Time's door without breaking glide. Deep inside his compound, the entrepreneur was beginning his walk through a room of priceless artifacts that he had meticulously collected over the years. In his hand–Jane's diamond bracelet.

As Time hobbled along, he passed display cases containing specially chosen items, uniquely preserved in his Hall of Artifacts. In a glass box on a pedestal, Red's first reindeer harness…worn leather, frayed on the edges, yet still freshly oiled. In another case, about four and a half feet tall, hung a complete elf outfit. It was Gerald's first uniform. The green fabric was faded, but the way the bells on the hat and the bottom of the vest reflected the light, it seemed as though they had been polished just yesterday.

Next, he came to a large six-by-four-foot table covered with real grass. Rows of small, four-inch-high white crosses stretched diagonally across it. It was the Graveyard of the Unknown Gingerbread Men. One cross, placed exactly in the middle of the table, had the name "Piet" inscribed on it. There was a toothpick-sized Dutch flag in front of the cross. A pair of scissors sat next to the table with hints of green showing on the blades. The grass was lightly watered and manicured on the daily. You could smell it. More than the grass, you could smell the depth of a period in time more powerful than any happening in The North, *before* or *since*. Heavy. Stand in front of that table, make you think about who you are for more than a minute.

Farther along, a large glass case held Santa's fuchsia suit. Beside it, a framed napkin, stamped with a red lipstick kiss from Vicki. Time shuffled along with labored breaths on his way through the most secluded room in his facility. It was quite a trek to get there. However, his shortness of breath was also closely tied to a release of emotions, knowing he was passing by memories of a different day. He rolled the bracelet around in his fingers as he passed a golden egg, sitting adjacent to a mint condition, first-edition print of Dr. Seuss's *Green Eggs and Ham* book.

Time walked deeper into the hall until his feet stopped as if immovable weights had been strapped to them. To his right, stood a seven-foot-tall glass case. Inside the case, hung a full-length heavily worn, black leather coat, with strips of dark fur running down, three inches to either side of the center buttons. On the top, a nameplate which read, "*Father Winter.*" Time opened the case, stretched out his arm, and gently placed Jane's diamond bracelet into the pocket of the coat. Then he shut the case, put his open hand on the glass... and bowed his head to pray.

Jane landed on a hillside and retracted her glider wings. She worked her way through light brush and intermittent groups of youthful trees until another opening was revealed. Then she yanked out her zip line launcher, reloaded it with a spear cord, and fired a shot across the gorge below her. After detaching the cord, she jammed the launcher into her bag. Then she secured the cord to a large tree and iced the line. Without hesitation, she pulled out the chrome handle, slapped it on top of the cord with both hands, and hopped forward.

Mountain elk paused to catch a glimpse of the white streak flying past them. High above, white owls observed Jane while swooping perpendicular to her path. CRACK, CLACK, CRACK! Three hundred feet below the elk, rock-solid rams locked horns with intruding rams. It was as if they were all competing to open up a pocket for Jane to land. She didn't need much space though. Jane knew there was enough room on that high post to go around. When she dropped into the rams' circle, she remembered an old message from Father Time. "*In all sincerity...it's not how much time you have...it's what you do with the time you have that matters...*"

At the same time, Santa's sleigh rested on top of a stretch of row homes nestled within a large city. The elves rapidly built chimneys on top of the houses and cut holes into the roofs. When the elves gave Santa the signal, he snapped a sturdy steel hook onto his sleigh. The hook was attached to a cable, which he latched onto his belt. After Santa gave the elves a thumbs-up, they proceeded to lower him down one of the freshly made chimneys with his sack of toys.

"Shhh. Down, down…"

As the crew swiftly dashed from one end of the row to the other, a rainbow of lights flashed along with them. They were finished in minutes. It was on to the next town!

Meanwhile, Jane had already popped out her skate blades, powered a stream of ice through the gathering of interested rams, and skated between them. She steered around and down the ledges of the cliffs as though she were riding a roller coaster. A hard turn threw her into a forest. And then another drop. Jane sailed downhill at a harrowing pace, her knees absorbing all the rattles and bumps the terrain would unveil. When the forest opened up, the frozen lake below became her sole target. CLAP! Her skates hit the ice. She ceased use of her ice spray, relying on her downhill momentum to carry her forward.

Massive polar bears galloped behind Jane's path. They would never dream of catching up to her, but one could tell they were totally down for a good time. They slammed their monstrous paws through the ice, launching fish into the air. With mouths open wide, they bouldered into each other, hoping to get a gulp of the downward descending snacks. The bears' raised lips exposed canines that could rip a bus open, yet most of us would contend, they were only showing their teeth for the sake of sharing a good meal and a laugh.

Jane shot off a ramped bank at the opposite end of the lake and fired off into the woods, leaving the titanic beasts, the flying fish, and the cratered ice in twisted mayhem. She landed without slowing her forward progress—even retracting her skate blades mid-stride. Slink, slink!

The memory of my guidance ignited Jane further. "*When you run, child...run like it means somethin'. If anything gets in your way...you just run right on through it.*"

Jane tore through the pine trees and bolted across the creek on foot. Once again, her route was stalemated by the formidable face of a jagged cliff. The wall of rock marked the literal end to the edge of the forest. Between the trees and the stone, there was barely a place for Jane to breathe.

"We going to do this again?" Jane asked the stone wall.

This time, she tilted both palms to the ground and sprayed an ice column out of each, hoping to achieve a semi-vertical ascent. However, Jane's icy spray came out in downward angles, tilting her body wildly to the left and right as she rose. Tree branches pointed daggers at her from behind while the massive wall of rock screamed by, directly in front of her face. Each tilt brought Jane inches closer to one fate or the other. She broke free of the rise and threw her strong hand out onto the ledge as soon as she could. Then she muscled herself onto the overhang with her forearm, before another serious injury could occur. She didn't need to push forward at this pace, but an *All Jane Event* was an *All Jane Event*. There's not much more I can say about that.

The broad arms of an aged oak tree held a protective cloak over her, but as Jane crawled away from the cliff's edge, her mother's voice of despair ran down her spine, "*She's ice. She's all ice! Snowflake, your heart is warm. Come back through your heart...come back through your heart!"*

Jane rose to her feet, shook out her banged-up arm, and cracked her knuckles. She lifted her brown eyes far across the snow-covered terrain, onto the next mountain. After taking a moment to revel in the extreme height of the cliff on which she stood, Jane confidently walked to within an inch of the rocky drop-off. Those white boots of hers showed more than a few deep scuffs, but their soles preserved a story of work...of fearlessness...of victory.

Jane's thighs held her steady. As a matter of fact, she took her trailing boot and placed the tip of it down, so it hung out *over* the ridge by a few inches. Massive boulders at the bottom of the gorge looked like tiny pebbles. Large birds of prey looked like floating black dots. Janey was *way* up on that mountain.

Her glossy white pleather pants stretched outward from her boots, up over her calves and thighs, pronouncing her sturdy definition. The cuffs on her jacket worked back onto sleeves that wrapped snug to her toned arms, showing off every muscle she had used over the previous thirty hours. Jane stood tall, surveying the ground hundreds of feet below. Only her breathing caused her chest to rise and rest. Rise and rest.

"If you were any other daughter, I could not make this sacrifice," the deep, bass-filled voice of Father Winter resurged through Jane's inner soul. *"If I wait just one day too long...the problem will be too great, for even me to mend."*

She would not whirl herself into flakes. She would not jump into open space. She remained in her human state, absorbing every thought and every emotion coming through her body. Finally, Jane turned her back on the ledge and faced the broad, experienced oak tree behind her.

She closed her eyes and allowed Santa's voice to pour into her mind, resurfacing a conversation she had with him many years before. *"Your father, like the truth, is the foundation of The North..."*

Jane took off running. She disappeared into the woods and swept through the villages, coating everything she laid eyes on with another layer of ice and snow. Flashbacks of Jane's childhood ran through her mind, including the vivid image of the day she ran home crying when Reggie told her he was going away. BANG! The glider wings expanded behind her shoulders. She flew high into the air. Jane would face the first light of Christmas Day head on... with something more valuable than all of Father Time's gadgets put together, mm-hm...*with the knowledge of who she was.*

XXXIII

A Polar White Mercedes SL 65 convertible whipped around the bend of a long driveway, kicking up snow from its rear tires as it hummed. The car swiftly moved with a mission until finally gearing down in front of a set of grand, wide stone steps. At the top of the steps rose a pair of majestic double-entry doors. Doors to a marvelous white mansion that waited for its owner on the other side of towering columns.

Two tuxedo-wearing butlers stood on either side of the doors. They also waited. The first butler, Brad, was a middle-aged white man with movie star looks. He had charming blue eyes, which were offset by a scruffy, dark brown five o'clock shadow. Deep brown roots flowed from the beginnings of his dazzling dirty blond hair. Put that in a tuxedo. *For sure!*

The other butler, Bradley, was stationed in front of the door to the right. Also a white middle-aged man. Dark brown wavy hair flowed back over his head...fine northeast-city-boy style. His blue eyes rose up over his midnight-shadowed beard. His smile was dapper, but his jawline was rigid and defined. Put that in a tuxedo. *Feel me?*

But who were they waiting for? Whoever it was, was about to step out of that Mercedes. First, one knee-high, white platform boot carefully placed itself onto the stone pavement outside of the sleek two-door. Buckles and stitching wove all the way up to the top of the boot. Next, the other leg lifted out of the bucket seat, knee first, before slowly lowering down onto the pavement. Perfectly white polished nails slid over top of the door...and Jane's beautiful face emerged...with the beautiful scar still intact just below her right eye. A sly smile gave a rare, tiny glimpse of her crisp white teeth.

From the top of the steps, The Brads followed every inch of her movement.

Jane's hair held no more exasperated strands. Only black tresses...all in rhythm. This time Jane's own beliefs swept through her mind...*her* work...*her* message. Thung. She shut the heavy door to the Benz, vacuum-sealing all of her personal thoughts...all of her personal feelings...her struggles...her triumph. Only to be opened on *her* terms, in *her* time.

The two Brads opened the ten-foot-tall doors, and watched Jane walk directly up the center of the steps. Not an inch to the right. Not an inch to the left. But straight. Up. The. Middle.

Yip! A black and white husky pup came barreling out of the open doors! Blond-haired Brad scooped it up with one arm just as Jane arrived at the top of the steps. He cradled the wriggly puppy, placed it into Jane's awaiting arms, and professionally stated, "You've created a *magnificent* white Christmas, Ms. Frost."

Jane kept her focus straight ahead past the entry, into her living room, where a large husky relaxed on a pristine white couch. She relinquished a grin, and returned a comment under her breath with swagger, "I have...haven't I?"

Then she walked past the two Brads, before pausing just inside the front door. A third husky circled in front of the large adult husky, and sat up with anticipation. Ice blue eyes, black and white fur...smaller and skinnier than his father, sitting on the couch behind him. The slender husky tap, tap, tapped his paws, anxiously trying to stay put, while the big guy lay still like a shadow on snow. Yes, Jane's babies were waiting for her too. They were about to give her all the hugs and kisses she had coming. But then her cell phone vibrated.

She put down the puppy, slid the phone out of her back pocket, and opened the message. It was a text from Rollo saying, "*TY*". Jane patted her heart and smiled. Then an ellipsis arose on the screen, which materialized as a follow up text from Rollo, "*I bet DR is happy he stuck around!*"

Jane sat down on the couch, crossed her legs, and reached her arm out. "Sergei," she called sweetly. Didn't take a second calling for the big husky to scooch over with his paws and put his large mushy head on her lap. "Yes, Player," she called out next. "Are you the baby?" The slender dog broke from his tap, tap, tapping, threw himself into the side of the couch, and poked his nose under Jane's arm. "Are you the baby? Are you the–"

BUZZZZ. Her phone vibrated again. This time it was a text from her pal, Tuesday, "*Guess what I'm doing? Eatin' sweet potato pie and watchin' your big snowflakes blowin' round!*"

Jane giggled and rolled her eyes.

BUZZZZ. Jane's phone was blowing up! "Orvil Lantern?" she sang out. "Whaaat?" She laughed as she read his text, "*If you could see the big smile on my face!*" Jane slapped her leg and toe-tapped the floor. "Orviiiiil!"

"*U crazy!*" she texted back.

BUZZZ. St. Patrick messaged, *"Someone put snow at the end of the rainbow! That's better than gold!"*

Jane flicked her head up to the ceiling. "Ha!"

Jane lost it when she read the next text. "No. Way." You wouldn't be able to guess who, if I spotted you the S-A-D! It was Sadie Hawkins! "Saaadie!" Jane yelled as she stood up. The dogs started yipping and hopping around. This sparked the curiosity of The Brads, who were still holding command of their post outside the doors. Jane could imagine they were dying to know what was going on, so she shouted out the text to them. "Sadie texted me and said, *'Does this mean you finally have a little free time?'*"

The Brads allowed themselves a moment to share in on the chuckle.

A lone white hawk took in an aerial view of Jane's mansion. Wings expanded…soaring…gliding into a bend. Didn't miss a thing. Yes, this was an exact replica of the mansion Jenny had sat at her desk and drawn, some two decades before.

Jenny placed the cerulean blue crayon back into the crayon box, picked up the picture, and pinned it to the wall. In the lower right-hand corner of the picture, the lead reindeer stood with confidence. It had antlers drawn with a blue glitter crayon…and down below, bright blue glittery hooves to match.

Jenny was good at putting her dreams on paper. Jane was good at making those dreams come true.

Jane could think now. She could try to make sense of all the events that had occurred over the past week. And she found warmth in what was cold. She looked out of the window, allowing herself to think back even further, to that little girl with big dreams.

As Rollo thumped his way across her snow-covered lawn, she saw him as that paper figure—the one with the fedora in the picture. Same smile now as he had in the drawing...waving to Jane in all his glory. The sidekicks took their places around Rollo. Seven small white cutouts with tall ears and fluffy white tails. They would never leave his side. Even the evergreens appeared paper white, as though Jenny had drawn a blueprint for what Jane was now living. Jane waved back to the boys, and returned a smile. Rollo tipped his hat to The Brads, who acknowledged the big, round snowman kindly, before softly closing the massive doors to Jane's mansion.

People wonder if Jane's home is made of ice and snow. I've never asked her about it. Never been inside. Can only tell you what we see through those open doors. As for The Brads, they're a vault... why they were chosen. Won't get anything out of them. And those doors were closed, now. But I can tell you what happened next, because Jane told me the story in such explicit detail, I feel like I was in there with her and those loveable snow dogs that Christmas morning. The way her eyes sparkled as she told it. Reminds me of her father every time she gets that look. *Surely does.*

So as Jane shared, the dogs were whirling around in circles, when Player bumped into the Christmas tree. She heard one of his claws scratch into paper. Of course, she wondered, *Is there a present under the tree?* Now, Janey hadn't even thought about it as a possibility when she entered the house. She twitched her head. Swiveled. Thought for a moment. Then she eagerly pushed herself up off the sofa.

Sure enough, there *was* a gift waiting under the tree for her. Jane could see a round white belly through the hole in the wrapping paper. She was filled with anticipation...with wonder...just as anyone is when they see a gift for themselves under the tree. Didn't have a clue of what it was, until she pulled the paper off...and uncovered a freshly boxed ROLLO DOLL! Just what she wanted. Jane studied it, marveling at the detail, the big round feet, Rollo's big snowy smile...and of course, his fedora. She ran her finger over the straight edges of the mint condition box, before putting it up to her cheek. It was cool. So cool. She pulled it away and inspected Rollo's face again. Then she lifted up the box to her nose and breathed it in. *Mmmm.* Jane was home.

She slid out her cell phone. But not to read another text. She wanted to play music through her house speakers. While Jane was searching for a holiday playlist to suit the mood, she tuned to a general radio station and let it stream in the background.

"DJ Krane, back at it again...with my Bonnie!"

"I swear you got fifty names for us."

"Okay, Kelly...Kelly T."

"Pssh. You gonna give 'em the weather?"

"Muuucho Friiiiio!" DJ Krane laughed.

"Here we go again. Not complainin' about the cold either. Your accents are just so bad."

"Alright, Kel, chill...I'm just tryin' to lightin' the people up a bit. 'Tis the season!"

"The weather..." Kelly stewed.

DJ Krane was hyped. "Thirty-degrees in Miami!"

"Thirty?"

"Yep."

"Sheesh."

"Brrrr."

"Tell ya this, Krane…sure beats the sun burnin' a hole through your skin."

"I know that's somethin' *everyone* can agree on! Here, check this out…I got one for you…"

Jane paused to listen.

And this time, the DJ played *her* song for everyone else to hear…

Jane Frost, without flaws of course,
The boss, movin' ice at all cost,
Snow white Benz, SL 65 her choice,
Makin' y'all hoarse…
Jane Frost.

Ice in the Alps, or a blizzard in Cali.,
Pray for it baby, better be up for the challenge,
C'when she bring it, she bring it, know she ain't playin',
Bit by the frost, a hundred it's Jane,
Crank up the heat, still got the chill on yo neck,
Free pass at the Pole, Rollo on text,
Layin' ice for sport, hope the truth don't hurt,
Theeeeere arrrre no lies in the North!
Benz pedal under foot, wolves on the wing,
Fearless in her stride, daughter of a king,
Thinkin' on the come up they could break her twice,
Slippin'? Put ya in that freezer for life,
They shunned, didn't want her around,
Layin' shade on Jane, complainin' through town,
Now they lookin', but she can't be found,
They beggin' the DJ to bring back the sound,

Jane Frost, without laws of course,
The force, the Voice of the North,
Passed the line you shouldn't have crossed,
Now you gettin' tossed...
Jane Frost,
Now you gettin' tossed...
Jane Frost...
Now you gettin' tossed...

Addicted to snow, then she's the one,
Allergic to ice, then you better run,
Frost on the windshield, snow on the lantern,
Freezin' out kingpins from Compton to Camden,
Doubt to no doubt she's turnin' the pages,
Beatin' the spread, like she was in Vegas,
Rippin' that spin, fightin' the cause,
fightin' for hers, fightin' for yours,
Blazin' a trail, but there's no need to follow,
Reppin' that soul, like cornbread and collards,
White twenty-fifth winter wonderland, check,
Families bond like her word, call it respect.
In the club, they wild, she droppin' it down,
In the hood, they cranked up, throwin' it 'round,
People talkin' that nonsense, but they all actin',
Questions like riddles, gotta know who's askin'?,

Jane Frost, without flaws of course
The boss, movin' ice at all cost,
Snow white Benz, SL 65 her choice,

Makin' y'all hoarse…
Jane Frost.

Broad stroke brush paint Jane as a villain,
Forgettin' God loves all his children.

Movin' ice, movin' ice,
Movin' ice, movin' ice,

Jane Frost,
Jane Frost.

Now, I know Janey's momma told her, *"You can't believe every-thing you read in books."* But you know *this* story is all true. Still have presents on Christmas morning. Still hear the, *"Ho ho ho,"* on Christmas Eve. You hear the jingle bells. And some of you, if you were lucky, have even seen reindeer fly. Did it snow today? Yes. And let you know, that was just Jane coming to pay you a visit. You *want* to believe, *I can feel it.* We all want to believe. Everyone does. Going the other way though, understand this…when times get a little rough and you begin to have self-doubt…maybe lose faith, lose your way…I'll tell you, up here in The North we believe in you…even when *you* don't believe in *yourself*…

…sure as that little snowflake Janey rested on the tip of your nose.